BREAKING TRAIL

A Tom Patterson Western

BREAKING TRAIL
•
Jerry S. Drake

AVALON BOOKS
NEW YORK

Published by Avalon Books,
an imprint of Thomas Bouregy & Co., Inc.
160 Madison Avenue, New York, NY 10016

Library of Congress Cataloging-in-Publication Data

Drake, Jerry S.
  Breaking trail / Jerry S. Drake.
      p. cm.
  ISBN 978-0-8034-7721-6
  1. Railroads—Employees—Fiction.   2. Union Pacific
Railroad Company—Fiction.   I. Title.
  PS3604.R35B74 2011
  813'.6—dc22
                                                    2010031117

PRINTED IN THE UNITED STATES OF AMERICA
ON ACID-FREE PAPER
BY HADDON CRAFTSMEN, BLOOMSBURG, PENNSYLVANIA

For Ginny, Peggy, Sue, and Nancy;
the wonderful women in my life

Chapter One

Gilford, Texas, 1858

The gangling youngster bent to pick up the second of three filled spittoons spaced at intervals along the front of the saloon bar. Just one of Tommy Patterson's jobs in the bar was to regularly empty and clean each spittoon during the afternoon and nighttime business hours. As he straightened and started to walk to the third, a foot stretched back from a patron at the bar and tripped the youth. As the boy sprawled forward, the two spittoons fell from his hands, and foul tobacco juice and spittle spilled to the floor with a goodly splash upon the tan leather boot of a customer at the bar.

"What the hell?" came the angry cry from the wearer of the boot, a thickset, middle-aged cowhand with a jowly, scowling face flushed from too many glasses of cheap whiskey. Nearly staggering with the effort, the heavy man kicked away the nearest spittoon and reached down to grasp the boy by the back of his shirt collar. "You clumsy little rat!"

"Warn't his fault, Ted!" a voice protested from the table area. "One of your pard's tripped the lad."

"He ruined my boots!" the angry man bellowed. "They was danged near new." He pulled the boy erect and shook him violently. "Look what you done, you little scamp!"

"Leave him alone, Ted!" shouted one of the saloon women, a buxom lady in a gaudy dress who rose from her chair, ignoring the restraining hands of her table companions. "Take it out on Ray, he's the one who did the tripping."

The fat man glowered at the woman and turned a fierce look on the smirking cowhand who had been named as culprit.

1

"Sure, come try it on me," the accused, Ray, taunted. "You ain't man enough to do me any shakin'."

Frustrated, the surly cowhand intensified his fury on the boy who was still struggling in his grasp. "He shouldn't have tried to carry them two," the cowhand argued. "He ain't nothing but a little bar brat. I'm gonna teach him better." Holding young Patterson with both hands, he started marching the writhing boy toward the café doors of the saloon.

As the drunken belligerent pushed the squirming boy through the saloon doors onto the boardwalk, most of the bar patrons followed. The struggle between man and boy brought attention from passersby on either side of the main street of the small settlement, and a few began to amble toward the tussle.

"Whatcha going to do to him, Ted?" one of the men asked.

"He's a dirty little critter," the portly man crowed. "I'll give him a bath, and then let him clean my boots."

"Let me go, you damned drunk!" Tommy shouted.

"I'll wash your mouth out while I'm getting at it."

Weaving slightly, the cowhand forced the boy toward the nearest watering trough, their abrupt approach causing two horses to lift their muzzles and back away to the length of their tethered reins. With a surge of adult muscle over the struggles of a scrawny twelve-year-old, the man lifted the boy, plunged him headfirst into the scummy water, and held him there.

"Let him up, Ted," the bartender said, standing in the saloon doorway. "You'll drown him, you keep on."

"So what?" Ted spat his contempt. "Mean something to you?"

"Just a kid I was trying to help," the bartender countered. "That's enough now."

"I'll say when's enough," the drunk bellowed.

"Let him up!" A voice came from a new direction.

All eyes turned to a stranger riding his horse on the town's central street toward the saloon. He was a large man, able-bodied, in his late fifties or early sixties, with a neatly trimmed beard and a bushy mustache that somewhat masked a lined, weathered face. He was a mature dandy with a near-new derby on his gray-haired head and a long linen duster over his cream-colored shirt, beige vest, and matching riding britches.

At the distraction, the boy struggled to raise his head above the water to gulp air before Ted forced him under once again.

"I said let him up," the stranger repeated. He swung down from his horse, threw back his duster from his right hip and, with astonishing speed, whipped an ivory-handled revolver from a holster and cocked it. "Do it now."

Ted was slow to react, and a bullet cut into the dirt between his feet. The now-frightened bully pulled his hand away from the boy's head and backed away in alarm. Horses whinnied, people uttered their surprise and wonder, and the youngster came sputtering up from the trough, wheezing and gasping for air.

"You ain't really gonna shoot me?" Ted questioned.

"You okay, boy?" the stranger asked.

Unable to speak, Tommy nodded.

"Climb out of there," the man with the gun instructed. "And you, sir," he cocked the revolver again and waved it at Ted. "Soon as he's out, you take his place."

"I ain't going to," Ted blustered.

"I'll hurt you if you don't," the stranger told him.

"Big talk, mister," Ted responded, his courage gathering.

In answer, the stranger put the second bullet into one cheek of Ted's ample buttocks. "There's times I don't suffer a fool who won't listen."

There was a delayed reaction until the pain of his flesh wound swelled into the drunken man's awareness. He yelped and began to shriek as he dropped to the ground, trying to reach his wound to ease the hurt from it. "He shot me," he yelped. "He done shot me."

"He'll be riding sidesaddle for a spell, I'll venture," the stranger said in a calm, cultured voice. He returned the showy

Navy Colt to his holster as the slightly injured man continued his whimpering. "I made sure it was nothing more than a little nick in his backside."

"You could've killed him," one of the onlookers said in a reproving tone.

"Hit just where I was aiming," the stranger said.

"Who are you, mister?" a bar patron wanted to know. "You ain't from hereabouts . . . whatcha doing here?"

Instead of giving an immediate response, the stranger reached his right hand into a vest pocket and drew out a silver dollar that he displayed in an exaggerated manner to the gathering spectators. He transferred the coin to his left hand and then tossed it high in the air as he flashed his right hand to the revolver once again. The handgun boomed, and the dollar dropped into the middle of the street.

"Missed!" one of the crowd jeered as an acrid smell of black powder hung in the air. "I didn't see it jump!"

"Pick it up," the shooter commanded.

One man scooted to retrieve the coin and raised it to examine it. "Hit it sure enough. See the dent right here on the edge."

"Bring it to me, if you'd be so kind." The stranger pocketed the damaged silver dollar, holstered his revolver, and nodded to the groaning man on the ground. "You know who you're dealing with?" He lifted his eyes to the assembling crowd and raised his voice. "Tell him it was the one and only world-famous pistoleer, Will Beatty, who has spared his life. And tell him next time I'll put one in his heart if he ever hurts any youngster while I'm hereabouts."

"You with a traveling outfit?" a well-dressed cattleman in a brown suit wanted to know. "Putting on a shooting show?"

"Just riding through, my friend," Beatty replied. Again, he spoke for all to hear. "However, I *do* entertain folks from time to time with my legendary pistol skills. Perhaps the residents of this fine community might enjoy a shooting demonstration." He paused. "Most places where I've performed my extraordinary marksmanship, the folks that see what I can do are mighty appreciative." Once more, he paused. "Of course, as I said, I'm merely a traveler passing through your fine town. Who knows whether I will ever pass this way again?"

Tommy Patterson heaved himself out of the trough soaking wet, still breathing hard, his mane of unkempt blond hair plastered down the back of his neck and over his face. He brushed the wet strands away, rubbing his eyes to clear the irritants from the polluted water.

"Where are your folks?" the gunslick asked.

"Ain't got none," the boy replied in his raspy voice.

"Can't be likely," Beatty said. "Who takes care of you?"

"I take care of myself."

Beatty chuckled and turned his attention back to the crowd. "Been on the trail a spell and I 'spect a drink or two of whiskey, if such was offered, might heal my saddle sores . . . applied from the inside out." He waited expectantly.

"Be my pleasure to serve you, sir. On the house." The bartender stepped out from the cluster of awed spectators. "That youngster works for me, and you done him a good turn." He turned to Tommy. "Did ya thank the man?"

Tommy shrugged but made no reply.

"That's quite all right, let him get his breath," Will Beatty declared munificently. "The generosity of you good people to a traveling stranger will be thanks aplenty."

"Ain't never seen such shooting!" a toadying member of the crowd crowed.

"Any chance we could get you to put on a show for us, Mr. Will Beatty?" asked a bald-headed man wearing a shopkeeper's apron.

"Well, I am on a bit of a schedule, but I might stay over here in . . ."

"Gilford, Texas," the bald-headed man informed him.

". . . for maybe a day or two."

"You ever kill anyone, Mr. Beatty?" came another breathless question.

"Just to defend myself," the pistoleer countered. "Not counting ferocious Indians, I've put down only bandits, killers, and scoundrels—blackguards each and every one of them."

With additional exuberant exclamations and fawning be-haviors, a knot of drovers, drifters, and town drinkers escorted the self-celebrated marksman through the café doors into the saloon.

After a minute passed by, Tommy moved to the doorway and opened one of the slatted doors partway to look inside. At the bar, the bartender was filling the stranger's shot glass while an idolizing audience pleaded for him to tell tales of dangers faced and bravely concluded.

Beatty responded, launching his first story with broad, theatrical gestures, his resonant voice rising and falling with dramatic emphases. "Four, now going on five years ago, I was riding scout for General Harney out of Fort Kearny in Nebraska territory. We were having a powwow with a Sioux chief who called himself Little Thunder. Well, gentlemen, all hell broke loose, and before we knew it, we were in a pitched battle with those bloodthirsty savages. I took down five charging braves myself, and it turned out to be a time those heathen Sioux were never going to forget . . ."

The boy stepped away from the doorway and looked down at his soaked clothing, the only outfit he had to wear. Rather than walk through the boisterous saloon and interrupt Will Beatty's story, he moved to the side of the building and turned down a narrow alley between the saloon and the next-door diner. At the back of the saloon, he took off his shoes and socks, stripped down to his underwear, and laid shoes, socks, shirt, and trousers in the sunlight on the back steps of the build-ing. He sat down next to his clothing, hoping the garments would soon dry under the blazing Texas sun.

It had been six or maybe seven months since he had arrived in this small Texas settlement—he wasn't quite sure. He couldn't remember his mother, and almost five years had passed since his pa had abandoned him in Houston, the drunkard disappear-ing without a word. Only seven at the time, he was picked up by a town constable and placed in an ugly, two-story ramshackle house that served as one of the community's few orphanages. The caretakers of the facility, mostly older women, ranged from strict authoritarians to near sadists in their treatment of the young ragamuffins plucked from the streets. Some sporadic attempts were made for schooling these little wildings, but the aversion to learning—born of the pupils' harsh treatment—made education nearly impossible.

At the age of ten, Tommy left his bed—a pile of blankets on the floor in the corner of a crowded upstairs room—and crept down the steps. Although the doors were bolted securely every evening, he had earlier unfastened a ground-floor window and, at two o'clock in the dark morning, he opened it and crawled outside. Shivering a bit from the night chill of early fall, he was elated at his new freedom. He glanced back at the dark house and shook his head at the beatings he had suffered, recalling the abusive words directed at him, the squalid living spaces, the dreadful food and the rancid smells. He walked briskly down the street, looking to find a better life somewhere else in the world. Hitching rides from place to place in Texas, he sought food and shelter, begging for or working for what people would grudgingly give or provide.

"Tommy?" The woman's voice was soft. "You okay?"

The boy turned to the woman who opened the screen door at the back of the saloon. It was the saloon strumpet who had protested his treatment by the ruffian. Once a pretty one, early middle age and a dissolute life had coarsened her face and fattened her figure.

"Yes, ma'am," he answered. "No harm done."

"Jacob was sorry he didn't interfere," she said. "He wants you to know."

"Yes, ma'am," Tommy repeated, only now aware that the bartender had failed to intervene.

"These the only things you got to wear?" she asked.

"Some underwear," he told her.

She hesitated, stepped out onto the porch and reached into the cleavage of her gaudy dress and drew out a small roll of dollar bills. She separated four of the bills from the roll and offered them to the boy. "Here," she said, her voice a command. "Soon as you get them rags dry, you get yourself over to the general store and buy some that's decent." She peered at his scuffed, worn shoes and then peeled off three more bills. "And new shoes too."

"I can't take your money, Miss Ruby," he protested, although his small hand was already reaching.

"I ain't got no problem in getting more," she said, shoving the money into his palm. "And you take yourself a bath 'fore you put them new duds on, you hear?"

"Yes, ma'am," he said for the third time.

"What do you say?"

"What do you mean?"

"Like . . . maybe . . . thank you, Miss Ruby?"

The boy nodded, eager to make amends. "I do thank you. I thank you a lot, Miss Ruby. Honest, I was going to say so."

A gentle smile came over the woman's painted face. "I knowed you were, Tommy. Come show me when you're all dressed up." She reached out her hand once again to touch the boy's damp head, almost a caress, then opened the screen door and returned to the saloon.

"New duds from the general store," he mused aloud. "Ain't I gonna be the swell?"

Chapter Two

Gilford, Texas, 1858

Tommy woke as the early sun slanted through the storage-room window and into his face. He rolled his head away, but his sleep had been disturbed enough to bring full wakefulness. He sighed and sat up on the cot, yawned, and rubbed his eyes. It wasn't much different than the sleeping arrangement in those dreadful days at the orphanage, but the difference now was an uncommon concern and an even exceptional kindness from his employer. Jacob McKay, the saloon owner and bartender, had rustled up a canvas cot and placed it among the beer barrels and liquor shelves. The man had also garnered a couple of blankets and even a feather pillow from the upstairs ladies of the establishment.

The boy dressed in his old clothes and stashed his store-bought shirt and trousers under the pillow, his new shoes under the cot; all saved for later. Barefoot, he rose, walked to the door of the saloon, and opened it to look through. The barroom was shadowy and silent, no sounds from the upstairs or from the adjacent kitchen. He closed the door softly and walked across the room to the outer door. He let himself out, descended the porch steps, and hurried up the alley to the main street.

The rural village of Gilford, thirty-eight miles east of Dallas, was situated in a shallow valley with a river running nearby. Low-rising hills surrounded the settlement and sheltered it from the strong winds that blew winter cold and summer heat out of the northwest from time to time. Fully grown leafy trees overhung much of the tiny town, giving it welcome shade on hot midsummer days.

Gilford's business district consisted of only seven buildings. On the south side of the central avenue, there was a general store, a boardinghouse that served permanent roomers and overnight visitors, a small eatery, and the saloon. Across the street, there was a blacksmith's shop, a livery stable, and a feed store. At some distance away on the short side, a church was under construction, although no one had yet decided its denomination. A few small houses, cabins, and even some tents were scattered along the road and behind the commercial buildings to house some of the settlement's ninety-six residents.

Tommy hurried along the road, waving his hand to an early-morning arrival, a man on his farm wagon coming into town. The driver returned the gesture and guided his team toward the feed store.

The tributary was Tommy's destination—precisely, the deep, eddying pool where a bend of the stream turned it away from the town. It was a place where boys could strip naked and swim without being seen by the townsfolk. There were stories that the comely Bannister sisters, both in their rebellious late teens, had been spotted in nothing but their birthday suits on more than one late night. Tommy regretted that his saloon chores, from afternoon to midnight, prevented him from seeing for himself such a wondrous sight.

Cutting across a field, he trotted to the procession of cottonwood trees that followed the flowing tributary, and then he raced along a streamside path. Seconds later, he went through an opening in the brush and down to the pool. A quick glance around assured that he was alone, no other males or females, young or old, in sight. He stripped out of his shirt, trousers, and underpants, and plunged into the cold water. He came to the surface, his teeth chattering from the frigid dip. After a minute or so, the chill dissipated and he swam out into the current, accepting the challenge of the force of the cascading water as the torrent beat against him, threatening to carry his bare body back near the town for anyone who would happen to see.

He swam back into the calm water pool and rolled over

on his back, floating lazily. He paddled occasionally to stay afloat, glancing up from time to time to seek the position of the rising sun filtering through the fluttering leaves of the over-arching cottonwoods. Out of the corner of his eye, he spied a ripple in the pond a few feet to his left. He turned his wary attention to the water moccasin until it continued on and disappeared from view. It would be a couple of months before the snakes swarmed. He knew he'd best keep away from the river while they were feisty.

He cupped water in one hand and scrubbed one armpit and repeated the process under the other. "There, Miss Ruby! I done had me a bath," he said aloud. He swam to the bank, crawled onto a large flat rock, and stood up into a full shaft of sunlight to dry. He felt the heat and the morning breeze envelop him and, after five minutes, he reached for his clothes.

He was buttoning his frayed shirt when he heard the first booming report of a gun and, instinctively, he crouched, wondering the location and nature of the unseen shooter. A few moments later, a second shot thundered, and this time Tommy determined that the activity was nearby, perhaps only a hundred yards or more upstream along the riverbank.

At the third gunshot, he moved through the underbrush and trees that rimmed the riverbank, heading toward the sound's source, a half-guess already forming in his mind as to the identity of who he would find.

He halted amidst the foliage at the edge of a clearing, a level expanse of ground atop the river's bank some ten feet above the swift-flowing stream. Will Beatty stood at the edge of the embankment, a revolver in his hand. He fired three more shots toward the river and then placed the revolver in the holster on his right hip. Tommy saw for the first time that Beatty, now without his concealing duster, wore a two-holster gun belt with a weapon in each.

"You can come on out, sonny," Will Beatty said without turning around. "I'm not going to shoot you."

"You knowed I was there?"

"Heard the crashing as you was coming along," the sharp-shooter said, his back still turned. "Nobody ever taught you hunting skills, I would suppose."

"How'd ya know I wasn't that feller you shot?"

"You were doing small-fry crashing. I'd have heard that big ox a mile away." Beatty swung around and waved the boy forward. "Come on out of the brush before you get some ticks on you."

"Whatcha shooting at?" Tommy asked as he stepped into the clearing.

"Practicing my trade," Beatty told him. "I'm doing an exhibition this afternoon for the good folks hereabouts." He looked around, appraising the river location. "This is a good spot . . . trees and brush between us and town should muffle the sounds and not disturb folks still in their beds." He took several steps and squatted down to reload the empty handgun from a canvas bag of supplies resting on a splintered tree stump. Moments later, working with swift precision, he charged the last of the cylinder chambers with powder and levered the final ball into place.

As he rose and stepped to the edge of the embankment, Tommy moved a few steps toward Beatty. "Can I watch?"

"Suit yourself," Beatty said as he continued looking down at the swiftly flowing river. He reached across his body for his second matching Colt, reverse-holstered with the ivory handle jutting forward. He drew and cocked it, extended his arm and aimed. He appeared to be tracking a floating object, a short section of a fallen tree branch swirling near a stretch of cascading rapids. As the driftwood entered the fast-moving current, it gained speed, bobbing up and down, making it a difficult target. Beatty swung his Colt to follow the object and squeezed the trigger. The shot-splintered branch jumped from the water, slammed to the opposite bank as the Colt's loud report blasted the woodland tranquility.

"Whooee!" Tommy exclaimed. "That's some danged good shooting!"

Beatty half-turned and directed his gaze to Tommy. "You ever handle a pistol, sonny?"

Tommy shook his head.

"Want to try?"

"Can I?" Tommy said, eyes shining as he moved to stand beside the shooter.

Beatty cocked the hammer and carefully placed the Colt into the boy's outstretched right hand. He smiled as the weapon sagged down a few inches until Tommy raised it level once again.

"Okay," Beatty said as he bent down, his head next to Tommy's. "Find yourself a target."

"What kind of a target?"

"Well, how about that tree across the stream?" Beatty suggested, pointing to a large cottonwood. "See if you can hit the trunk."

"What do I do?"

"Just hold it steady, aim at it, and squeeze the trigger."

Tommy closed his left eye, sighted along the barrel, and jerked the trigger. With an explosive sound, the revolver bucked hard, kicking up, and he nearly lost his hold on it. Beatty caught Tommy's hand and the Colt, and took it from him.

"Did I hit it?"

"I don't rightly think so," Beatty said. "You don't need to close that left eye, and you need to *squeeze* that trigger, not jerk it."

"Maybe I ain't cut out to be a shooter," the boy groused. "I betcha I didn't hit a danged thing."

"How old are you, son?"

"Folks think I'm twelve or more. I don't know for sure."

The gunman was silent for a few moments, then: "There's a war coming in our country. At your age, most likely it'll come your way." He cocked the Colt again. "Let's try 'er some more."

With a half hour of gun instruction—consisting more of Beatty's patient explanations of weapon handling, stance technique, and philosophy rather than shooting—Tommy fired two more shots, with one striking the tree trunk.

"Getting better, ain't I?" the boy asked hopefully.

"Handgun's a little heavy for you, but you'll grow into it," Beatty said, taking the revolver from the youngster. He checked the remaining load in the Colt, turned again to the river and snapped a shot at a bobbing tin can riding the current.

"You missed!" The boy cast a wondering look at Beatty.

"I've still got a pretty good eye, but I'm not perfect."

The boy stared at him for a few moments. "I wasn't looking when they said you shot that silver dollar yesterday." There was an element of skepticism in his voice.

Beatty regarded Tommy for several moments, a contemplative look on his weathered face. Then he spoke: "I suppose you want to see me do it?"

"Yes, sir, I surely would like to see that."

Beatty walked a few steps into the center of the clearing and holstered the weapon. He reached his right hand into his vest pocket, took out a silver dollar and, re-enacting his theatrical manner, held it out for Tommy to see. He closed it in the palm of his left hand, dropped the arm to his side, and then tossed the coin into the air.

Tommy tracked the high arc of the silver dollar and then lost it against the sun. Out of the corner of his eye, he saw Beatty's right hand whip the Colt from his holster and heard the loud report of the weapon.

As the coin fell to the ground, Tommy rushed to retrieve it. "I couldn't see . . . didja do it?" he asked. Picking it up, his mouth dropped open in wonderment as he eyed the impact dimple. "By jiminy, you sure done 'er." Then he cast a questioning look at Will Beatty. "How come you hit this 'un and missed that big old can that was just a-floating by?"

Beatty didn't answer for a long time. "If I show you a secret, can you keep your mouth shut?" he asked finally, a sly smile showing through his beard. "You promise not to tell a soul?"

"I guess so," Tommy said. "What kind of a secret?"

Beatty glanced down at the revolver, half-cocked the hammer, rotated the cylinder, uncocked the weapon, and returned it to his holster. As he had done the day before, he reached for his vest pocket and, displaying another silver dollar, he transferred the coin to his left hand and tossed it high. Again, the Colt flew into his hand. He cocked it and pulled the trigger, but there was no sound other than the click of the hammer on an empty chamber.

"Fetch it," Beatty said as he holstered the Colt.

Puzzled, Tommy moved a few steps and retrieved the coin. As he examined the dollar, his perplexity turned to confusion. This one showed a dent near the center. "I don't . . ."

Beatty opened the palm of his left hand and showed an undamaged silver dollar. "Never left my hand. Tossed a banged-up one. Always into the sun so folks can't see there's no hit."

It took a long while for Tommy to grasp the fraud. "Then . . . you ain't for real. You—"

"Fooled you?" Beatty cut in with a shrug. "Tricks of the trade." He reached again to his vest pocket and took out three more silver dollars, each flawed with an impact dent. "Oh, I've done it a few times, but it's always been a fluke. These . . . and the two you're holding . . . that's five of them that I've really shot out of the air."

"But you let on that you can do it every time!" Tommy declared. "That's cheating!"

"No, kid, that's making a living when you haven't got much else to offer," the man said. "I'm good, but I'm not the best. Now, I could hire out my gun for a killing. I'm plenty good enough for that. Or, at my age, I could put my weapons away and, maybe, herd cows or sweep out barns or saloons." He shook his head. "What I do is put on a show and entertain folks. If I fool them, so what? They believe they've seen something very special, so who's to say they didn't get their money's worth?"

"Why are you telling me?" Tommy asked.

"I don't rightly know," Beatty admitted. "Maybe because you're a good kid and . . . and sometimes, I just hanker to tell somebody."

"Since you done told me," Tommy asked gravely, "you still gonna put on your shooting show?"

Again, Beatty smiled. "I don't think you'll give me away."

" 'Cause of me in the horse trough?"

Beatty cocked his head and then nodded. "Well, there is that . . . maybe you *do* sort of owe me." He took a deep breath. "You and me, we've sort of gotten to know each other this morning." He paused. "So . . . what about it?"

"I won't tell. That's a promise."

Again, Beatty nodded. "I believe we're finished out here. How about getting back into town and having some breakfast?"

At two o'clock that afternoon, Will Beatty entertained thirty-nine men, women, and children for nearly an hour. Tommy Patterson, wearing his brand-new clothes and shoes, was in attendance, given permission by the saloon owner at the behest of Miss Ruby. At the edge of town, Beatty stood handsomely dressed all in black, with his pair of ivory-handled Navy Colts set off in a shiny black-leather holster belt. The early part of the show consisted of gun handling and fancy twirls of those revolvers—Beatty spinning them, separately and together, in and out of his holsters with an aloof air of disdainful expertise.

He called a young cowhand out of the crowd to take the part of a dastardly outlaw in a play-act situation. Supplying the cowhand with a supposedly loaded handgun, Beatty smartly disarmed him with a flick of his derby hat brim against the unfortunate young man's wrist. He continued to thrill the on-lookers with quick draws and skillful shots, demolishing fifteen glass bottles set at various distances. Nervous volunteers held playing cards at arm's length while Beatty blasted them from their hands. Astride his horse, he fired at five tin cans atop a line of fence posts, hitting all but one as he rode along at a casual pace.

For the grand finale, with a wink at Tommy, Beatty tossed five silver dollars into the glare of the sun and appeared to shoot each one out of the air, a feat that brought wild applause. As the show came to an end, he took off the derby and passed it among the crowd to collect a hesitant yet sizable donation from most of his audience.

On his way back to his chores at the saloon, young Patterson gave a small wave to Beatty who, turning his attention from surrounding admirers, returned an acknowledging nod of his head.

That was the last time Tommy saw or heard of the man.

Chapter Three

Tyler, Texas, 1863

There he is!"

On the loading dock, Tom turned at the shout to see the three rowdies rounding a back corner of the feed store building. Teenaged bullyboys, near his own age—he knew them well from their taunts and jeers whenever they spied him on the street. The name calling included "tramp," "trash," "riffraff," "bastard," "hobo," and a great many vulgar and obscene variations of the same sort. At each instance, there had been a mocking challenge, but the odds were always against him; four or five to attack, all at once. No fair-fight rules would be at hand; it would be brutal and hurtful. He had ducked the anticipated brawl at each encounter, although realizing that his avoidance surely emboldened them—his good sense was viewed as cowardice.

Tom hoisted a hundred-pound feed sack from a large stack beneath the dock cover and placed it among others on the unattended wagon parked next to the dock. He wiped the sweat from his brow, then walked to the edge of the dock and jumped down, ready to face his advancing antagonists. Today, under the hot midmorning sunlight, fisticuffs would be unavoidable, and he had known it was coming. The fact that there were only three to face probably gave him his best chance to avoid a serious beating.

Besides, he considered, *I've been looking forward to this.*

The leader of the trio, swaggering a few steps ahead of his cronies, was a trim, muscular, and handsome youth named

Jimmy Gordon, son of the wealthiest man in Tyler and brother to a pretty sister.

"You been talking to my sis, ain't ya?" Jimmy Gordon made the question an accusation.

"We've been talking, that's true," Tom admitted.

"Wilma wouldn't talk to trash like you," young Gordon snapped. "You . . . you . . . accosted her. That's the word, all right."

"She said 'Good morning' and I bid her the same, and we talked a while. Nothing more than that," Tom said, steeling himself for what was to come. "Wanted to know how I was getting along, and I told her I was just fine."

"You're a lying—"

Tom easily ducked the roundhouse blow that he had expected and punched hard into Gordon's midsection. As the surprised bully doubled over in gasping pain, Tom chose the better of the remaining two, a husky young brute. Judging the youth slow to think and slow to react, he jabbed his left fist three times into the youth's pudgy face and followed with a hooking right. With one bloodied and staggering, another still wheezing and trying to stand straight, Tom turned to the third of his assailants.

The youth ran.

Tom turned to young Gordon just in time to avoid another sweeping right hand aimed at his head. With the street-fighting savvy acquired in Texas village after village, Tom kicked a boot heel at his opponent's right kneecap. With a howl of pain, Gordon fell to the ground, hugging his knee with both hands, the fight gone out of him.

With his fists held high and cocked to strike, Tom whipped about to face his remaining antagonist. The battered young tough backed away and held up both hands, palms facing skyward in surrender. Tom shrugged his indifference and walked toward the loading dock.

"That was some fighting, youngster," said a man standing at the back door of the building. "That was a sight to be seen."

The voice came from his overall-clad employer, Cyrus Nagle, an amiable rail of a middle-aged, thin-haired man. Despite his lanky build, Nagle was wiry-strong, and he often helped Tom buck the heavy sacks and supplies coming in and going out of the store.

Tom gave an apologetic shrug, glanced back at his fallen foe, and then looked up at Nagle. "Warn't my idea, Mr. Nagle. They came a-looking, and I had to oblige."

Nagle reached a hand down to Tom's to assist him up onto the dock. "I knowed they been spoiling for it. Heard them calling you names once or twice." His face turned sober. "I 'spect it's gonna cause trouble for you."

"His old man?"

Nagle nodded. "He's a man of property, and he'll likely sic the law on you."

"Just fer giving his kid a licking?"

Again, the slender man nodded. "That brat of his ain't never been licked before." He paused. "I'll stick up fer ya, but you gotta know I ain't got the clout Old Man Gordon has."

In the back lot, Jimmy Gordon's two cronies had reappeared to help him to his feet. Placing the limping youngster between them, they assisted him to the corner of the building and moved out of sight.

"Why don't you take a rest for a bit?" Nagle suggested. "Finish loading the wagon a little later."

"I'm fine now," Tom responded. "Not a scratch on me."

With a nod of appreciation for his employer's support, Tom walked to the pile, lifted another sack, and carried it to the wagon bed.

"You got a choice here, sonny." The local magistrate, a middle-aged man with a thick head of black hair and a long, matching beard, directed his edict to young Tom. "Army or jail." He continued with just a hint of mockery: "For what you've done to Jimmy and his pals over there."

Tom glanced over his shoulder at the three youths, two of them scuffed and scraped. They were sitting with their fathers in the front-row chairs of a small courtroom. In the center of the six, Jimmy Gordon sat with his larger and much stouter father.

"Not quite fair, Arnold," Cyrus Nagle said as he rose to his feet. "I've been sitting here a spell waiting to tell Tom's side of it. Can I now?"

"Go ahead," the magistrate said.

"The three of them," Nagle said with a cock of his balding head toward the three battered youths, "they started it. They been laying for Tom . . . and they got better'n they could give." He paused. "That change anything?"

"Nope," the magistrate said. "He's still a vagrant, and that's cause enough." He turned toward Tom. "How old are you, sonny?"

"Somewheres around seventeen, I reckon," Tom said, then hastily added, "Your Honor."

"That's old enough for soldiering," came the response.

"Needs to go to jail!" the elder Gordon thundered.

"Don't push it, Hiram," the magistrate warned. "'Less you want Jimmy-boy marching off to war with him."

The hearing ended with Tom ordered to report on that very day to a visiting recruitment officer of the Confederate Army.

"Sorry, Tom," Nagle said as they walked from the building. "I'd have liked to have you full time, but I'm not that important in Tyler."

The three youths and their fathers were trailing behind, smirking in their victory, voices loud enough that the insults could be heard.

"Never mind them," Nagle continued. "Someday, some way, they'll each get their comeuppance. I've seen them that was spoiled in early life, and it ruins them for the rest of it." He paused and reached out his hand. "Take care of yourself in the war. Come see me sometime after it's over."

"Mr. Nagle?" Tom began as he shook the thin man's hand. "Can I ask a question?"

"Hope I can answer it."

"What's the war all about? I don't rightly know."

Nagle gave a tight smile and slowly shook his head. "North's got their way of life, we got ours."

"Which one's right?"

"Maybe neither one," Nagle said and drew a deep breath. "Good luck to you, young man."

Chapter Four

Spotsylvania Wilderness, Virginia, 1864

The spring day began with warm sunshine and a nearly cloudless sky. Minutes after first light, Tom's cavalry platoon was once again in the saddle. By midmorning, twenty-two other riders of his group were scattered as they moved through the dark and treacherous woodland. The ominous stillness of the shadowy woods marked a contrast to the distant sounds of crackling rifle fire and the occasional boom of cannons somewhere off to the east.

As a conscript, Tom had been assigned as a replacement soldier to a company of a Texas Cavalry Brigade fighting in Virginia. In the late fall of 1863, he and fifteen other young Texans had arrived near the small settlement of Spotsylvania and joined the Confederate Army of Northern Virginia.

During the winter, General Grant had amassed a battle force of more than one hundred thousand Union soldiers spread wide across Virginia. Now a massive offensive had begun, with the Army of the Potomac driving toward Richmond.

With blue-uniformed soldiers on the move through the forest, Confederate infantry and cavalry companies, including Tom's platoon, had been ordered into the gloomy wilds to repel the Union advance. Today the conflict continued in the dense woodland of what was known as the Spotsylvania Wilderness, a huge tangle of close-standing trees choked with thick, clawing underbrush.

"Stupid . . . this ain't no place for horses," Tom muttered softly as he and his companions urged their mounts through the thorny bushes.

23

The day before, Tom's squad, along with others, had struck at a long supply wagon train bringing provisions, equipment, ammunition, and weaponry to the great mass of Union soldiers advancing in this area. Streaking in with rebel yells, suffering no casualties of their own, they had succeeded in exploding two ammunition wagons and killing or injuring a dozen or more of the train's guards.

Today, as they moved slowly and warily through the forest, Tom held a massive Le Mat revolver at the ready in his right hand, another fully loaded pistol in his gun belt holster, and a carbine sheathed in his saddle scabbard.

The Le Mat revolver had been a death-related bonanza. In a skirmish with a Union cavalry patrol several days before, a fellow rebel, mortally wounded, had dropped the weapon and ridden a few yards away to die. After the body had been lashed to the man's horse for transport back to camp, Tom had returned to search for and retrieve the remarkable French-designed pistol.

In scarce supply, but popular in the Rebel ranks, it was a heavy, double-barreled handgun. An oversized cylinder that held nine .45 caliber balls fed the upper barrel, providing an extra three-shot advantage for Tom in close combat on horseback. A second benefit was a movable hammer that, when switched to a different position, allowed the discharge of a .20 gauge shotgun load from the lower barrel, a deadly surprise for near-range foes.

"Gonna kill my horse in them danged bramble patches," a nearby rider, Sam Gallagher, complained to Tom as they emerged at the same time into a small sunlit clearing. He was a young man of twenty, two years older than Tom. "I ain't never seen such a hell of a place," he continued.

"Mine's pretty tore up too," Tom said and leaned to examine the fresh bleeding scratches on the neck, shoulders, and then the withers and flanks of his dark chestnut stallion. Star, a nimble horse issued to Tom, had been so named for the forehead marking. Tom ran his hand in a caress on the side of Star's head.

The animal had been taken along with many others in a daring raid in an opening phase of the Chancellorville battle of a year ago. Twenty-five thousand Rebels had swooped out of this very forest into the bordering territory to capture four thousand Union soldiers who, at suppertime, were caught totally surprised and offered no resistance. The raid yielded a treasure trove of provisions for the underequipped Confederates. Food supplies, bridles and saddles, handguns and even a number of new Spencer repeating rifles were confiscated, along with plenty of much-needed powder and ball ammunition.

Today's a different go 'round, Tom reflected.

"Lincoln boys are thick as flies," Gallagher said. "They's everywhere, and it ain't easy to get a clear shot at 'em in this danged jungle."

Tom searched the surrounding woods, peering into the deep shadows. Enemy sightings were almost continuous; Union foot soldiers wending their way through the trees and thickets. Over the past hour, the sounds of combat had grown louder as the battle pushed deeper into this murky tract.

"We'd better get the hell outta here," Tom said, "if'n it ain't too late already."

At the sound of hooves, Tom quickly swung his Le Mat pistol to aim as a Confederate horseman rode into the clearing.

"Whoa there, youngster!" Sergeant Casey Beckman exclaimed, reining his sorrel mare to a standstill. "Others coming in behind me."

Matt lowered the handgun, and, seconds later, eighteen men of the platoon crowded their mounts into the clearing.

"Where's the Looie?" Tom asked, his eyes seeking their commanding officer. "And the others?"

"Lost, shot dead, or maybe already skedaddled outta this hole of Hades," Beckman responded, his tone dismissive. "We're pulling back, boys. We may be already cut off."

"Ain't we close on our own lines?" Gallagher asked.

"I don't rightly know," Beckman admitted. "Maybe a hundred feet back, maybe a mile."

"How about heading southwest?" one of the cavalrymen asked. "I don't hear no shooting that way."

Beckman shrugged. "I think we're being flanked. We can try that way, but we may have to fight our way out." He waved his hand. "Let's not waste time chawing about it . . . let's ride." He lowered his voice. "Walk your mounts slow and quiet, and no talking. If we're lucky, maybe we'll get clear 'fore the Yanks catch us out."

The cavalrymen guided their horses out of the clearing, and, moving as a group, they threaded their way in a southwestern direction. Tom held the reins in his left hand, using his knees to urge Star forward, letting the stallion find his way between tree trunks. Gun at the ready, he swept his eyes into the gloom of the forest, ready to fire at any enemy appearance. Star shied suddenly, hooves dancing, and Tom caught a glimpse of a copperhead slithering beneath a mossy log.

"How the hell did I get myself into this?" he muttered under his breath, and he gave Star a pat of reassurance as he urged the skittish stallion on.

Moving through the trees, Tom glanced from side to side and saw fleeting glimpses of blue-jacketed men moving closer through the forest. There were shouts of discovery as Tom's outfit was sighted, and the repeated smacks of rifle balls into nearby trees galvanized the Rebels into a cantering pace through the thick underbrush. Behind them, the activity seemed more of confusion and hasty shooting rather than coordinated proficiency. Tom and his fellow cavalrymen held their fire, not wasting ammunition on improbable targets.

After ten minutes of fearful flight, Sergeant Beckman raised his hand to halt the riders at the edge of a long, wide swath of open land. Tom and the others moved their horses close together, some men darting anxious glances back into the forest.

"We gonna cross, Sarge?" Gallagher asked, pointing at the extensive exposed meadow. "Out in the open?"

The sergeant gave a nod to his right. "There's a creek over that way, how deep I don't know . . . and we'd be easy pickings getting caught in the middle of the water." He turned his eyes left and surveyed the distant curve of trees that ringed the broad clearing. "We could stay in the woods and circle 'round to the other side or—"

"Or why not make a dash across?" Gallagher cut in. "I'm for it! I ain't staying in these spooky woods any longer than necess—"

"Take the long way round, Sarge," Tom interrupted. "We're dead out there without cover."

"I don't know, kid," Beckman said. "They're right behind us." Suddenly, without another word, he dug his boot heels into his horse's sides, prodding the mare into a gallop into the meadow.

Then, as one, the remaining members of the platoon whipped and kicked their horses into a frantic pursuit, each horseman urging his mount to a greater speed.

Tom rode wide of the rest and bent low over Star's neck, expecting rifle fire as his stallion raced over the meadowland. Sergeant Beckman's horse was two lengths ahead of the following platoon, all riders on their mounts at full gallop across the wide field.

They were over halfway across when the first shell from a Napoleon 12-pounder shrieked and blasted the ground behind Beckman's horse and ahead of the rest of the riders. The front-running animals in the clustered group slid to a stop, reared, and bucked in terror, throwing their riders from their saddles, then bolting away, right and left. A second shell whistled and exploded in the center of the churning confusion.

Tom was nearly unhorsed by the shock wave. He heard the whistle of shrapnel cutting through the air about him, but he felt nothing touch him. He glanced first at his body and next to his horse to confirm their mutual survival. Then he looked at the cloud of black smoke, now dissipating, drifting up and away to reveal the bloody consequence.

The sights and sounds of the carnage seared Tom's soul. Surviving riders, in shock and turmoil, milled around the dreadful slaughter, trying to control their frightened steeds.

Tom's first impulse was to ride to help those injured comrades, but another shell dropped near the site of the slaughter. Tom wheeled his horse away, self-preservation overcoming his concern. He spurred Star into a gallop toward the deep forest ahead. The other cavalrymen, now wary of the lethal danger of staying close together, spread apart and rode furiously for the shelter of the woods ahead.

Tom breathed a sigh of relief as he slowed Star a few yards from the edge of the forest and the promise of safety in the surrounding trees. The relief was premature—a hail of bullets sped from that very refuge and, immediately, he felt Star falter. He swung from the saddle and threw himself to the ground as the animal slowed to a stagger, front legs buckling as the wheezing stallion fell forward and rolled onto its side.

Hating himself, Tom crawled to the wounded horse to use Star as a shield from the continuing fire. He stretched his hand over the dying stallion to retrieve his carbine. He looked around and saw, several yards to his right, Sergeant Beckman lying flat in a shallow hollow. Close by, two gray-clad bodies lay still, and other fellow cavalrymen were on foot, crouching low, trying to find protective hillocks or depressions. A couple of men, like himself, were hunkered behind dead horses while surviving animals were running free in different directions.

Tom felt the last shuddering breath go out of Star, and he laid his rifle barrel across the body. He took a quick glance behind him and saw a solid line of blue uniformed soldiers edging out into the open field. Although an advancing danger, they were too far away for his immediate concern.

"Into the trees, boys!" Beckman shouted. "Ain't good, but it's better'n out here."

"Just as bad in there!" came a shout that Tom recognized as Sam Gallagher's.

"Go in shooting!" Beckman shouted. "Only chance, only chance!"

Tom pulled the trigger of his carbine again and again, aiming blindly into the trees and underbrush fifteen yards in front of him, hearing a fusillade of gunfire from his comrades. He tossed the empty rifle aside, rose to a crouch, and, with the Remington revolver in his right hand and the Le Mat in his left, he charged forward. He felt a bullet buzz an inch past his right cheek and another tick at the cloth on his left shoulder. He fired the Remington repeatedly as he dashed toward the forest, tossed it away when empty, and transferred the Le Mat into his right hand. Then he was in the woods and crashed into a cluster of incredulous Yankee riflemen.

As they swung their weapons toward him, he fired the Le Mat as fast as he was able, five of his nine shots striking down soldiers. The two unharmed bluebellies grinned at the click on the Le Mat's empty chamber. Standing side by side, deliberate in their movements, they aimed their Spencers at Tom.

Tom flipped the hammer to the lower position and triggered the shotgun charge into the torsos of the surprised pair. As they fell lifeless, he whirled, first to his right, then to his left, now with an empty handgun and no ammunition. He peered into the gloom of the forest, sure he would see more of the enemy and, in disbelief, did not.

Emotion surged through him, his eyes welling with tears, and a choked sob escaped. He drew several deep breaths, wiped his eyes with the right sleeve of his uniform jacket, and walked slowly forward, not knowing what now he should or could do. He trudged on until he came to the bank of a small river tributary. The water was hued with blood, and there were Union- and Confederate-uniformed bodies on both banks, a few lying facedown in the shallows of the stream. He heard only the soft, rippling sound of the brook's flow close by, muted gunfire at a distance. He stood in the hushed sanctuary of the forest next to a fallen log. Thinking of nothing better to do, he sat upon it and waited for whatever might come.

Several minutes went by.

"Patterson?" It was a soft call, almost a whisper.

Tom sighed. "I ain't no ghost, Sam."

Gallagher stepped from behind a tree and, behind him,

Sergeant Beckham hopped into view, helped on either side by two cavalrymen. They eased him to the ground as eight surviving, dispirited Rebels emerged, one by one, from the woods.

"We've got to give it up, boys," Beckham said to the gathering as he pressed a crimson rag against a bloody wound in his right leg. "We got no choice."

Chapter Five

Spotsylvania Wilderness, 1864

Exhausted, Tom stumbled, stopped running, and leaned against a tree. He gulped for air, pulling long wheezing inhalations into his labored lungs. He rested for another five minutes and waited for his strength to return.

"Soldier?"

Tom turned, relieved to see a gray uniform, not a blue one.

"Soldier?" the Confederate junior officer repeated. "Where's your unit?"

Tom shook his head. "Shot to hell, sir," he said in a hoarse whisper. "Maybe all gone."

The officer regarded him for a few moments and then gave a sidewise motion of his head. "Join up with our company back there."

Tom managed a salute that the officer returned before briskly striding away. Drawing another deep breath, Tom looked down at his shabby uniform, ripped in many places from his dash through the undergrowth thorns and stained with the mud and slime of the places where he had fallen. Worse, the uniform was spattered with the blood of his murdered companions, men shot to death by their Union captors.

I surely look a sorry sight, he thought to himself.

His forage cap gone, he hand-combed his blond, tangled, and dirty hair in a futile effort to better its appearance, and then walked through the trees to pause at the crest of a ridge. He stood for a while and looked down at a large Confederate Army battle-staging site in an open field.

It was a hub of frenzied activity, with a horde of gray-uniformed soldiers rushing at their precombat preparations. There were men unloading wagons, helping mules pull howitzers over the rough ground, and squatting and kneeling to load rifles and muskets. There were pockets of temporary rest and repose: young Rebels gathered around small cooking fires, eating their skimpy meals, and battle-weary warriors sat on the grass, a few sleeping through the tumult surrounding them.

Tom walked down the slope into the military camp and looked for a commissioned officer or noncom. As he moved through the bustling activity, he spotted one of each standing at the edge of the traffic flow. The officer—a tall, trim lieutenant—was speaking earnestly to a strongly built subordinate who wore sergeant stripes on his uniform sleeve. Both men seemed focused and confident, the officer making thrusting gestures toward the Union-infested woods. The sergeant nodded in agreement most times, with only an occasional dissent.

Tom walked toward the two men and came to a stop at a respectful ten-foot distance, close enough to be noticed but not near enough to intrude. He stood facing them and waited as the pair continued their conversation.

Finally, the officer took notice. "Can we do something for you, soldier?" he asked with curt authority.

Tom stepped forward, came to attention, and saluted. "Permission to speak, sir."

"Granted," the officer said with a return salute. "What is it, son?"

"Separated from my unit in battle, sir," Tom said. "Forward officer told me to report here for reassignment."

"Tell you who to report to?" the lieutenant asked.

Tom shook his head. "No, sir. Whoever'll have me, I 'spect he meant."

The sergeant glanced to his superior who gave him a quick, permissive nod. "Cavalry?" the noncom questioned. A husky, red-haired man in his early thirties, he carried his authority with size, muscle, and assurance. "What happened to your outfit?"

"Captured and executed," Tom replied. "Most of 'em killed, I reckon."

"Executed?" the officer broke in. "How do you mean?"

"We didn't want to give up, sir, but when we did, a damned Yankee captain started the killing. He shot our sergeant first; then shot the others in the head, one by one, right down the line. Them of us that still could, we run for it," Tom said bitterly. "They was firing after us as we run . . . and I guess I got lucky. Can't say about the others."

Neither the officer nor the sergeant responded immediately, their faces turned hard at Tom's account of the atrocity.

Finally, the lieutenant looked Tom up and down, and a slight smile played across his face. "Well, soldier, you may not have been shot, but from the rips and tears in that uniform, you must've run into a wildcat or two."

"I was scooting through a passel of them thorny bushes, sir," Tom explained solemnly. "Surely felt like wildcats."

The officer turned his head away to hide a wider smile.

"Before you was running through them prickly bushes," the sergeant questioned, "did you do any real fighting?"

Tom nodded.

"Do any damage to the other side?" the sergeant persisted.

Again, Tom nodded. "Think I done a goodly share."

"Get him outfitted and give him something better to wear, Ben," the officer said to the noncom. "I'm Lieutenant Kepner." He bobbed his head to his subordinate. "This is Sergeant Benjamin Haley . . . he'll be your new NCO 'til we can get you back with your own unit."

"I surely thank you for that, sir," Tom said.

"What's your name, boy?" Sergeant Haley asked.

"Patterson, Sergeant, Private Tom Patterson."

"Well, Private Tom Patterson, follow me," Sergeant Haley said as he beckoned Tom forward. "We'll see if we can't put you back together."

"Boys, hear now!" Sergeant Haley announced as he and Tom, now wearing a serviceable, near-new uniform, came out of the night into the firelight. They approached the cluster of twenty soldiers of the rifle platoon circled around a low-flame campfire in an earthen hollow. "This here is young Tom Patterson, going to join up with us foot soldiers 'til we find a way to send him back to his Texas cavalry."

"We already heard . . . you the yellow-bellied rabbit that run out on your buddies?"

Tom shifted his eyes across the campfire to the standing man who had spoken the derisive words, a brawny man in a badly dyed butternut jacket that poorly served him as a uniform tunic. The insult brought guffaws from three soldiers who sat on the ground at the feet of the grizzled speaker. There was a noticeable gap separating the majority of the soldiers from the powerfully built antagonist and his toadies.

"Shut your mouth, Biggs," Haley said in a loud voice. Then the noncom turned to Patterson. "Sorry, son, but there's usually a sour apple in every peck." He nodded to Biggs. "He's ours . . . best steer clear of him."

Tom nodded without comment.

"We keep hoping a Yankee ball will get him," a seated soldier nearby, a corporal, said in a low voice. "Sarge is right; he'll go for you just 'cause you're new."

"Thanks for the warning," Tom replied to the corporal, and he gave another nod to Sergeant Haley.

"Settle in. This is your new outfit 'til we getcha back with your regiment," Haley said. "You a good shot?"

"Passable," Tom replied.

Haley nodded, turned, and walked away as Tom propped his newly issued Enfield rifle against a tree and placed his battered haversack next to the stock. He squatted and then seated himself next to the sympathetic soldier.

"Corporal John Meriweather," the soldier introduced himself and offered his hand. "You'll be in my squad."

"Tom Patterson, Corporal."

"What's your outfit?"

"Fourth Cavalry."

"Biggs said it; we *did* hear. True what happened to your bunch? Slaughtered?"

Tom nodded.

"Murdering bluebellies," Meriwether said with a slow shake of his head. "Born nasty, I guess." He nodded across the campfire to Biggs, who was still glaring at Tom. "Although I do 'spect a man on our side like Biggs would do something mean same as them."

Tom turned his head and locked his eyes with Biggs in a steady, unyielding stare. For a long time, neither man looked away. Finally, the big man uttered an oath and sat down with his cronies.

"You look like you can take care of yourself," Meriweather said. "That's the kind Biggs likes to take on, figgers himself cock of the walk, I guess." He chuckled and looked down at his slender frame. "He don't much bother with them of us that's on the scrawny side."

Tom shrugged. "He's the least of my worries."

Meriweather considered Tom's statement for a while before he nodded his head in understanding. "General Longstreet's bringing his army up from Gordonsville, may be here by tomorrow," the young corporal said. "You can bet it'll be a different story for them Lincoln boys from now on."

"Should've been here yesterday . . . today might've gone different," Tom said as he stretched out, looked up at the stars for a few minutes, and then closed his eyes seeking sleep.

"On your feet, on your feet!" Sergeant Haley shouted, walking to each man sleeping on the ground surrounding the cold fire site. He kicked the boots of a couple of soldiers slow to awaken as he moved through the faint starlight of the predawn that filtered through a wind-swirled, smoky haze. "We're moving out, moving out fast. Get your gear and get going."

"What the hell's that smell?" Meriweather said as he sat up, his head raised, sniffing the air. "Smoke?"

Haley paused to stand over him. "Cannon fire lit up the woods. We got a forest fire nearby . . . bad 'un."

"How bad?" Tom said as he rose to his feet.

"Caught soldiers on both sides, burned 'em to death 'fore they could clear out of where they was sleeping." He kicked Meriweather's boot. "It's coming down on us, so hurry."

The soldiers were now all standing, stuffing their light blankets and personal belongings into their haversacks, several beginning to cough from the intensifying fog of acrid smoke, a near panic showing in their frantic actions.

"Hurry up, boys," Haley said loudly. "We move in two minutes. You're on your own if you ain't ready."

"Which way is it coming, Sarge?" The question came from a slender silhouetted soldier a few feet away.

"Look for yourself," Haley told him.

As one, the entire group turned their heads, seeking and finding an orange flush flickering over the trees to the west.

In less than two minutes, the soldiers had the haversacks strapped to their backs and their weapons in their hands.

"Wind's behind it and blowing pretty hard," Haley said. "We're joining up with Lieutenant Kepner and the rest of the company. We're moving southeast and try to get around it. Let's go!"

"It don't look good," Meriweather said as he fell in beside Tom, his eyes turned toward the glow now brightening in the sky. "No, sir. It don't look good at all."

"We've got to turn south," Tom said, his gaze fastened on the approaching forest fire. "There's water that way." He hurried to catch Haley. "Sarge, we can't make it this way."

"We got orders, Patterson," Haley said gruffly. "Fall back. We're meeting up with our officer."

"It's coming too fast," Tom persisted. "We're heading right into it."

For a few moments, the noncom continued walking, although he too, was now studying the sky, seeing flames now flaring above the treetops. He paused and held up his hand, bringing the column to a halt behind him. "You're right," he said to Tom. "Kepner's probably already cooked."

"There's a little brook about a quarter mile south," Tom told him. "I know 'cause I came a-running from that way."

"How deep?" Haley wanted to know, anxiety now apparent.

"Three, four feet maybe," Tom answered. "We can dip under and maybe stay alive."

"You know the way—let's go!"

Turning to the south, the men of the platoon began to struggle through the close-clustered trees, shoving their bodies through the clawing bramble bushes, stepping over and stumbling on fallen limbs, forcing their way through the heavy growth of shrubs that blocked their tight paths between the tree trunks.

Behind them, the fire burst into full view, flames leaping and swallowing the pines. Tongues of fire snaked through the underbrush and torched the base of tree after tree, igniting each into a blazing pillar.

The sight of the wind-driven, pursuing inferno brought instant fear to the soldiers, who shed their backpacks and rifles as they ran for their lives.

"We ain't gonna make it!" Meriweather screamed as he tripped and nearly fell. "It's coming too fast."

"Shut up and run!" Haley commanded as he snaked his way through the trees and then turned toward Tom, who was running nearby. "How far?"

"We're almost there!" Tom shouted as he ran.

With the firestorm right behind them, eleven of the men of the platoon reached the slant of the riverbank and dashed into the stream. High, howling screams of pain came from those too slow to outrace the flaming hell that caught and engulfed them.

Tom, Meriweather, and Haley flung themselves into a shallow pool, and, glancing back at the flames now racing up and crowning the trees on the riverbank, they dove in and ducked under the surface.

Tom, thankful for the three feet of water to shield him from the fiery whirlwind that roared above, held his breath. Rising to breathe would be fatal. Blistering hot air sucked into his lungs would be a searing, agonizing death. He rolled over on his back, looking up through the water at the canopy of fire that arched over the stream. Knowing he could hold his breath no longer, he paddled near the bank, seeking some area where the overhead flames seemed not so fierce. He reached for and slathered his face with mud, pulled his shirt over his nose, and inched it barely above the surface.

The air was hot, very hot, but it was borderline breathable, and, before it worsened, Tom sank again beneath the cool water. Again and again, with long periods of breath holding, he repeated the process. From his underwater point of view, he watched the progress of the fire above, seeing the flames eating away the limbs, many blazing and falling into the stream and raising great plumes of steam.

At long last, he ventured to bring his head above water and looked at the blackened forest on either side of the tributary. Thick clouds of smoke hung in a choking mist just a foot above the river's surface. Another head rose, and it was Sergeant Haley, with a mud-caked face and, above his forehead, hair nearly all scorched away.

"You okay, Sarge?" Tom managed to ask before a fit of coughing rendered him speechless.

The noncom nodded and then gave a sidewise cast of his head to Meriweather's fire-scorched body floating partially submerged a few feet away.

Tom looked down the river and saw one more head arise amid other floating cadavers.

"Biggs, wouldn't you know," Tom managed to whisper.

Chapter Six

Spotsylvania Wilderness, 1864

With the sun high over the battlefield, there came a lull in the fighting. The crackling of rifle fire diminished to the report of an occasional shot, and the sounds of the heavy artillery bombardment ceased.

Sergeant Haley, his uniform tattered and discolored, rolled to his side and removed his cap. He tenderly touched the top of his head, exploring his scalp, where the fire had created a large, blistered bald spot. "Raised up outta the water right under a danged burning limb," he muttered. "Stupid of me."

"That hurt?" Tom asked. "Still pretty sore looking."

"Not too bad now, just kinda like a sunburn," Haley responded. "Never had me a sunburn up there." Haley's hands roamed over the uneven stubble of what remained of his red hair. "Reckon it'll grow back?"

"You'll be a funny-looking jasper if it don't," a nearby soldier said and followed it with a cackle. "Pardon my saying so, Sarge, but you surely are a mighty sorry sight."

"More a scary sight than a sorry one," Lieutenant Kepner said with a sly grin. "Even so, bluebellies get a look at our scarecrow, they'll run for their lives." He chuckled. "Stick your head up, Ben, and send them packing up north."

Nine soldiers, a squad assembled from what was left of Tom's platoon, lay prone behind a grassy ridge in an open field surrounded by the forest. Each man was keeping his head down, well aware that a sizable number of Union soldiers were behind a similar ridge, no more than forty yards away. Tom, Sergeant Haley, and Lieutenant Kepner were huddled close at one end of the line while, to their temporary gratification, the surly Biggs lay at the other.

The three survivors had emerged from the river and made their way through the pockets of persisting flames and the choking smoke of the smoldering woodland into the welcome greenery of the untouched forest. They had wandered for more than a mile until they stumbled upon the main body of their army. To their pleasant surprise, they had found their platoon officer and the remaining members of their decimated unit.

The general command of the army division, with no sympathetic regard for their fiery ordeal and consequent casualties, had immediately ordered the men back into the unending battle. For five exhausting days, they had alternately advanced and retreated in skirmishes against the enemy. Casualties were horrendous for the opposing armies, and neither North nor South could claim victory.

"Hey, Rebs!" came a distant shout. "Reckon we can have a little bit of a truce? Stop the shooting long enough for a little lunch?"

Sergeant Haley cast an inquiring look to Lieutenant Kepner. After a few moments, the officer shrugged and nodded.

"You honor bound to do the same?" Haley called.

"Fine with us!" It was the same voice. "You boys got enough to eat? If ya don't, come on over and we'll share!"

"Kind of you, but we got ourselves some Virginia ham steaks, green beans cooked in good ol' bacon grease, corn bread and butter . . . all we can eat!" Sergeant Haley responded.

"Sure ya have, Reb! More likely it's hard old field corn and wormy biscuits."

The taunt was very nearly the truth. Hunger was a constant in their ranks. Infrequent meals prepared by the quartermaster cooks were skimpy at best and, every day, Southern soldiers with growling stomachs foraged for wild onions and bush berries for meager nourishment.

"Where you from, Yank?" Haley asked, changing the subject.

"Proud state of Maryland!" the voice answered.

"Why, hell, boy! That's right next door to the South!" Haley called. "That ought to make you just like us! You outta be soldiering over here, not with them Yankee scalawags!"

"Don't see it that way, Reb . . . but it's a pure fact, I *do* have some kin living down there in your secess country." The voice was friendlier now, the earlier sarcasm missing.

"Now, you see there!" Haley declared. "For all you know, you might be shooting at your very own folks. How'd you feel about that?"

"Well, friend, even be that so, it maybe don't much matter. You Rebs are making a good fight of it, but we figure the war is just about winding down . . . and that's got to be a blessing no matter what side we're fighting on." There was a pause. "Let's just say a prayer that we both make it home safe and sound!"

Haley raised his head to answer, then lowered it and gave a shrug. "Sound's like a right nice feller over there . . . that is, for a bluebelly."

"I 'spect he's right about the war," Tom said softly. "Things just ain't going so good no more."

"That'll be enough of that kind of talk!" Lieutenant Kepner spoke with crisp authority although there was little of a reprimand in his tone. With a sigh, he threw a sharp look at Haley. "Let's leave 'em to their lunch time, Ben. No more of your jawing back and forth."

"Yes, sir," Haley said and turned away. On his stomach, he heaved his body higher, lifting his head to peek over the crest of the ridge, then raised his right hand and waved.

Suddenly, the loud report of a nearby rifle shattered the tranquility of the woodland.

"Who the hell?" Lieutenant Kepner exclaimed, his head whipping to his right. "Biggs?"

At the end of the line, a fine haze of powder smoke curled into the sky from Biggs' rifle. He lifted his eyes to meet his officer's glare and a smirk appeared on his face. Then he turned his attention to reloading his Enfield.

"What happened?" Tom asked, bewildered.

Haley slid down the embankment, his face nearly as ruddy as his blistered scalp. "That fellow who was doing the talking," the sergeant said in fury. "He was just waving back."

"Damn you, Rebs!" came a new voice from yards away. "Damn the murdering lot of you!"

A barrage of rifle fire began—a constant hail of bullets pounding into their protective grassy mound, many shots buzzing overhead, some ricocheting into their very midst, dangerously close. Tom and his fellow soldiers hunkered down, not daring to rise into the furious fusillade to return fire. A few minutes later, the war resumed with all its ferocity; distant gunfire chattered in the surrounding woods, artillery shells whistled overhead and then fell to explode near their position.

"Biggs," Tom whispered, his face pressed into the grass. "Wouldn't you know."

Chapter Seven

The door opened as two Union officers stepped out into the courthouse corridor and started walking slowly down the hall toward Tom Patterson and Benjamin Haley, who were seated on a wooden bench. The older of the two officers, Colonel Neville Slade, was the prosecuting attorney, a judge advocate. Tom well remembered the second man, Wallace Noland, who was now a captain, as a horrified junior officer at the Spotsylvania woods murders.

"Don't look good," Tom said in a low voice to his former sergeant. "The way they're walking, it don't look like it went well at all." He and Haley rose to their feet as the officers stopped in front of them.

"Gentlemen," Colonel Slade said. "It isn't exactly what we wanted, but it isn't all bad either."

"They let the bastard go?" Tom asked.

Both officers shook their heads.

"Like he said, Mr. Patterson," the junior officer added a comment. "To some degree, justice *was* served, but I'll let Colonel Slade explain."

"The defense held that Captain Noland's testimony was a case of jealous retaliation against his former commanding officer," Slade told them. "A couple of men from Captain Portee's company held that your Confederate soldiers were killed in action and that no atrocity was committed."

"They lied!" Tom exclaimed.

The colonel nodded. "It was *your* testimony, Mr. Patterson, that made a difference. Your description of the event gave

43

considerable credence to Captain Noland's account of what really happened on that day."

"What's that mean?" Haley asked. "Considerable credence?"

"Patterson's statement, as an independent eyewitness, lent a significant credibility to the murder charges," the military attorney said. "It matched Captain Noland's account and cast a great shadow on the story that Captain Portee told of the incident . . . and it *did* help that the witnesses for the defense were not very good on the stand."

"Thanks to the good work of Colonel Slade," Noland interjected. "He really took them apart. He caught both of them in one contradiction after another."

The colonel smiled his appreciation for the compliment, and then his face became solemn. "Unfortunately, your testimony as a former enemy combatant was a bit of a nullifying factor."

"That mean they didn't believe me?" Tom's face twisted in anger.

"Oh, they believed you," Slade hastened to say. "It just went against their grain to have to accept the truth from a member of the Army of the Confederacy."

"They ain't going to punish him?" Tom asked. "He's getting away with what he's done?"

The senior officer shook his head. "No, he won't hang, and by rights he really should . . . but he *will* be stripped of his rank and dishonorably discharged. He's a proud man, and he'll carry this disgrace for the rest of his life."

"It ain't enough!" Tom said. "*They* don't kill him, *I* will!"

"I couldn't blame you," Slade said without rebuke. "Keep in mind, however, that it would make *you* the victim once again. Take revenge, and it would be *you* swinging at the end of a rope."

"He's right, Tom," Haley said, placing a hand on his young companion's shoulder. "Maybe for a man like that, everybody knowing what he did . . . shame is gonna be worse than dying."

"For what it's worth, Mr. Patterson, I'm so very sorry for what happened," Captain Noland said. "It was my fault for not seeing it coming and not being quick enough to stop it." He paused. "I'll carry those mistakes for the rest of my life."

"You ain't to blame, sir," Tom said. "I saw you knock his gun away when he was aiming at me."

"I wish I could've saved more of your fellow soldiers."

The two officers thanked Tom for his testimony and, with courteous nods, turned and walked away.

"Let's get out of here, kid," Haley said. "I ain't too comfortable in a Yankee courthouse."

Donning charity-given coats and stocking caps, they descended the stairs to the building's entry doors and walked out into the pale sunlight of a hazy January sky. Union soldiers were everywhere in sight and only a few threadbare gray uniform jackets were glimpsed. Most of those garments were the only coats retained by impoverished, defeated men to ward off the damp Virginia cold. Nearly all of the former Rebels on the streets of Norfolk walked with their heads down, doing whatever the vanquished could do to exist under the harsh conditions visited on them by their victors.

A small article in a Richmond paper concerning the upcoming court martial of Captain Edward Portee of the Union Army had caught Tom's rapt attention. Despite an initial rebuff by a hostile military bureaucracy, Tom's persistent demand to testify had, finally, been welcomed by the prosecutors.

Before and after their discharge, Tom's former sergeant had become his friend and mentor. He and his older companion had become close during the waning months of the war, a camaraderie born of codependency during times of great danger. The pair and most of their new squad, including Biggs, had survived the battle of the Spotsylvania wilderness and made it safely through subsequent lesser skirmishes. After Lee's surrender in the spring of 1865, both Tom and Haley had remained in Virginia, trying to survive as homeless, destitute veterans. The two of them had vied with former comrades for menial jobs: cleaning stables, washing dishes, loading trash and garbage on foul-smelling wagons—whatever low-pay tasks they could find and obtain.

"You've got no family to go home to?" Tom asked.

Haley shook his head. "No wife, no kids. Old folks, they's both gone. They was sharecroppers, and there warn't no house. Got a no-good brother somewheres, but I don't claim him—or him me."

As they walked along the sidewalk, they were jostled and deliberately bumped by a throng of blue-uniformed soldiers who challenged them with mocking stares and then moved on with contemptuous smiles and raucous laughter.

"Ever since that actor feller shot Lincoln, seems like they think we was *all* in on it," Ben said, stepping aside to avoid an intended collision.

"I'm thinking we gotta get out of this part of the country," Tom declared, seething with anger as they strode along the street. "I ain't gonna be ground down under some damned Yankee's heel!"

"Ain't gonna be easy. Getting anywhere, it'll hafta be on shank's mare," Haley argued. "We got no money. Not even enough for a meal today, much less any wherewithal for road traveling." He sighed and looked down at his feet. "Wherever we go, we'll be walking in these sorry-looking brogans with holes in the soles big as goose eggs. We've ain't got no where-withal for a train or stagecoach . . . not even a red cent to buy a broke-down mule to carry us."

"That being so, we'll still head west," Tom said with determination. "We can hitch rides on wagons and maybe rely on good folks to share their eatings."

Haley shuddered. "We was poor, but I never begged in my life."

Tom cast a sidewise glance at Haley and grinned. "I've done it *all* my life. We got no choice."

"Where out West you planning to go?" Haley asked. "Texas?"

"Maybe, 'though I'm pretty much shut of that," Tom said without enthusiasm. "There's other places I'd like to see." He frowned in thought as he marched along. "How about Colorado?"

"Whooee!" Haley crowed. "Now, that's a far piece for walking to."

"Or hitching to," Tom reminded him.

"Or hitching to," Haley repeated dutifully. "And what are we gonna do once we get there?"

"Gotta be better than here. Maybe we can work some cattle."

"I don't rightly know that line of work."

"You know how to ride," Tom told him. "That's the main thing. I can teach ya how to rope and what else you need to know."

"We get there dead broke, how we gonna buy us horses to ride? Tell me that."

They continued to walk, moving out of the business district and onto a street lined on either side by warehouses, sheds, barns, corrals, and cattle pens. When they reached the city's edge, they turned off the road and walked single file along a path that wound through trees along a meandering creek. After trudging for a quarter mile, they came over a rise into a clearing where a cluster of tattered tents, shabby bedrolls, and frayed blankets served as a forlorn encampment for a gathering of two dozen raggedly clothed men.

Tom and Ben hurried down the slope to join a group of five unkempt former Rebels who, in the remnants of their butternut-colored uniforms, were warming themselves around a small fire. Nods were given as spiritless greetings, but no words were spoken, no inquiries as to jobs, coins, or vittles found.

Tom moved close to the fire and stooped down to lean into the warmth, rubbing his hands to restore circulation in his cold-stiffened fingers. After a few minutes, he rose and walked a few feet to a space of earth between two men lying prone, not sleeping, but awake and curled into their frayed blankets.

"Who's got mine?" Tom questioned brusquely. He turned to the man on the blanket to his left. "You said you'd watch it."

"Just borrowed it while you was gone," a voice said from behind him.

Tom turned to see a slight young man removing a wool blanket from over his head and shoulders as he came forward. "Warn't stealing it, mister." Hatless and wearing only a thin shirt and denim trousers, he offered the blanket to Tom.

"Keep it on for a while longer," Tom said grudgingly. "Got to have it back come nightfall."

The young man nodded his gratitude and quickly re-wrapped the blanket around himself. "I thank you, mister . . . I'll wear it for just a minute or two more."

"How are you sleeping?" Tom asked.

The young man, not much more than a boy, canted his head toward one of the tents. "They let me sleep in there part of the night." He looked down, ashamed. "Laying up close to each other to keep warm."

"Ain't nothing wrong about that," Ben said. "Body heat'll keep you alive." He paused. "What's your name, soldier?"

"Jason Fuller . . . but they calls me Jace."

"Well, Jace, when's the last you had something in your belly?" Ben wanted to know.

"Three days . . . going on four."

Ben threw a quick glance to Tom and then looked back to the young man. "Maybe we can find us some furry critter to eat out there in the woods," he said, pointing to the surrounding trees. "Got me a pistol hid out with a couple shots left." He looked again to Tom. "We get anything . . . maybe we can share."

Tom nodded.

"Want me to come with you?" Jace asked.

Ben shook his head. "Stay close to the fire. Stay warm."

Tom and Ben turned from the young man and, unhurriedly, ambled toward the nearby stand of trees. Once out of sight, Ben led the way a short distance to the broken stump of a fallen elm. Bending, he brushed away a covering of leaves from the nearby log and reached his hand into a space beneath it. He withdrew a cloth-wrapped object and undid it to disclose a Remington revolver. He sat on the log and examined the weapon, then nodded his satisfaction at its condition.

"Former comrades in arms, they may be," he said as he rose and stuck the Remington inside his belt. "I 'spect they'd knock me over the head to get hold of this . . . so I hid it."

Tom chuckled. "Didn't even tell me you was carrying."

"Lucky I got a coat where you couldn't see."

"Yankee patrol catch you with it, they'll slap you silly."

"Well, it may be all that's 'tween us and empty bellies," Ben said. "Let's see if we can't potshot us a tasty rabbit, possum, or even a squirrel."

"Long as it ain't no skunk."

Shadows were deepening as Tom and Ben walked along a wide path in the woods on their way back to the camp. Tom carried a large hare by the legs in his right hand—the rabbit a relatively clean kill by Ben's accurate pistol shot. Their conversation was, for a change, cheerful with the anticipation of a decent meal.

Suddenly, they stopped still at the sudden eruption of loud shouts and excited outcries blended with the pounding of horses' hooves and occasional gunshots straight ahead.

Tom looked to his companion. "What in the name of—"

"Flush-out raid!" Ben cut in. "Damn them Yankees!"

They moved forward to the edge of the clearing to stand and observe in the shadows of the woods. A dozen blue-uniformed riders, screaming curses and yelling their hatred, were charging their horses back and forth through the encampment. With deliberation, firing their handguns into the air, they guided their mounts over the tents with disregard to anyone inside. They rode through the small fires, scattering the coals and knocking cooking pots yards away. The Rebel vagrants were helpless against the onslaught, doing their best to dodge the galloping animals, some slammed to the ground to be trampled by other riders.

"Look there!" Ben said, pointing.

Tom's eyes followed the direction just in time to see a bluecoat riding in pursuit of the hard-running young Jason Fuller. Overtaking him, the Union soldier reached out and down to club his victim repeatedly about the head with the revolver in his hand. As young Jace fell to his knees on the ground, the soldier circled his mount, clearly intending to continue the beating.

"Leave him alone, damn you!" Tom shouted.

The Federal soldier reined his horse to a halt, his eyes looking straight toward the woods.

"Now you've done it!" Ben muttered. "And he's a-coming!"

The soldier held his revolver high, wheeled his horse, and spurred it toward the two men.

Ben drew the Remington, cocked it, and aimed.

"Save your last load, Ben," Tom said softly. "He's mine." He stepped to one side, moved back into the woods, and motioned for Ben to move in the opposite direction, to leave an open path into the thicket between them.

He waited until the soldier's horse charged into trees, the rider looking right and left for a target. As the animal pounded close, Tom sprang from concealment and swung the rabbit hard at the startled soldier's head.

The blow knocked the rider from his saddle, his revolver flying from his hand as he arced into the bordering trees, slamming his head against one as he fell to the ground. The horse galloped a few more yards and then slowed to a standstill.

"Any more coming?" Tom asked in a soft voice.

"Don't see none," Ben said as he emerged from the shade. He walked toward Tom, bending down to pick up the Yank's Army Colt revolver. "Is he dead?"

Tom walked to the motionless body and leaned close. "Still breathing," he said. "Maybe he'll be okay."

"Don't care one way or the other," Ben said as he came to stand over the unmoving Yankee. "What happened to our rabbit?"

"'Round here somewheres. 'Spect I tenderized it a bit."

"Reckon it don't much matter to find it," Ben said, cocking his head to listen to the continuing tumult. "Camp's wiped out, and it ain't no place now for cooking supper." He hefted the revolver, then handed it to Tom. "What we got is another gun."

"And a horse," Tom said with a nod to the now grazing animal. "If this jasper comes to, I 'spect him doing some walking might help clear his head."

"Take his ammo and, long as we're at it, see if he's carrying any greenbacks," Ben said.

"That'd be stealing," Tom said wryly as he took the belt, holster, and the ammunition.

"And what do ya call the horse and the gun?" Ben chuckled. "Call it spoils of war. The blue and the gray's still fighting, so it's okay whatever we take."

Tom shrugged and bent to search through the soldier's pockets, extracting two bills. "Just a couple, not worth much."

"More'n what we got," Ben said. He nodded to the horse. "We'll hafta ride double."

"Better'n walking," Tom said. "Let's skedaddle."

Chapter Eight

Norfolk, Virginia, 1866

Just got the one horse 'tween ya?" The question came from the large and thickset middle-aged man who ambled forward in a rolling gait to examine the animal. "Good animal, but I suspect that's a Yankee-issued saddle on her."

"So what?" Ben said. " 'Spect it ain't so all-fired different from what you've seen before."

The fat man shrugged and stroked his heavy black beard. "Long as no bluecoats see it."

Following a grapevine rumor of railroad work to be had, Tom and Ben had led their purloined animal to a livery barn on the outskirts of Norfolk. Able-bodied in contrast to a near-dozen scraggly men clustered nearby, they stood for inspection by the portly Union Pacific representative.

"You boys look like you've missed some meals, but maybe you're fit enough for ordinary work. Don't know you'd be any account at hard labor like laying rail." He nodded to the group of thin, wasted men shuffling about in the yard. "Now, that's a sorry lot, the bunch of 'em." He sighed and shook his head. "Be different if both of ya had a ride. We looking for guard fellers, and we favor hirees to have their own mounts and carry their own weapons," the man said. "Since ya got one horse, maybe I could hire just one of ya."

"One of us could ride and the other would do the rails," Tom said earnestly. "I'm young and strong enough for that."

The portly man shook his head. "Well, you don't look like no sissy-guy, but . . . 'sides, we getting our full load of husky fellers . . . Irish, Polish, even them freed slaves . . . who can

52

do that kinda work. What we need is ex-soldiers that can handle their horses and are mighty handy with their shooting irons."

"Well, we've both been soldiers, got pistols, and know how to use 'em," Ben persisted. "Tom here is a crack shot and so am I. Looks like that'd count for a lot . . . with or without another danged horse."

"Whatcha need them gun shooters for?" Tom asked.

"Doing some herding, but mostly riding guard duty. Working through Indian country out West," the man replied. "There's been trouble, attacks on settlers and war parties jumping on our crews. We need fellers for outriding while the surveyors are out ahead and work gangs are laying track." He gave the pair a speculative look. "Tell ya what . . . bring your one horse 'round back. You fellers said you were good with guns . . . so let's see." He waved the pair to follow and sauntered to the corner of the barn, ignoring the surly, envious looks from the waiting job seekers. "I'm Bill Gentry," he introduced himself as they moved along the side of the barn. "I'm recruiting for the Casement brothers—them the new fellers that's running the whole track-laying shebang that's heading fer California."

"Whatcha got in mind for us to do, Mr. Gentry?" Tom asked as they came to a corral at the back of the barn.

Gentry nodded to Ben. "Your redheaded pal here said something about both ya both being crack shots. Now, if you're anywhere near as good as ya say, maybe we *can* find another horse once ya get out there to Omaha."

Gentry walked to the back of the barn, rummaged through a trash barrel, and brought out an empty tin can. "I'll set this up some good distance away, and we'll see if your aim is as good as your bragging."

"Set 'er up then . . . and don't make 'er too easy," Ben said.

Gentry smiled and walked toward the corral, passing the first upright post, the second, and the third, and finally placed the can on the flat top of the fourth post. "See it all right?" he called.

"I'm reading pork and beans right off the side of it," Ben called back. He raised his Remington and aimed. "You might want to step off a ways, Mr. Gentry. A bee might sting me just at the wrong time."

Gentry laughed and took five steps to his right. "Fire away, sir!"

"That's a far distance for a handgun, Ben," Tom whispered.

Ben nodded and took a deep breath, held it, and then squeezed the trigger.

At the boom of the revolver, a small wisp of wood fragments sprayed from the side of the post a half foot below the can.

"Can I try 'er again?" Ben called.

"Oh, I think that shows me enough," Gentry responded as he walked to the post and examined it. "Now, what about you, young feller?"

Tom took his newly acquired Colt revolver from its holster, cocked it, and waited until Gentry, again, walked five steps to the side.

"You're the crack shot, I hear!" Gentry said loudly. "Show me!"

Tom aimed the revolver and slowly tightened his finger on the trigger.

His shot barely ticked at the side of the can, sending it into a spinning wobble atop the post before falling to the ground.

"Not bad, fellers! Not bad at all!" Gentry exclaimed as he ambled toward them, his manner casual and detached. " 'Course it's just target shooting, and there ain't nothing here I ain't seen before—"

"Begging your pardon, Mr. Gentry," Tom cut in quickly. "With your permission, I'd like to show you something a little extra."

Gentry paused in his step, his face turned stern at the interruption. "Better be good, youngster."

Tom holstered his revolver, reached his right hand into his pocket, and took out a silver dollar that he held up for the railroad man to see.

"A danged silver dollar?" Ben whispered. "Been holding out on me, boy?"

"Later, not now," Tom muttered. He transferred the coin to his left hand, closed his fist around it, dropped his left arm to his side, and then hurled a coin high into the direct blaze of the morning sun. His right hand flashed to the revolver, drew and cocked it, and fired into the sun.

A moment later, the target coin dropped into a patch of grass adjoining the corral.

"Good try, youngster," Gentry said with a wintry disdain. "Missed it, I believe."

"Did I?" Tom said.

The expression on Gentry's face changed to wonderment, the man intrigued by the assurance in Tom's voice. He turned and shuffled to the grassy area and reached down for the coin. "My, my," he said, obviously awed as he examined the dented dollar. "My apologies, son . . . now this here is something I ain't *never* seen before 'cept in a carnival show."

Gentry handed the damaged coin to Tom as he joined the two men. "Gents, I reckon you're what you say you are and who *I* say we need. Put your horse in the barn . . . you're hired."

"You mean . . . right now?" Ben asked, his face wreathed in a smile.

"As of right now," Gentry said. "Got a place to sleep?"

Neither Ben nor Tom responded.

"Find a place in the barn," Gentry told them. "Train heading west tomorrow. You boys be on it."

He shook their hands before returning to the front of the barn while Tom and Ben led their horse through the back entrance to the stable.

"You gonna tell me how in tarnation you did that?" Ben asked, more a demand than a question.

Tom grinned. "Well, me being a crack shot like you was saying—"

"You two just get hired?"

As one, the pair turned to the man standing in a dark corner of the barn as he stepped into the sunlight streaming through the wide doors.

"Biggs?" Ben exclaimed.

"Wouldn't you know!" Tom muttered under his breath.

Chapter Nine

Omaha, Nebraska, 1866

Shut that danged door!" Ben commanded. "Gotta be hell below zero out there."

"I think I seed something upriver that might be Omaha," a lanky man said as he shoved the freight car door closed, cutting off the frigid wind whipping inside. He gripped his wool blanket around him and scurried along a narrow aisle through the maze of boxes and crates of rail-building supplies that jammed the space within the unheated boxcar. In a pocket surrounded on three sides by such containers, a four-foot-high mound of straw had been heaped against the forward freight car wall. He burrowed in close to four other men huddled at one end of the pile, all seeking warmth beneath the covering of grain stalks, their blankets hooded over their heads. These five, including Tom and Ben, were former Rebs and now new companions. Half-buried in the straw three feet away, two former Union soldiers, still in their blue uniform jackets, kept their distance—their comments short and seldom uttered.

Leon Biggs sat by himself in a niche across a narrow aisle, clutching his blanket around him. Choosing to sit by himself, making a show of disdain for all other boxcar occupants, Biggs was being the disagreeable Biggs.

They had ridden this freight car for days as it had been switched from rail line to rail line, crisscrossing the country. They had traveled six different railways to make their way to St. Joseph on the eastern bank of the wide Missouri River. As yet, no bridge crossed it at any point, and servicing the headquarters of the Union Pacific in Omaha, Nebraska, was a difficult and costly endeavor.

The heaviest loads from eastern factories—such as machinery, locomotives, boxcars, and flatcars with hundreds of tons of rails, joining plates, nuts and bolts, picks and shovels, etc.—were first shipped by freighters to New Orleans. There, rail cars and substantial materials were transferred to cargo steamers and barges on the Mississippi, then reloaded again to flatboats and flat-bottomed barges to travel up the shallower Missouri. Still other shipments, including boxcars with lighter loads, came to St. Joseph, Missouri; the nearest railhead, it was one hundred and sixty miles downstream from Omaha.

On this early March morning, turned glacial by a Canadian cold front, these eight were still riding the boxcar. It was one of two loaded aboard a big flatboat that had large paddlewheels on each stern side as it steamed up the waterway from St. Joseph. Capable of carrying up to thirty tons of weight, the flatbed boat featured only a small pilothouse at the stern, with just barely enough room for the crew. For the newly hired Union Pacific recruits, the boxcar remained their only shelter from the bitterly cold wind blowing across the icy water.

Earlier in this day, Tom, Ben, and two other men had ventured out to the deck to watch the slow advance up the river. Shivering, they were awed by the sight of shelves of ice encroaching from either bank and leaving only a narrow channel of clear water through which the barge plied its progress. Their outside stance in the cold lasted only a few minutes before they all retreated once again to their straw piles.

"Heard that in a hard winter the ice gets so thick they can drive a full-loaded ox-cart clear across it," one of the Union soldiers said, the first of the pair to make casual conversation.

His blue-jacketed companion turned his head sharply, as did Tom's fellow Rebs. All were stern-faced, not one showing approval of this Yankee's overture.

Tom took a few moments before deciding to respond. "I heard another 'un, though I don't put much stock in it." He paused. "Some say they done laid ties and rails across the ice and took a danged engine across the river."

There were hoots of derision from the gathering.

"That's a fool notion," Ben said, a rare chastisement of his young companion. "Too foolish to be nothing but a stupid story."

"True or not, I sure wouldn't be on it," the blue-jacketed young man said. "One of them engines would crack plumb through it and take everyone down to a danged cold death." He hesitated for a long time before moving closer and offering his hand. "I'm Bill Seymour."

The silence lasted for a long while.

"I ain't sure I want to shake no bluebelly's hand," Tom said finally.

"Suit yourself," Seymour responded and dropped his hand to his side. "We're gonna be working 'longside, so I figgered we might just as well get the hard feelings said and done if we can."

"We got a lot of friends cold in their graves 'cause of you Lincoln boys," Ben said. "You're right about them hard feelings."

"We lost a lot of our fellers too," Seymour's comrade joined in, an edge to his voice.

Again, there was a long silence.

Then Tom reached out his hand to Seymour. "Tom Patterson."

The Yankee nodded and shook Tom's hand.

Behind him, Ben swore under his breath, then reluctantly extended his hand, first to Seymour and, next, to his friend. "War's over," he said brusquely. "Ain't likely we'll ever be friends, but I reckon we'll have to make do."

Even so, with the exception of Tom, Ben, and Bill Seymour, the rest of the men remained silent, aloof, and unreceptive.

"That surly fellow over there?" Seymour said as a question with a nod to indicate Biggs. "One of yours?"

"In our outfit and come with us, but we don't claim him," Ben answered in a low voice. "You can shoot him if you want."

"We wouldn't hold that against you," Tom added.

A wry grin played on Seymour's face. "We had our good-for-nothings too." He touched his gloved right hand to his forehead in a half salute and scooted back beside his companion.

Three hours later, the flatboat nosed into position at the Omaha dock and unloaded the boxcars onto a side spur on the Nebraska bank. Minutes later, a switch engine maneuvered the cars to couple onto a string of others. The newly assembled train began to move, and Tom felt the wheels beneath the car pass over a rail switch and recognized a resultant slight change of direction. After a half hour of slow-moving progress, the train shuddered to a stop, and immediately there came a pounding at the car's door. "Omaha!" an outside shouter announced. "Everybody out!"

As soon as the door opened wide, five of the men leaped to the ground, Tom and Ben following, with Biggs a swaggering last. They were standing on a wide swath of hardpan earth, a freight-handling area in a good-sized rail yard. In this section, in addition to the distant depot, there were a number of small and large buildings with loading docks. Tom could see several rail spurs with parked boxcars, a hopper, flatcars, and a chugging switcher locomotive moving a string of cars.

Up and down the length of the train, an industrious scene of varied activity was now in motion. Men were placing slant boards at the livestock cars, preparing to bring horses and mules to the ground. Others were positioning wagons at the doors of boxcars to unload the hardware of railroad construction as well as supplies for the town's residents and the present and arriving railroad workers.

If the chill of the boxcar journey had been daunting, the bite of the frigid prairie wind was overwhelming. One of the men scrambled back onto the boxcar and began handing out the left-behind woolen blankets. Each man wrapped himself against the bitter cold. Tom cowled a fold over his head, holding a part of the fabric against his lower face, leaving his eyes uncovered to search for whatever was next to come.

"You sissy boys expecting a warm welcome?" a sarcastic voice exclaimed. Stepping out from between two boxcars behind them, a rangy man of middle years came chuckling before the shivering group. He was wearing a sheepskin coat, gloves, and a ten-gallon hat with earmuffs beneath the wide brim. "Maybe ya fancy some hot tea and them . . . whatchamacallits . . . crumpets?"

"A gallon of coffee, a beefsteak, and my backside to a red hot stove, if it's just the same to you, sir," Tom responded merrily, his unexpected retort bringing laughter to the group and a slow smile to the newcomer.

"Right up there to that big warehouse," the tall man instructed, pointing to a large, one-story structure in the rail yard with two plumes of black smoke rising from a pair of rooftop chimneys. "I'm Charlie Bonniwell . . . and I am your welcoming committee." He waited. "Well, you gonna stand here all day?"

Immediately, the eight men began a hurried scramble toward the building, with Bonniwell trailing behind. A double dozen men from other cars were now heading in the same direction, all in quickstep, in search of warmth and, hopefully, stomach-filling sustenance. As they strode past the locomotive of their train, to his left, Tom saw a couple of flatcars parked on an adjacent rail siding and a stream of men walking to and fro in the space between.

"Busy place," Ben said as they rushed ahead.

Crowding through the door of the warehouse, with others before and behind, Tom felt the wash of warm air envelop him. The spacious interior of the building had been configured into a temporary mess hall. Two big coal-burning stoves were located twenty-five feet in from each of the end walls, stovepipes stretched up to and through the roof. Tom followed heat to the nearest stove where he, Ben, and the other six of his group joined five other men circled around it. At the opposite end of the warehouse, a like number ringed around the duplicate heater.

Between the stoves, narrow rectangular tables, positioned end to end, formed three long rows, with benches on either side. From the number of tables, it was apparent the mess hall was designed to handle a much larger number than this group now inside. At the back wall, directly in front of the tables, was an unoccupied, foot-high platform.

Along the near side wall, a long table featured coffee urns and mugs, soup and goulash kettles, bowls and platters of food—a midday spread for the cold and hungry newcomers.

Flushed now from the welcome change of temperature, Tom counted the number of men in the room. There appeared to be thirty new arrivals, plus a dozen men he presumed to be Union Pacific supervisor employees. Standing beside the platform, four older men of obvious higher rank were engaged in earnest conversation.

One of the four—a diminutive, bearded man wearing a long fur coat and a tall fur hat—caught Tom's eye. "Who's the pipsqueak ferner over there in the big fuzzy hat?" he asked, turning to Bonniwell standing behind him. "Looks like one of them Russkies."

"Watch what you say, my boy," Bonniwell warned in a soft voice. "*That's* your new boss."

"*My boss?*" Tom's incredulous question brought the attention of Ben and two others, who turned to face Bonniwell.

"That's General Jack Casement," Bonniwell told them.

"General?" Ben's voice was scathing. "Why, hell, he ain't half high enough to be a general of anything."

"Lot of your fellow Rebs found out plumb different during the war," Bonniwell countered. "And don't think he can't handle them that's twice his size."

Tom rolled his eyes and grinned. "You say so, so be it." He nodded toward the food table. "Any of that meant for us?"

Bonniwell nodded. "Yours for the taking, soon as your backside's warm enough. Hot coffee and soup, beef and potato goulash . . . sandwiches . . . just dig in."

Chapter Ten

Omaha, Nebraska, 1866

An hour later, the newcomers were warm almost to the point of sweating. They were also sated and satisfied after ample mouthfuls of coffee, soup, fresh baked bread, and goulash, topped off with wide wedges of apple pie.

"Gentlemen!" the undersized Jack Casement said as he stepped up on the platform and walked to a center point to address the gathering. With his Cossack-styled hat removed, he was, at most, a little over five feet tall. Nonetheless, he carried his slight frame with an air of self-confidence and authority, without the testy bravado so often seen in small men. "I know you've had a miserable journey to join us. I do hope we've managed to make up for your discomforts with the warmth of these surroundings and the nourishing vittles in your bellies."

There were murmurs of agreement from the seated men as Casement paused with a wide smile on his face and then continued, "It is now just after two o'clock. In a little while, you'll be shown to your quarters and given the rest of this day and tonight to settle in. Tomorrow, you'll be outfitted with whatever you need, and your work will begin."

He paused to take a deep breath. "From California, the Central Pacific is laying rail toward the east. Here, from Omaha, the Union Pacific is charged to lay track westward to meet and join our rails with theirs. With this dreadful war now behind us, it is our mission to create a transcontinental railroad to tie this great country together once again." He shook his head. "I'll mince no words about the status of our part of the contract." He thrust out his arm, finger pointing to the west. "Forty-five miles, gentlemen! That's *all* the track that has been laid in two years! I find that unbelievable and unacceptable. We've got to do better . . . and we will."

Casement began to pace, anger now in his face and words. "Out there, a part of our concern is the problem of marauding Indian tribes. The Cheyenne, the Sioux . . . especially a particularly troublesome fellow called Red Cloud and his Sioux warriors . . . they are constantly probing, always a danger, tearing up ties, harassing our surveyors and graders, even attacking and killing settlers. Most likely, they'll soon be killing *our* people." He walked along the front line of seated men. "The Army has set up posts to help, added more soldiers and more patrols to keep the Indians away, but they can't be everywhere every day, every time there's a threat. That's why you're here . . . you're *special* recruits."

At the end of the front line, he reversed his direction, pointing as he walked. "You and you and you . . . will ride and protect our surveyors and advance work parties. You and you and you . . . will guard our main work body at the front and at the rear as we move across these plains." He walked to the center once again. "Some of you were Johnny Rebs, some were Union bluebellies. That war is past. You are a handpicked group of skilled combatants, hired to fight a new battle. The men who will build this essential railroad will depend upon each of you to see they build it in the safety of your guardianship." He paused. "Once again, gentlemen, welcome to history . . . the history you will start making tomorrow."

The large room was quiet, only the hiss of the flames and the occasional tumble of coal clinkers sounding in the silence.

Casement turned to his cadre of supervisors. "Get the men to their quarters." With a wave, he stepped down from the platform, donned his tall fur hat, strode to the door, and left the building.

Tom and Ben rose and, at Bonniwell's beckoning, walked to join him. The railroad overseer gathered half the newcomers, while a second company man assembled those remaining.

Bonniwell waved his cluster to follow and led them out of the building and into the frigid Nebraska afternoon.

As Bonniwell led the group back into the rail yard, Tom noticed a sizable number of husky men working at various tasks. Most were warmly dressed for the cold weather: heavy coats, caps, and gloves.

"Any chance I can get something warmer to wear?" Tom asked as he fell in stride with Bonniwell.

"You ain't the first that needs," Bonniwell told him. "We got the means to outfit ya at a dirt-bottom price."

"Where are we going?" Ben asked as he hastened to join the two. "Ain't there a bunkhouse or barracks or something?"

"Town's full up. Ain't no place left fer time being 'cept on the train," Bonniwell informed him.

"You mean . . . back in one of them danged boxcars?" Ben complained.

The Union Pacific supervisor crossed the tracks in front of the train on which they had arrived. With a clutch of followers striding close behind him, they came in view of a strange sight.

"What in the name of . . . ?" Ben exclaimed as he and the group came to an abrupt stop, eyes wide and mouths agape.

"Never seen nothing like this, nothing at all!" Bill Seymour marveled. "Never in my life!"

"Your new home, people," Bonniwell announced. "For many a month to come."

The scene before them was a long series of odd-shaped railroad cars with a locomotive and its tender positioned far at the rear. Coupled behind two commonplace flatcars, two undercarriage frames were topped with wooden, single-story house-like structures, both crowned with peaked roofs. A smokestack poking through the shingles of the latter indicated a transportable kitchen.

The next three rolling stock entities were tall, windowless, rectangular structures, each one twice as high as an ordinary boxcar. Further down the long line, there was a mixture of standard boxcars, hopper cars, and flatcars interspersed with more of the houselike fabrications; another pair of the tall top-heavy units; and a couple of open-sided cars with peaked shingled roofs.

"Town on wheels," Bonniwell said, walking as he turned to address his followers. "Kitchen cars, dining cars, blacksmith shop, carpenter shop, water tanks, cars for picks and shovels, general store . . . everything riding the rails . . . following close behind on the tracks as we're laying 'em down."

He came to a stop at the first of the three tall boxy structures. "Dormitories . . . that's what General Jack calls 'em," Bonniwell explained as he swept his hand at the top-heavy unit. "This here is where you'll sleep and pass your idle time." Then he chuckled. "You won't be having much of that last."

Upon entry into the dormitory car, a pungent smell of coal smoke and rancid sweat assaulted their nostrils. They found an interior with three-tiered bunks lining the walls on either side of a middle aisle. Centered in that aisle, a potbellied stove promised excessive heat for those bunked nearby and scant warmth for those at a distance. Most of the lower bunks appeared to have been already taken, with their occupants' meager belongings on top of the beds and garments hanging close by. The remaining empty bunks, the majority on the second and third tiers, were scattered throughout the dormitory car.

As the other newcomers scrambled to find and claim their berths, Tom found an empty lower bunk near the far end of the car that he graciously offered to his older friend.

"Thanks, sonny," Ben had acknowledged with a wide smile. "Ain't decrepit, but I ain't as spry as I once was."

For himself, Tom found a bunk in the second tier on the adjacent stand. A rolled wool blanket had been placed at one end of his bed: a pillow for summer, a covering for winter. It was no surprise for Tom to see Biggs select a lower bunk near the center of the car, sweep the personal belongings already on it to the floor, and replace them with his own.

"Hope that belongs to one of them big Irishmen we've seen," Tom said, bringing laughter from those around him.

Sure enough, in the early evening, a strapping young Irishman appeared and roared his anger to find his property on the floor and Biggs in his bunk. Gripping the intruder by the front of his shirt, the outraged man swung him out and into the aisle, and then threw his possessions after him. As Biggs tried to rise to his feet, the infuriated Irishman's heavy boot thudded into his buttocks and sent him even further down the central path.

Cursing and vowing under his breath to get even, Biggs gathered his scattered items and retreated to a high bunk in a distant corner.

Ben gave a quick smile and a nod before changing to a sober expression. "That fellow better watch his back," he said. "Biggs will likely put a ball in it some dark night." He turned his head as his eyes roamed the huge barnlike boxcar facility, the sleeping quarters for over a hundred men. A wry smile came to his lips. "It ain't much, but I reckon we'll stay warm."

Tom wrinkled his nose at the pungent mixture of foul odors. "Maybe back to the boxcar might be a mite better . . . specially when winter's up and gone away."

Chapter Eleven

Omaha, Nebraska, 1866

Upon rising, Tom and Ben went to a corral to identify their horses. Before their journey west had begun, Tom had given the lively and responsive stallion the name Duke. A second horse, a gelding named Blaze for its forehead marking, had been issued to Ben. The animals were kept by day in one of the several rail yard corrals. By night, many were quartered in a large barn, while others were reloaded onto the numerous livestock cars.

Their next activity was a visit to a general store in the business district of Omaha. Each carried a small slip of authorized paper to identify him as an authentic employee of the Union Pacific.

"Seem like it ain't as cold this morning," Tom said as they walked out of the store and turned toward the rail yard. He carried a large bundle containing a few new things as well as his old clothes. "Seem that way to you?"

"They say that you get feeling warmer when you're freezing to death," Ben responded blithely. "Or maybe 'cause of them new duds we're wearing."

Tom nodded with a look down at his just-acquired apparel: a warm mackinaw coat, new jeans, and a flannel shirt. New boots and a new, wide-brimmed hat completed the ensemble. He glanced back at the store. "I ain't gonna see a cent fer a while. Charging my outfit against my pay, it's gonna cost me right near a half month's pay for this stuff."

Ben touched the sleeve of his new coat, a match to Tom's. "I warn't needy as you, but they'll be docking my pay for a spell, just the same." He turned his gaze toward the flatlands to the west. "Well, we got regular pay and regular meals. We got ourselves outta Yankee country, and we're on our own. Oughta count our blessings fer that."

"Hmmph," Tom snorted.

The Omaha frontier community had become a boomtown as it swelled with industry and commerce, all because of the Union Pacific railroad endeavor. As they trod the boardwalk, the clamor of construction sounds was all about them. There were many hammers and saws at work in carpentry shops, building special needs for the railroad, and coming from machine shops, the squeals and pounding of metal being fashioned into different shapes for the rail project.

Out-of-work men had flocked to this hub of activity, including ex-soldiers from both the North and the South, freed slaves, and immigrants from European nations, including Germans, Swedes, and, especially, Irish. All, in these depressing postwar days, had been drawn by the lure of steady employment at an average and fairly decent wage of thirty-five dollars per month. With months ahead in the relatively unpopulated prairie regions, and with few places to spend their wages, many men hoped to accumulate goodly funds for the future, even if it meant long separations from their families.

Following the men and their money had come the inevitable crowd of gamblers, medicine wagon shills, card sharks, thieves, confidence men, attorneys, shady ladies, and dangerous felons. Robbery and murder were not uncommon in the burgeoning community and, as more and more dodgy people arrived, the lawlessness posed a threat to the town's citizens and a constant distraction for the railroad and its workers.

"Watch out fer yourselves in town, boys," Bonniwell had warned them. "Some'll fleece ya if they can, and them ladies will promise you a good time and steal your money outta your pants on the end of the bed."

Passing a pair of comely strumpets out for a morning stroll, Ben noticed Tom's interest. "Got yourself a girl somewheres?"

Tom returned his gaze to Ben with an embarrassed grin on

his face. "Twice, maybe," he answered. "Never in one place long enough for anything to matter." He paused, reflecting. "None you'd call a proper girl."

As they approached their dormitory car, Ben nudged Tom and nodded to the trio of men coming their way. Two tall men, one of them Bonniwell, flanked the familiar small, bearded man in the lead.

"General Jack," Tom said softly. "Should we salute him or something?"

"How would I know?" Ben countered.

"You, there!" Casement called. "Young fellow there!"

"Me?" Tom asked and stopped still, Ben doing the same.

The small man was, again, wearing the high Cossack-style hat. His short jacket was open and revealed a huge revolver in the belt at his waist.

"You the one who can shoot silver dollars out of the air?" Casement asked, more a demand than a question.

Tom didn't answer.

"Well?"

"I guess . . . sometimes I get lucky."

"Like to see you do that," Casement said crisply. "Like to know what my sharpshooters can do."

"Well, sir, I'm not sure—"

The little man cut in. "I'm waiting. Show me!"

"Sir, I . . . ah . . . well, I surely would, but not having no silver dollar—"

Casement's right hand reached into his pocket and brought out a bright silver coin. "Here's one."

Tom handed his clothing bundle to Ben, then felt in his own pocket for one of the shot-damaged coins. "Well, I guess I could try—"

"I'll toss it," Casement said, swinging his hand down to his side. "Tell me when."

Tom touched his teeth to his lower lip. *I'm a goner!*

"You ready?" Casement repeated impatiently.

Tom lowered his right hand to his holster revolver. "Let her fly."

Casement's hand swung up and the bright coin spun and glittered in the sunlight.

Tom drew the revolver, cocked it, aimed, closed his eyes and fired.

The coin jumped a dozen feet to the right and fell to the ground.

"Son of a gun!" Bonniwell exclaimed, hurrying to pick up the coin and examine it. "He did it!"

No one noticed Tom opening his eyes.

"Good shot, young man, great shot!" Casement complimented. He turned to his associates. "Outstanding, really outstanding!"

With an abrupt wave forward, he motioned the men to follow and strode on his way, the men behind mincing their steps to keep pace.

"You surely do amaze me, young Mister Tom," Ben said, shaking his head in awe, his eyes aglow. "Proud to be your pard!"

Chapter Twelve

Omaha, Nebraska, 1866

I thought we'd be riding guard," Bill Seymour complained mildly. "Not just cowhands riding herd."

Tom gave a short laugh and heel-kicked Duke to maneuver two wandering steers back into the large body of shorthorn cattle grazing on the grassland beyond the Omaha outskirts. The animals would be driven alongside the work train as it moved west, a meat source for the brawny workmen as they hammered tracks across the prairie. Four riders in addition to Tom and Seymour were ranging slowly at different points at the perimeter of the herd.

To Tom's surprise, he had taken a liking to the easygoing former Yankee soldier and, in a sense, felt they had forgiven each other for whatever their wartime duties had required. Most of the other former soldiers, North or South, had also established peaceable working relationships. Many did so grudgingly, but many others appeared willing to let go of the past. Even so, most of the workers tended to flock together in their own groups.

A few, like Leon Biggs, stubbornly retained their hostility. A small and separate faction of former Confederates, they swaggered their belligerence and persistently swore their hatred. Most of their fellow employees found them tiresome and offensive to a high degree. Both Tom and Ben opined that Biggs and others of their bad-tempered sort would soon be weeded out of the Union Pacific work force.

By the latter part of the month, winter softened into spring, and the hard, frozen ground of the rail yard became mud. Jack Casement marched daily through the muck, supervising every aspect of preparation for the rail expansion task ahead. Often, his brother, Dan, the railroad's on-site payroll and financial manager, accompanied him.

While the Casement duo were finalizing their plans, and as the laborers waited for the main work to begin, there were too many idle hours in which these restless men drank, brawled, gambled, and caroused with the saloon ladies and bawdy women. Some of the guardian personnel were temporarily assigned to assist the local law in keeping order.

"Your partner working the town?" Bill asked, urging his horse forward to ride beside Tom.

Tom nodded. "Tonight. Things get rowdy after sundown."

"You had a turn at it?"

"Not yet," Tom replied. "This is Ben's second go-round."

"Reckon that's because he's older . . . him being a top-kick sergeant and all."

"Reckon that's right. Ben's cool as a cucumber and handy when some of them bullyboys start hard drinking." He tucked his lower lip under his upper teeth. "I *do* worry about him."

"He'll be okay," Bill assured him, and changed the subject. "How soon you figure we'll be laying track?"

"General Jack, feisty as he is, 'spect it'll be any day now."

"Looking forward to it?"

Tom shrugged. "I'm already getting a sour head sleeping in that stinky car. Lordy, no, I ain't gonna, come summertime."

"Others are saying the same. Tenting out seems best."

"We're about grazed out here," Tom said. "Some better-looking grass up ahead a bit. Let's move the herd."

A little after ten o'clock that night, Tom came awake as a hand shook his shoulder urgently.

"Pull on your pants," Bonniwell commanded. "We're needed in town."

"For what?"

"We got us a goldanged donnybrook a-going," the big man told him. "Hurry up!"

Tom rose, donned his shirt, then his pants, and sat again to pull up his boots. "Sidearms?"

"Carry, but don't use," Bonniwell said crisply. "We're breaking out pick handles five cars down."

A dozen men were on their feet getting dressed, some grousing about the loss of sleep, others excited and eager for action, no matter good or bad, to allay the daily boredom.

Tom was one of the first out of the dormitory car, and he sprinted down the line to a freight car, where pick handles were being dispersed. He stepped into the lantern light coming from the car's interior and was immediately handed a hardwood bludgeon.

"Let's go, boys," Bonniwell commanded. "Let's knock some sense into some hard heads."

With a wave forward, the big man led the group toward the town center, his long strides just shy of a trot. The followers, especially the shorter ones, had to run to keep up. A few moved wide and practiced swinging their clubs, whistling them through the air with fierce intensity.

"Careful with them bonker sticks!" Bonniwell shouted. "Don't kill nobody or lame 'em too bad! We need these fellers fit to work once they sober up."

"Beats herding cattle," Bill Seymour said as he fell in step with Tom, his eyes shining with excitement.

"Herding this bunch gonna be a hell of a lot harder," Tom responded, remembering a childhood spent in many saloons. "Watch your backsides. Bar fights ain't no fun."

It took less than ten minutes for the men to reach their destination, a building with a sign, THE ROUNDHOUSE SALOON, hanging over the open-door entrance. The melee was not confined to the interior of the tavern; multiple fistfights had spilled out onto the boardwalk and into the street. Two Omaha deputies were vainly trying to break up the most ferocious scuffles between the shouting, swearing, and drunken bruisers.

As Bonniwell led the new group of club-toting enforcers into the fray, Tom looked for Ben. He didn't see his friend involved in any of the outside brawls, but he could see, through the open door of the saloon, a furious fracas in progress inside.

"You fellers sure are a welcome sight!" A tall, ruddy-faced man rushed to meet them, pulling his vest aside to show the badge on his plaid shirt. "Most of 'em are your people, and they're a plumb handful."

"This here's Sheriff Tucker," Bonniwell said hurriedly.

"Ain't no time for introductions," the lawman said. "Wade in and let's break this thing up 'fore somebody gets killed!"

"Pick your fight and do what you can!" Bonniwell shouted as he reached for the collar of a nearby brawny fighter and swung him away from his smaller opponent. As the surprised fighter wrenched free to face this new adversary, Bonniwell jabbed him hard in the midsection with his club. The blow doubled the man over to gasp and clutch at his stomach, the fight gone out of him. With contempt, Bonniwell kicked him to the street, where he lay writhing in pain. Then the big supervisor waved the pick handle at the still-standing smaller combatant who lifted his hands in inebriated surrender and staggered away.

"Going inside!" Tom shouted to Seymour. "I'll need help!"

Seymour nodded and waved three men to follow as Tom dashed into the saloon.

Just inside the door, the five stopped to survey the riotous scene. The barroom was in shambles, furniture upended and broken, one of two overhead chandeliers dark with smashed lantern units. Paintings of scantily clad women were hanging askew, and a large mirror behind the long bar was shattered, with a few glass shards still clinging inside the frame.

The fights outside had been spaced apart, but in here the struggles were jammed close together. Fists were swung first to one man, then to the next nearby. The brawlers were shoulder to shoulder as the many battlers staggered and wheeled, both from inebriation and the blows that crashed them over tables and chairs. Liquor bottles were jarred from shelves to smash on the floor as fist-swinging opponents crowded into the narrow aisle behind the bar. Two bartenders, standing back to back in the center of the space, were wielding blackjacks at any fighter who ventured into their reach.

Tom scanned the room for Ben and saw him in a corner with a chair held defensively to fend off two men menacing him. He shoved his way through the struggling fighters and found an easier path along a wall toward his embattled friend. He saw that Biggs was one of the men, and that he and the second man were brandishing lethal combat knives. He also saw that Ben's holster was empty. Dancing from side to side, both of the aggressors were looking for an opening to thrust their ugly weapons into their cornered victim.

Biggs caught Tom's approach out of the corner of his eye and started to turn, but Tom slapped the pick handle onto Biggs' right hand, the Bowie knife dropping to the floor. Wincing in pain, Biggs fumbled at his holstered revolver with his left, but Tom swung the handle to the back of the man's head, a sharp blow that felled him immediately.

Without a pause in his rhythm, Tom turned to the second man, his first swing of the club slamming into the rib cage as the assailant tried to turn away. A swift second blow just above the ear dropped this brawler unconscious to the floor.

"You okay?" Tom asked.

"Cut me a little on the side," Ben said, his hand touching a bloody stain on his shirt. "Not bad, just a lucky poke in my fat side." He paused. "Thanks for coming. I was surely in a fix." He took a few steps one way, then circled around, sweeping his eyes on the floor. A few circles more and he reached down with a smile of triumph and lifted his revolver. He inspected the handgun critically and returned it to his holster as he came back to stand with Tom.

Around them, the superior number of the newly arrived enforcers was bringing the wild disturbance to a tapering halt. Together with the town's lawmen, the railroad guardsmen were manhandling the fighters, pushing, shoving, and stepping between struggling individuals to drive the adversaries apart.

"How did this get started?" Tom asked.

Ben pointed across the room. "See them two Irish fellers over there?"

Tom's gaze followed the pointed finger. Two burly men were leaning against the middle of the bar, one showing great concern for the bruises on the other man's face.

"I didn't see it myself, but I heard tell that them two blockheads always hanging out together, they started a fuss with each other. Bad drunk they was, and then they started swinging." Ben paused with a rueful smile on his face. "Then some other feller 'cided to help one of 'em. He jumped in and, by thunder, both them Irishmen started beating on *him*." Again, Ben paused. "And that's when things got dicey. Whole place began hitting on one another."

At that moment, Sheriff Tucker walked over to gaze down at the two inert figures on the floor. Behind him, Bonniwell was wending his way through the straggling drunkards still resisting eviction.

"Saw your action, young feller," the lawman said with a nod of approval to Tom. "You got grit, way you waded in and handled them two rascals."

Tom shrugged at the compliment.

"This was your doing?" Bonniwell asked as he joined them, giving a bob of his head at the two prone ruffians.

"That I did," Tom admitted. He reached down and picked up one of the combat knives. "They was trying to stick Ben here."

The sheriff cast his gaze at Ben's bloody shirt. "Looks like they got him. You bad hurt, Ben?"

"More blood than hurt," Ben said. "Nothing that won't heal up."

"Best go see the company doc and have a stitch." Bonniwell leaned down to peer at the unconscious Biggs. "Ain't this Biggs a part of your crew?"

"Him?" Tom responded. "Not by our choosing."

"He was in our squad during the war," Ben chimed in. "Mean as a copperhead, he was . . . and still is."

"Always had it in for Ben," Tom added. "Ben being his squad sergeant and all."

"Who's the other guy?" the sheriff asked.

"One of 'em that hangs out with Biggs," Tom told him. "No-accounts, the bunch of 'em."

Bonniwell turned to the sheriff and motioned to the two men, who were moaning and beginning to stir. "You fixing to charge 'em?"

Sheriff Tucker pursed his lips in thought and then shook his head. "Nobody got killed and I'd reckon a judge would say they was just mean drunk and turn 'em loose again. Of course, if the railroad was to run 'em clean out of Nebraska, it might be the right thing to do."

Bonniwell tapped the toe of his boot on the top of Biggs' head, a warning to lie still. "Well, we sure don't need no trouble-makers working for the Union Pacific. If you got empty cell room, stick 'em down at the jail 'til morning. Soon as they're clear-headed, one and all, they're gone, any of his bunch." He turned his head to survey the wrecked saloon. "They ain't getting no pay neither. Somebody's got to pay for this mess."

"The railroad?" Sheriff Tucker asked.

"Hell no," Bonniwell said. "We'll dock the pay outta every knothead in here who was fighting."

"Maybe 'cept that jasper over there," Ben cut in hastily, pointing to a slight, middle-aged man sitting at an upright table near the back of the large room. "Sat there quiet and peaceable all through the whole shebang. Drinking his beer like nothing was going on."

"You ain't serious!" The sheriff peered at the solitary figure at the table who was lifting a half-filled schooner of beer to his lips. "That the same beer?"

Ben nodded. "Didn't spill a drop."

"Well, that's surely a tale to be told," Bonniwell said in awe.

"Told, but not likely to be believed," the sheriff opined.

Bonniwell nodded. "Even seeing with my own eyes, I can't rightly believe it myself." He turned his attention to Ben's side, his eyes fastened on the blood seeping through his shirt. "Help your pard over to the railroad infirmary for a patch up. I'd go right now cause I 'spect them other banged up fellers will be coming long right soon after."

"Ain't no need to get the doc outta bed," Ben groused. "I'll mosey over in the morning. Tomorrow's soon enough."

"Getting the doc outta bed is what we pays him for," Bonniwell said. " 'Sides, he's got himself a right pretty nurse."

"How pretty?" Tom asked, his eyebrows lifting.

Bonniwell chuckled. "Enough to turn up her nose at the sorry sight of you."

"Liked the way you handled yourself, young feller, like to have your name," the sheriff said to Tom, then glanced to Ben. "I know Ben . . . you fellers work as a team?"

"Usually, it's the kid getting in trouble and me getting him out of it," Ben said with a grin. "He's Tom Patterson."

"Who can introduce himself, *old* friend," Tom said cheerfully.

"Well, you two boys ever get tired of railroading and want to do some full-time deputizing here in town, we could use more help these days," Tucker told them. "If you get such a notion, come see me."

"Much obliged," Ben said. "We'll keep it in mind."

Tom placed his hand under Ben's elbow and hurried him across the room and through the entrance doorway.

"You got any hankering to be a full-time lawman?" Tom asked as they walked.

"We just got started on this job," Ben said with a grimace of pain. "If getting cut up is your idea of full-time work, I'll say 'no thanks.' "

"Better'n getting scalped or tomahawked by some wild Indian," Tom countered. " 'Sides, I thought tonight was kinda fun."

Ben gave him a reproving look.

They turned from the street and entered the Union Pacific rail yard, now dark and silent.

"Take it a mite easy," Ben growled as Tom increased his pace, hurrying Ben toward the small, dark building that housed the Union Pacific medical clinic. "Like the man said, she ain't likely to fancy a homely young buck like you."

"Maybe so, maybe not," Tom responded as he touched his face and grinned. "I'll still give her the first chance at me . . . 'fore them better-looking fellers take a run at her."

Chapter Thirteen

Omaha, Nebraska, 1866

Shortly after dawn, Leon Biggs, carrying saddlebags, entered the dormitory car at the west end, accompanied by two stern-faced town deputies. Few of the car's occupants were still sleeping, the majority of men already, or getting, dressed. Under the watchful eye of the deputies, Biggs gathered his meager possessions and stuffed them into the saddlebag pockets with angry thrusts. As he finished, he looked up, his eyes searching the far end of the car.

"Looking for me?" Tom said as he stepped forward out of the shadows. A moment later, Ben moved up to stand beside him.

"The pair of ya," Biggs said gruffly as he nodded toward Ben. "There'll come a day . . . and it'll be your last, you can count on that." Without waiting for a response, Biggs turned sharply and walked swiftly to the opposite end of the car, the two deputies close behind.

"Whoooeee!" exclaimed Bill Seymour, looking down from a third-high bunk nearby. "And that feller used to soldier with you?"

"True comrade-in-arms," Ben said with a smile. "Had him ride point every chance we got, but you bluebellies warn't never good enough shots to take him out."

"Best watch him, Ben!" another voice called. "He's a back shooter if I ever saw one."

"I'd appreciate you boys helping me if that being the case," Ben responded. "You see him sneaking up on me and Tom, be kind of ya to let us know 'fore he gets there."

"Time for breakfast," Tom said as he reached for his new hat. "Biggs had his chance at us more'n once and didn't have the nerve. We ain't gonna worry about him."

"Gimme a minute 'til I get my boots on," Seymour said. "I'll go with you."

A few minutes later, Tom, Ben, and Seymour walked the center aisle to the door at the car's end and stepped down to the ground. Seymour fell in step beside Tom as they walked between the rail spurs toward the mess hall building. In the time since their arrival in Omaha, Tom and the former Yankee had formed a sort of camaraderie, being close in age. Ben, however, was still standoffish, not openly hostile to a former enemy, but noticeably reticent.

"How'd it go with that young lady last night?" Seymour asked.

A grin came across Tom's face. "Went okay."

"Like how?"

"She paid me no never mind at first, a little snippy to tell the truth," Tom admitted. "After a while, when her old man was patching up Ben's side, she lightened up, and we talked a bit."

"Doc Scofield's her pa?"

Tom nodded. "She told me when her ma passed away, she kinda took over her nursing duties." He paused. "Name's Mary Beth."

"Is that all that's gonna come of it?" Seymour questioned. "Just a little talking last night . . . or is there gonna be more?"

"It might be more," Tom told him.

"You gonna see her?"

"Maybe."

"You two get over mooning about that nurse girl," Ben said crossly. "She sees a hundred or more just like you down-and-out drifters ever day. She might give you a pretty smile and a little talk, but her old man's gonna see she marries class, not some railroad riffraff."

Tom gave Seymour a wink and then said, "We'll see."

"Don't go making plans," Ben warned. "Word is we'll be on the plains long before the young miss takes a shine to you."

They met Charlie Bonniwell, coming from a different direction, at the door of the mess hall. Their supervisor gave them an acknowledging good morning nod. "They ran your Biggs and his buddies out of town a few minutes ago," he said as they entered the building. "Sheriff and the town marshal took 'em to city limits."

"Good riddance," Tom said. "Which direction?"

"Heading east," Bonniwell informed them.

"Hope we've seen the last of him," Ben put in.

"Enjoy your last meal here in Omaha," Bonniwell told them as they seated themselves at one of the long tables. "We're moving the train this morning."

"Been expecting it," Ben said. "Weather's warming up."

"How soon?" Tom asked.

"Nine at the latest," Bonniwell answered. "Plan to start laying track right after noon. Ben, you being an army noncom and all, I'm putting you in charge of some of the men, including these two. Get your gear together right after breakfast and start the cattle west."

Ben nodded. "Been getting kinda itchy waiting to get going. We need to put this wild town behind us."

"Speak for yourself, old man," Tom spoke in jest. "Getting kinda attached to Omaha. Kinda hate to leave."

Seymour flashed a quick, knowing smile to Tom, one that Bonniwell didn't miss.

"Making eyes at that young Scofield girl?" their boss questioned, showing a perceptive smile of his own. "Well, you ain't the first and you won't be the last. She ain't gonna take up with the likes of you, young feller."

"Just exactly what I was telling him," Ben interjected. "Time for romancing gonna come when this railroad's built and you got a wad of money in your pockets."

"Let's get her built in a hurry then," Tom said with a laugh.

As Bonniwell predicted, the work train began rolling a few minutes before nine o'clock. The movement was a celebrative send-off—a gathering of Omaha citizens and town-based

Union Pacific employees at the station platform cheering as the rear-positioned steam engine chugged its odd rolling stock westward. Aboard the train, standing on flatcars and sitting on the slanted rooftops, the husky laborers waved their enthusiastic farewells.

As the train traveled toward the horizon, dozens of wagon drivers snapped their buggy whips and clucked their teams forward. Horseback riders opened the gates of corrals and began herding the horses and mules to follow the way west.

Tom, Ben, and Seymour were already moving the cattle as the work train came puffing along and moved slowly abreast of the herd. Again, the rail workers on the train waved and shouted their hurrahs until their strange-looking transport moved past, gathering speed.

They turned as one at the sound of approaching hooves to see Charlie Bonniwell bouncing awkwardly on a trotting horse.

"Mr. Bonniwell!" Ben called a greeting. "Figgered you'd be riding that train 'stead of horseback."

"Had my druthers, I'd be on her," Bonniwell admitted as he reined the horse to a stop beside them. He gestured to the train, diminishing in sight as it rolled into the distance. "They'll be at rail's end long 'fore we get there. We'll bed down the herd and ourselves tonight, and likely tomorrow's night too. There's a chuck wagon coming up with a cook and fixings for our supper and morning breakfast."

"We gonna be trailing these shorthorns all the time, Mr. Bonniwell?" Seymour asked.

"Off and on," Bonniwell replied. "Guard riding will likely start once the Indians see that we're working again." He paused, then added, "They'd prize a few of these beeves, so guard them just as you would our workmen." He kicked the sides of his mount and tugged at the reins to turn the horse. "I'm heading back to check on the wagons. I'll see you tonight."

As the big man rode gawkily east, Tom chuckled. "Hope he don't fall off."

"Man ain't sat a horse much, if ever," Ben agreed. He

turned to face the western plains. "You young fellers fan out now and tend to the herd 'fore they scatter. We ain't doing any good all sitting here together."

"Yes, sir, Sarge," Tom said with a mock salute. "Good to have you in charge again."

A wide grin appeared on Ben's face as he snapped a return salute and cocked his head at Seymour, his smile fading. "What about you, bluebelly?"

"Yes, *sir,* Sergeant Reb," the young man responded with a grin as he touched his right hand to the brim of his wide hat.

Ben's smile returned and a low chuckle came from his throat. "Son, I do believe we're gonna get along." He waved his hand at the herd. "Let's earn our pay."

"How old are you, Ben?" Seymour posed the question. "That is, if you don't mind my asking."

They sat on one side of the campfire, tin cups of hot, strong coffee warming their hands and scalding their lips. Ben didn't immediately answer, but finally said, "Thirty-four next birthday."

"You're a right good-looking fellow," Bill went on. "I'd have thought you'd have a wife or a girlfriend somewheres by now."

"None of your business, sonny," Ben responded.

"You ain't even ever told me," Tom said.

"None of your business neither," Ben admonished.

They sat for a while, no one speaking. There were four others on the opposite side of the fire engaged in their own conversations. Three absent members of their contingent were riding early watch on the cattle. The night was calm, with only a zephyr of wind from time to time, and the herd was settled and quiet.

"I was married for a little while," Ben said, breaking the silence unexpectedly. "I was going on nineteen, and she was two years younger." He paused. "She died in childbirth . . . baby boy went too."

Now the silence was uncomfortable.

"Wasn't none of our business," Tom said finally. "Didn't mean to bring up a hurt, Ben."

"You asked, now you know," Ben said. "Maybe there'll be a time and another woman for marrying, but for now, we ain't gonna talk about this ever again."

Across the fire, one of the four men spoke. "Ben, how much time left?"

"Three, four hours, I reckon," Ben answered. "Get a little shuteye 'fore you're up." He turned to Tom and Bill. "Same for you two. You're riding watch from dark to sunup."

"We're getting graveyard?" Tom exclaimed. "When didja come up with that?"

Ben gave them a wide grin. "Long about the time you young whippersnappers started asking personal questions."

Chapter Fourteen

Eastern Nebraska, 1866

As the days warmed into summer, with bright sun and blue skies, the transcontinental railroad construction moved west, the track crews laying rails at an average of a mile a day. Compared to the Central Pacific butting its way east through the coastal mountains, the Union Pacific had an easier go of it on the plains.

Tom, Ben, and Bill Seymour had regular duties now as outriders, roaming within sight of the lead crews preparing the roadbed. Not far behind, the track-laying crews placed ties and rails into position. Moving up from time to time on these newly laid rails, a locomotive pushed the string of cars that constituted the work train. Workers slept uncomfortably in its sweltering dormitory units and had their meals served in a mess car, the food prepared in a separate kitchen car. A little after daybreak, the men received their tools and supplies from the boxcars for their twelve hard hours of labor each day. The string also included carpenter and blacksmith shop cars. When the Casement brothers were on site, they traveled in the slanted-roof office car near the head of the train.

Ties and rails were unloaded from the flatcars and transferred to horse-drawn wagons. Driven in continuous relays to the forward end of the tracks, ties were unloaded and placed into position on the roadbed, heavy rails then carried forward and spiked into place.

Fanned out on one side of the train, the cattle herd grazed languidly, while on the other side, there were several remudas of saddle and workhorses, mules, and even a few donkeys.

This bustling hive of construction activity was an incongruity in the sun-baked, lonely isolation of the surrounding prairie. Accompanying the work train, a crew with wagons was erecting telegraph poles, the installed lines stretching to the east.

Even further back on the newly laid rails, a second train was slowly approaching. This train, sent out from Omaha on a regular schedule, brought replacement tools, materials, and supplies to the ongoing workplace. Once unloaded, it would back its way to Omaha for more.

"Ain't that a sight and a half?" Bill asked as he rode up beside Tom's horse, his eyes on the industrious panorama. "Like some sort of a doggone machine, the way they're working."

"Some other 'uns are giving it a look-see same as you," Tom responded, his gaze steady in a different direction. "Visitors just the other side of that ridge."

"Hostiles?" Bill turned his head sharply. "Where?"

Tom nodded his head to the high ridge that, for miles, paralleled their westward path. "Maybe not," he offered. "Maybe just Pawnees looking to steal a cow or two."

"Can't much blame 'em, poor as church mice," Bill said. He paused. "I 'spect they're fixing to cut out a critter or two at night so their folks can have something to eat."

"Way they're keeping outta sight, I'm figgering it's a Sioux dog-soldier party out there," Tom said.

"How many?"

"Well, I really didn't see no Indian riders. Saw a lot of dust through that cut back a ways, enough for maybe a good-sized raiding party."

"Told anybody?"

"'Spect it's time to do that right now," Tom answered. "You ride ahead and tell Ben; I'll ride back."

As Bill rode forward, Tom turned his horse around and urged the stallion into a trot along the long perimeter of the rail-laying project, reining to a stop beside the first outrider.

"Seeing dust over to the north," Tom told the man. "Could

be Red Cloud or one just like him. Way they're keeping out of sight, I don't think they're friendlies."

"I'll keep my eyes peeled," the rider told him. "Thanks for coming to say."

Tom rode on until he reached the end of the second train, delivered his message, and then trotted Duke back to resume his original guard position where Bill waited.

"Anybody tell Bonniwell?" Tom asked.

"Ben said they already knowed it. Said it could just be nothing but buffalo."

"And what if it ain't?"

Bill shook his head. "Ben said they'd keep a watch."

"You and me," Tom said conspiratorially. "Scout it out?"

"You mean—"

"Go see if maybe it's just buffalo dust or a raiding party."

"And if it's Red Cloud and a couple dozen war-painted savages and they see the two of us?"

Tom laughed, turned his horse, and dug his heels into Duke's sides to urge the stallion into a gallop toward the distant ridge. After a moment's hesitation, Bill urged his mount to follow.

"Maybe we ought not be out here," Bill whispered. "General Jack told all of us not to stir up any trouble with the Indians." He shook his head. "And we left our post. We're supposed to be looking out for the lead crews."

"There's others doing that. I just like to know what we're up against," Tom countered. "And I don't see no reason why we can't come out to take a look-see."

They were hunched down behind a knoll, looking down through a gap in the ridge; their horses were secluded in a gulch thirty yards away with their reins secured under rocks. They had dismounted and crept low through the hip-high brush to this vantage position to see what was on the other side of the elongated ridge. They counted eighteen Sioux braves riding bareback on their ponies. Tom and Bill were close enough to see the expressions on the Indians' unpainted faces, to hear their chatter, and to observe their behavior. Some were bare-chested with leggings, some wore only breechclouts, and still others were fully clothed.

It crossed Tom's mind that this could be nothing more than a hunting party. From the Indians' frequent gestures in the direction of the track-laying operation and their overall agitation, however, he believed them to be eager for raiding and killing. "Few rifles, some pistols," he whispered. He stretched his head higher for a better view. "Bows, tomahawks, and skinning knives."

"Well, we come to see what we needed to see," Bill said in a low voice. "Now let's get the hell outta here."

"Think they're gonna make a run at our outfit?"

Bill shrugged. "I'd say there's too many of us and too few of them. Still, they just might be dumb enough or mad enough to try to take some of us down." He paused. "Like the two of us dumb enough to be out here by our lonesomes."

"Look at it this way, Bill. General Jack ought to 'preciate us spying 'em out and telling how many there is."

"He'll likely bullwhip us fer leaving our posts," Bill countered. "Let's skedaddle."

A sharp *whoohist* in the air accompanied the flight of an arrow that sped over their heads. Another whistled and spiked its sharp point and shaft in the ground in front of them.

"Run for it, Tom!" Bill shouted as he sprang to his feet. "They've spotted us!"

Tom was already sprinting toward their horses, Bill a step behind him. They could hear the excited cries of a group of oncoming braves, and the sound of pounding hooves. Tom looked over his shoulder as he ran and saw four near-naked horsemen charging into view and turning their mounts after them. Tom reached Duke, yanked the reins free from the rock, and vaulted into the saddle. With his eyes on the pursuing braves, he drew his revolver while Bill mounted.

"Damn it, they're on us!" Bill yelled as he wheeled his horse about.

They prodded their horses to a furious gallop on a direct line to the distant work train assemblage. The four braves veered their mounts to intercept, bellowing their exultation.

Tom shifted his revolver to his left hand and, with his right, whipped the reins against Duke's flanks. He bent forward to urge greater speed into the stallion's ears and thrilled at the new surge he felt striding beneath him. He glanced to his right, worried to see Bill's horse lagging a length behind.

The Sioux warriors cut in just behind the fleeing riders, only a few yards of separation between the lead brave and Bill. The leading pony was coming up on Bill's left, the howling rider with a tomahawk in his right hand poised for a killing stroke.

Tom jerked the reins of his mount to the right and turned Duke back into the path of the fast-closing pursuer, the near collision of the animals swerving and slowing the pursuit. For a moment, the brave struggled to stay astride his mount, his tomahawk hand as well as his left clutching the mane. Recovering balance and now riding side by side with Tom, the warrior swung the ax across his body at Tom's head.

Tom ducked, the tomahawk slicing the air scant inches from his face and came as close again as the brave reversed the blade in a backhanded slash. Before he could swing again, Tom swerved Duke toward rather than away from his adversary, his revolver now in his right hand. The young brave's brutal expression instantly changed to comprehension and alarm. As he tried to veer away, Tom turned and fired a shot, hoping for, if not a kill, at least a distraction. Sure enough, the brave's pony slowed momentarily until the Indian renewed his pursuit.

Tom kept his eyes fixed on Bill riding just ahead, knowing that the safety of the work train operation was still a worrisome distance away. He knew the braves were directly behind him, the sound of their horses' hooves pounding so very near. He dug his heels into Duke's sides, acutely aware that death closely tracked his flight.

Tom ducked at the sound of a shot, but quickly realized that it came not from the rear, but from a distance ahead. He looked up in grateful relief to see six of his fellow guardsmen on horseback charging from the outer reaches of the work area. Another shot sounded, then another and, behind him, he could hear the Sioux braves abruptly slow their ponies to a halt.

He looked back as the braves turned their mounts and reversed their direction, trotting their ponies out of pistol range, although it appeared that the rescuing guardians were making no effort to effect a kill. He reined Duke to a slow walk to match Bill's mare and swiveled in his saddle to see the Indians now at a distance.

"That was close," Bill said with a great sigh as he reined to a stop.

Tom turned his attention back to his friend, reined up, and then looked to the half dozen armed men who circled around them. None of the riders spoke, but each was stone-faced, with no expression of support, nor disapproval.

One of them was Ben. "The big boss wants to see the pair of you," he said, his expression grim, his tone of voice grave. "If you were still living."

"How'd you know we was out here?" Tom asked, directing his question to Ben.

"Someone saw you leave," Ben replied. "Told the general." He paused. "We was coming to look for you."

In silence, the mounted group walked their horses across the remaining stretch of prairie to the fringe of the rail-construction operation. As they moved toward the front end of the train, they saw both of the Casement brothers standing in wait, and Charlie Bonniwell hovering nearby. There was no work in progress, the tie and rail carriers standing stock-still and watching their approach. No wagons were moving, no spikers were pounding; the entire community of workmen was standing in static, silent, and awed observance.

When they reached the two brothers, Tom and Bill dismounted and stood before them. Ben swung down from his horse and joined his two young friends.

Jack Casement, carrying a bullwhip, stepped forward and swept his hand at the motionless work site. "Look what the hell you've done!" he snarled. "You've brought the entire outfit to a damned standstill, no track laid while you were out there putting on a circus show!" He uncoiled the bullwhip and swung the length of it high in the air, then snapped the tip, the sharp report triggering a frightened start in all those nearby.

"Back to work! Everybody back to work! Now!" He snapped the whip twice more as the workmen broke from their stationary stances and hurried back into their labors. In no more than two minutes, the mechanism of the rail-laying endeavor was in full action once again.

As his brother remained close by, Jack Casement coiled his whip and moved to confront the pair standing before him. "You men left your posts. Why?"

Red-faced and acutely aware of all the eyes upon him, Tom cleared his throat. "We saw dust beyond the ridge and—"

"We knew about that bunch trailing us," Jack Casement cut in sharply. "Our Pawnee scouts . . . they're sworn enemies of the Sioux and it's their job to tell us about them, not yours." He stepped face-to-face with Ben. "Ben Haley, Charlie Bonniwell tells me you once were a Rebel noncom. These were your men, your responsibility."

"Pardon me, sir . . . General," Tom interjected, his voice strained and tentative. "It was my fault . . . not Ben's. It wasn't Bill's either . . . I egged him into it."

"Still his mistake," the construction manager snapped. "He should've just let you get yourself killed. Stay his post, we'd lose just one young fool, not two." He paused. "Catching the pair of you out there and doing you in stirs up the hostiles, makes them hanker for more scalps. You're not fit to ride guard duty on my outfit." He started to turn away. "Get rid of both of them."

"Tom's my friend, General," Ben said, his voice strong. "Like you say, he's young and maybe that makes him a fool, but he's saved my bacon more than once. Just 'cause he makes a young 'un's dumb mistake, ain't no reason for you make one too." He hesitated, then said, "I never soldiered with a better man."

"You talking up for the other young fool too?" Casement questioned brusquely.

Ben threw his shoulders back and nodded. "Yes, sir. From what I've seen, he needs a second chance right along with Tom. They'll be more good to you staying than kicking 'em away."

Jack Casement stood in contemplative silence for a long time. Then he turned to his brother. "Well, what do you think, Dan?"

The brother stepped close to speak in a lowered voice. "Bad example if we don't punish. Maybe not too big of one."

Jack Casement considered the statement and then nodded to Ben. "Leave it up to you. What do *you* think is a proper punishment?"

Ben didn't answer right away, his lips tightening as he considered his reply. Then he nodded. "Take 'em off guard duty and give 'em a week carrying iron."

"Nonsense!" General Jack exclaimed. "Takes skill to position the rails and—"

"Pardon me, General," Ben interrupted. "Didn't mean positioning . . . loading from the flatcars to the wagons. That's work that'll raise a sweat and cure 'em of foolishness."

General Jack turned his eyes to appraise the two young men. "They ain't strong enough for that heavy work."

"They can do it," Ben persisted. "They'll have to."

"They fold up, start dropping iron, they're gone!" General Jack snapped. "On their way back to Omaha—no pay, and we confiscate anything Union Pacific has provided."

Tom started to speak, but Ben gave him an elbow in his ribs.

"I think that's a fair deal, Jack," Dan said calmly. "The good side of this is that these boys can tell us just how many braves are trailing us, what weapons they're carrying . . . that sort of thing."

Jack Casement began to pace slowly, five steps to his right, five more to his left, his eyes focused on the three men before him. When he stopped, he gave a curt nod. "All right! Find out what they've seen over there, write it down, and get it to me in the next half hour."

"When do they start hauling iron?" Ben asked.

"Thirty-five minutes from now."

Chapter Fifteen

Nebraska, 1866

Last day," Tom said aloud with a deep sigh. He wiped the sweat from his face and neck and glanced up at the scorching early-afternoon sun.

"We hope," Bill Seymour said. "I'm plumb wore down, and it ain't anywhere near quitting time."

Tom bobbed his head in agreement. "Gotta hand it to these guys, ain't no fun way to make a living." Again, he sighed. "Here comes another."

Four husky men aboard the adjacent flatcar were lifting a six-hundred-pound rail from a large pile, two men at the ends and two in the middle. They walked it to the platform edge and handed it across the narrow space where Tom and Bill, along with two strong and practiced black men, received it aboard the horse-drawn open cart on which they stood. Tom and Bill, stationed in the center, strained under the heavy weight as the four of them lowered it to nest among several others on the floor of the long cart.

The two men working on the cart with Tom and Bill were hard-muscled, bare-chested former slaves who had often smirked at, but had little to say to, their new, inexperienced helpers during the past punishment week. Aboard the train, Michael Donnell, a hulking Irish immigrant with little education and a cheerful attitude, seemed to be the lead man on his crew. He was teamed with another migrant from Eire named Shawn, a Swede called Ollie, and another former slave who answered to Arthur.

"We're full up!" Tom called out. "Take 'er away!"

The four on the wagon jumped to the ground as the driver started his single horse forward. They squatted and watched the heavily loaded cart as it lumbered toward the rail-laying activity many yards ahead. The men on the flatcar sat and hung their feet over the flatbed side, taking a short rest in the time it would take for an empty cart to arrive and be maneuvered into position.

"Would you be wanting to do this all the time?" Donnell called in his thick brogue, a gently mocking tone accompanying the wide smile on his face. "You lads are getting quite good at it, if I do say so my very self."

"At least we only dropped the one," Bill responded, wiping the sweat from his face and neck with his kerchief.

"We'll keep that misfortune to ourselves," Donnell said. "Lots of us, we've done the same when we was just started to handle iron."

"If General Jack don't tack on another week," Tom said, "I'd like to think we'd be in our saddles come morning."

"You still have the bottom of the day to finish your chores," Donnell reminded him. "Aye, here's the next one."

Tom, Bill, and the two black men rose from the ground and walked out of the way as a driver expertly guided his horse to bring the cart bed a half-foot away from the flat car. This driver, another Irishman, gave a friendly wave and stepped down to move to restrain his horse. With a firm grip on the animal's harness, he would stay there to ensure no erratic movement of the cart would occur while the rails were transferred from the train.

With more sighs and grumblings, Tom, Bill, and their co-workers climbed up on the cart while their counterparts on the train rose to resume their strenuous labors. Again and again, the men on the flatcar lifted and carried each rail and transferred it to the waiting hands of the sweating receivers.

"I ain't seen no curved rails," Tom said to Donnell as they laid another rail on the wagon bed. "What do they do when they got to go 'round a bend?"

Donnell and his helpers picked up a rail, moved to the edge

of the flatbed, and handed it across. "There it is, my fellow," Donnell said and pointed to the rail.

"Where is what?" Tom was perplexed as he and the others lowered the rail to the cart floor.

"They take that straight one, lay it over a couple of stacked ties, and pound the devil out of it 'til she's the right shape for going 'round wherever it's a mind to go."

"I never saw 'em do that," Tom said, his tone skeptical.

"You lads been riding them hobbyhorses out there on the prairie," Donnell said. "Next time they bend, you come take a look and listen to what a dreadful din the pounders do make."

The hard work continued for most of the afternoon, the last load driven to the railhead at about seven o'clock in the evening. Donnell shook hands enthusiastically with Tom and Bill, and the rest gave them reluctant nods of farewell.

With the sweat dried into their clothes and onto their bodies, Tom and Bill hightailed it directly to a nearby small stream, where they stripped naked and bathed with dozens and dozens of other workers. Although the train carried a large supply of water, it was mainly for drinking and cooking rather than bathing. The supply was replenished at the streams and rivulets wherever encountered. Finishing their baths, Tom and Bill also scrubbed their underwear, and even their shirts and denim trousers, in the cold water before dressing in them again, delighting in the wet comfort they continued to provide.

"You boys ready to behave?" Ben asked as the duo entered the area where tents had been pitched under the shade of a five-tree grove near the work train.

"Saying we're sorry, it's been said too many times already," Bill put in. "We okay now with the boss?"

"You got their attention," Ben replied. "They'll be watching you close, so don't do nothing to bring 'em down on you again."

In the heat of the summer, nights in the dormitory cars were impossible to endure. Turned into ovens by the sun during the day, with scant air circulation inside, the cars were not livable.

In addition to the sweltering sour-stench atmosphere, the beds were infested with bedbugs and lice. The men ventured inside rarely, only to retrieve certain items of their belongings.

On both sides of the rail line, moveable campsites had been set up and advanced every few days to stay abreast of the track-laying progress. Some slept in tents, others in bedrolls or on blankets on the hard ground. Meals were still prepared aboard the train, and the tables in the sweltering mess car were uncomfortably attended for morning, noon, and supper-time meals.

Less than a mile behind, another mobile tent community followed the Union Pacific work force. Gamblers, con artists, whiskey sellers, shoddy-merchandise vendors, and prostitutes flocked to the railroad-building enterprise. Laborers, with regular pay and no other place to spend their cash, were enticed to make frequent visits to the canvas saloons, shops, and brothels. This close-traveling bazaar of corruption and licentiousness spawned a phrase of notoriety for the entire track-laying undertaking—the *Hell on Wheels Train*.

With the setting sun just above the horizon, some men in their camp were already leaving and walking east.

"They win in any poker game, they'll be lucky not to get knocked out of their senses and robbed on their way back," Bill said.

Ben nodded his head in agreement. "They're plumb fools anyway. Walking lonesome in Indian country . . . let alone tempting any of them cutthroats in that tent city back there."

"Why don't General Jack clear 'em out?" Tom asked.

"Oh, they tried it a couple of times," Ben responded. "They all scattered, but a day or two later, they was all back and more of 'em than ever."

"I'm steering clear of that outfit," Tom said with a tinge of righteousness. "Got more'n four months pay, more'n any I ever had in my life."

"Had your supper?" Ben asked as the threesome settled down in front of a small campfire, a flame for light rather than warmth.

Tom nodded. "Grabbed supper after dunking in the stream." He made a face. "Maybe I *will* walk over there to that sin city and see if anybody there knows how to cook."

The comment brought chuckles from the dozen or more gathered around the fire.

"Any more dealings with the Sioux or the Cheyenne?" Tom asked, his question posed to all within hearing.

"Heard a bunch tried to jump one of surveyor crews," one man said. "Couple of our boys and the crew had better weapons and run 'em off."

"Anybody hurt?" Tom asked.

"Nope," the man answered. "Just a lot of yelling and shooting—nobody either side came close to hitting a danged thing."

The conversations continued well into the night before the fire was doused and this small contingent of guards prepared for sleep. Although Tom, Ben, and Bill had a small tent to share, all three laid blankets outside of it, seeking the comfort of an occasional breeze to stir the humid air.

Like every other man in their mini-camp, Tom took off his shirt and trousers to spend the night on his bedroll in his summer underwear. He hung his still-damp clothing on a nearby tree, where the same light breezes and the night heat would have the garments dry by morning.

He lay down with his back on the thin bedding and looked up at the great vault of the starry sky. For a time, he marveled at the enormity of it and let that take away his dismays and discomforts. After a full seven days of hard labor, his muscles were sore from the heavy lifting, his sinews stinging with muted pain from unaccustomed strain. He rolled on his side to avoid the sight of space splendor and closed his eyes. His body said exhaustion, but his mind refused to acknowledge fatigue.

The physical discomfort of punishment was not the major bother at all, but the dressing down in front of everyone by General Jack still rankled. Perhaps the iron-willed headman had some reason for that angry public scolding, although it could have been done in private. As to leaving their posts, it seemed to Tom that the train was adequately surrounded by guardsmen, and, in their scouting venture, he and Bill were just doing their jobs.

If General Jack knew about them Indians trailing his outfit, why hadn't the word been passed to us outriding sentries? And if the Pawnee scouts were so good, why was it up to me and Bill to tell 'em how many there was and what weapons they was carrying?

Over the past week, these thoughts and dark others came fleetingly into his daylight hours and, at night, roiled in his mind before he could find sleep. For the hopeful dreamers, the politicians, the rich and the powerful, this was a grand and glorious project. For most of these laborers, employment on this railroad was a godsend, albeit a hard and difficult way to make a living. For hundreds of them, it meant long separation from family and friends, yet it provided a much-needed bit of money to send home.

For Tom, it was different. As with most employments in his nomadic life, this was merely a job to do and then move on. With the humiliation just suffered, perhaps it was, again, time to look for his future elsewhere.

Chapter Sixteen

Nebraska, 1866

A month later, the tracks had moved deep into the Nebraska Territory, the crews continuing to lay rails on an average of a mile a day, and often two or three. There were slowdowns; the paucity of hardwood trees on the plains meant importing ties from the East, involving shipping delays and higher costs. Eventually, ties were cut from softer woods and creosoted to add the strength necessary to hold the rails in place.

The further the operation moved from Omaha, the more additional problems surfaced. For two paydays in a row, inadequate cash had been supplied and, while some workers were paid on time, many others were skipped entirely.

"Got a new chore for you," Charlie Bonniwell announced one evening as he walked into Ben's camp. "We got us some troublemakers making a fuss about their pay." He paused. "I'm going over to try to make 'em see reason . . . but I'm gonna need you all to watch my back."

There was no immediate reaction; the men in Ben's small band waited for additional information.

"What are we supposed to do . . . watching your back?" Ben asked.

"Just make sure nobody gets rowdy, that's the gist of it," Bonniwell said.

Again, there was a long silence.

"Why us?" Ben asked.

"Why not?" Bonniwell countered. "You're trained for trouble."

"Is this *our* kind of trouble?" Tom asked.

"It's walking distance," Bonniwell said, ignoring Tom's question. "I'll need the bunch of you. There's maybe fifteen of them soreheads camping out on the other side of the train and there's, what, ten of you? That ought to be aplenty."

"I'm not too comfortable 'bout this, Charlie," Ben said. "Watching for Indians and herding duties, that's okay. Being hard with our own guys, I don't know."

"It just don't pay for me, alone, to go in there," Bonniwell said. "I don't 'spect no hassle if you all are walking with me."

"Well, I still—"

"That's an order, Ben." Bonniwell cut him off and turned to address the men, now all clustered close by. "Like I said, I ain't 'specting no problems, but you fellers bring what you need to deal with it if it goes nasty."

"You talking pistols?" Tom asked.

Bonniwell nodded. "Yes, sir, bring 'em along."

A few minutes later, in the dim light of dusk, Bonniwell led the group of ten guardsmen to the train where, one by one, they stepped over a coupling between cars and reassembled on the other side.

"There's their fire straight ahead," Bonniwell said, his hand pointing to a low flame in the midst of a large huddle of shadowy silhouettes seated on the ground. "Let's go."

"I don't like this," Tom said to Bill in a low voice. "There's not just fifteen there . . . more like thirty at least."

"What choice we got?" Bill whispered.

"Choose to be careful," Ben interjected softly. "Don't let any temper take hold of ya. You start something, they'll likely finish it for ya."

As the lesser band made its approach, the dark figures rose to their feet and, even in the gloom, the gathering exuded a quality of belligerence. The shadowy assemblage moved slowly forward and, as they came closer, their faces became distinct. Tom could see that it was a sizable grouping of large laborers, consisting of several different ethnic backgrounds; mostly Irish, but also including a few Poles, Swedes, and Germans. Notably, there was not a single person of color in the throng. As the distance closed between groups, three of the shadow men stepped ahead to intercept the intruders.

One of them was Michael Donnell.

Tom saw the big Irishman's eyes flick to him instantly and then shift back to Bonniwell. In this meeting, there was neither a smile nor any attitude of friendliness. Donnell was not the leader of the trio. Apparently, he was one of two muscled enforcers who stood with a slighter man in between them.

"What do you want?" the center man asked. He was older than his two companions, in his middle-thirties compared to their twenties. He was of a slender build, yet his bare arms showed the sinewy strength earned from a life of hard work. He had a thick head of black hair with just a scattering of premature gray at the temples. His face was narrow, his features craggy, and there was a feral quality in his manner. His thin lips were drawn in a tight smile that had no humor in it.

"You Danny McConaughey?" Bonniwell asked, his tone belligerent.

The man nodded. "I am and you surely know it."

Bonniwell swept his right hand to indicate the entire assembly of men behind the three. "What are you all up to?"

"Minding business of our very own." McConaughey's reply came with the Irish lilt, but the tone of it was surly. "Perhaps you should be minding that of your own."

"Starting trouble is more like it," Bonniwell said, his anger escalating at the slender man's mocking manner. "I'm hearing you're fixing up a work stoppage."

"That it could be, if there's no payday this week when the train comes," McConaughey said. "Some have been paid, but many of us have not."

"You'll get your pay . . . we'll give you vouchers, but there'll be no slacking off," Bonniwell said.

"No, it'll be cash we'll be getting, not your promise papers," McConaughey countered. "No work unless it's the sort of pay what we can spend."

Bonniwell muttered a word beneath his breath.

"Did you call me a blasphemous name?" the slender man asked.

"Never mind," Bonniwell said and stepped to one side to look past the three at the large group of men behind them. "You blockheads! You break it up now and head back to your own work groups!"

No one moved.

Bonniwell turned to Ben. "Break 'em up! Stamp out their fire, and pistol whip any dumbbell that gives you trouble."

No one moved.

"Did you hear me?" Bonniwell hissed. "Do it!"

"Take it easy, Charlie," Ben muttered. "Just walk away and let things simmer. They'll go their way on their own tonight when they're tired of talking. Come tomorrow, when they ain't a big bunch, we can talk sense to 'em, maybe one by one."

"Do it!" Bonniwell spat the words, his fury mounting.

Ben drew his breath and let it out with a sigh. "Charlie, just let it—"

Suddenly, Bonniwell reached for his revolver, his thumb cocking it as he drew it from his holster. As his right arm came up, McConaughey reached out to slap it to the side and the revolver fired. There was a scream of pain from someone in the crowd and an immediate roar of outrage from the surly men.

"Damn, now we're in for it!" Ben shouted as he backed away.

Tom remained in place, his eyes fixed on the action directly in front of him. Donnell and the other big Irishman had wrestled Bonniwell to the ground, and McConaughey had torn the revolver from his hand. As the protest leader raised the gun to fire, Tom leaped forward and chopped the edge of his right hand against McConaughey's wrist and knocked the revolver away. He followed with a sharp blow to the startled man's jaw that stunned and staggered him.

Tom took a step to retrieve the fallen weapon, tucked it in his belt and turned to the two men who were pummeling

Bonniwell with hard punching blows to the face and torso. "That's enough, Michael!"

Donnell checked his jabbing fist and looked up, a frown on his face for the interruption. Beside him, the second aggressor ended his strikes as well, his eyes turning to Tom.

"You kill him, you'll hang for it," Tom said to the pair.

"Didn't mean to shoot anybody," Bonniwell managed to mutter through his bloody mouth. "Warning shot."

Before anything else could be said, the horde of angry protestors rushed the guardsmen and enveloped them. Some of Tom's comrades had drawn their revolvers and were trying to club their attackers with them and fight their way to a retreat. Tom saw Bill swinging his Colt right and left as he backed away from two aggressors.

Tom directed his steady gaze directly into Donnell's eyes. "I'll take Bonniwell out of here, Michael. You'll give me no trouble, will you?"

There was no answer.

"And none from your friend here."

"Take him," Donnell growled. "We shan't stop ya."

Tom gave a curt nod and reached for Bonniwell's shoulders, easing the injured supervisor first into a sitting position, and then assisted him to his feet. "Can you walk?"

"Some, I guess," Bonniwell said through swollen lips. "Get me out of here."

Around them, the melee continued, fistfights pitting two and three or even four brawlers against each solitary guardsmen. Tom could see Ben with his back against a companion's as they tried to ward off the blows of a surrounding ring of beefy fighters.

Supporting Bonniwell with his left arm under the battered man's shoulders, Tom drew the revolver from his belt and aimed it skyward. He pulled the trigger twice, and the boom of each shot brought the skirmish to a standstill.

"Those were warning shots!" Tom shouted. "If I have to, I'll kill!"

There were shouts of derision and defiance.

Tom fired another shot into the air to silence the boisterous dissent and then bellowed, "We're backing out of here and any-one tries to stop us, he's dead."

"We already got a man dead!" a shout came from the crowd.

"That was an accident, and your own man caused it!" Tom countered. "Back away, or there'll be more of you on the ground!"

A hush fell and, in the calm, the men began to separate and shuffle in silence to regroup with their own. In the space be-tween, a figure lay sprawled and unmoving.

"We've got a dead one of our own!" Ben exclaimed solemnly.

Tom left Bonniwell to stand on his own as he walked to and knelt down beside the dead man, looking first at the hilt of the huge knife protruding from his back. Already knowing the iden-tity, he reached for and gently turned the head to see the empty eyes in the anguished face of Bill Seymour.

"Two dead, several hurt, including you, Charlie," Jack Case-ment said to the small group in the work train's office car. It was close to midnight, and Tom and Ben were standing close to a desk where Dan Casement sat in silent observance and a band-aged Charlie Bonniwell sat in discomfort in a chair nearby.

General Jack was pacing, as was his mien during high agi-tation. "What a frightful mess!" He stopped directly in front of Tom and Ben, his eyes switching angrily from one to the other. "You two, again!"

Ben started to speak.

"Don't!" General Jack said sharply. "When things go wrong, you two are always there." He turned his attention to Bonni-well. "Tell me what happened, Charlie."

The battered supervisor coughed to clear his throat. "We went over to talk reason with them fellers who was figgering on stopping work 'cause they said they ain't getting their pay on time." He paused. "We went about it okay, but this feller, McConaughey, he caused the commotion and, well, it all went bad. Things got out of hand."

"We'll take care of Mr. McConaughey, hang him if we need to," General Jack declared. "Who stabbed young Seymour?"

"Nobody knows," Bonniwell admitted. "We're trying to find that out."

"Shots were fired and a man was killed," General Jack said. "Who was firing shots?"

No one answered, but Bonniwell glanced at Tom.

"Now, wait a minute," Tom protested. "That ain't what went—"

"Shut up!" General Jack cut him off. "Charlie, I'm not pleased with your part in this, but these two trigger-happy Rebs, I want them off our job tomorrow morning."

"Hold on there!" Ben exclaimed. "This ain't fair . . . Charlie wouldn't be living if it hadn't been for Tom here."

Casement looked sharply at the injured supervisor.

Bonniwell shrugged. "He helped some, I guess, but I'd have been okay."

"Well, if that don't beat all," Ben said in disgust.

"Gentlemen," Dan Casement said unexpectedly. "Jack's made the point that these two young men have a habit of being where trouble begins. Now, maybe there's more to this story, but I agree. With these two out of the way, we'll take a hard look at any others who were involved in this fiasco." He looked directly at Tom. "I'm told you were actually threatening to kill some of our workmen."

"I said that just to get us outta there," Tom protested hotly. "And nothing other than that!"

"Dan's right," his brother said, dismissing Tom's outburst. "We'll sort things out as we go. Any of the men that were taking part in this will either go back to work tomorrow without complaining, or they'll walk all the way back to Omaha or wherever." He pointed to Tom and Ben. "As for you two, you're gone. I understand you came with one horse between you and carrying your own sidearms. That's what you'll leave with and nothing more. We'll cash you out minus expenses."

"I'll have my say," Tom said with grim determination.

"You'll have no such—"

"*You* shut up, General," Tom interrupted. "Charlie Bonniwell *ordered* us to bust up that meeting tonight. Ben, here, told
him not to push it and to let things simmer down and deal with
it when it was a better time. Charlie wouldn't listen, pulled a
gun and it was *him* that fired the first shot, the one that killed
the Swede."

Jack Casement eyes flashed anger and he opened his mouth
to respond.

"I'm not through yet," Tom said harshly. "He said it was an
accident, and I guess I believe him, but the only shots *I* fired
was warning shots to stop the fracas . . . and I did." He
paused. "It bothers me that Mr. Bonniwell tells things his way
and you let him, but you wouldn't let us tell our side."

General Jack bit his lower lip, but a small grin tugged at the
corners of his mouth. "You got sand, youngster, I'll give you
that." He looked to his brother. "Maybe we ought to sleep on
this before making up our minds."

"I ain't speaking for Ben, but I don't want you giving me
back no job," Tom said. "General, you're a hard man, and I
'spect that's what it takes to stretch a railroad 'cross this country. You may need to run roughshod over them that works for
you, but I'm not one to be trampled on."

"Me neither," Ben put in. "Tom and me, we're partners, and
we come as a team and we go as a team."

Tom suppressed a smile and directed his next comment to
Dan Casement. "If Ben's serious about quitting, he needs his
horse. We ain't riding double out here in Indian country."

"That's a better-than-average gelding," Dan said. "Worth
maybe what one of you has coming in your pay."

"Make it mine, then," Ben said.

"You've got quite a mouth on you . . . anything else you'd
like to say, Patterson?" General Jack said, the sarcasm steeped
in his voice.

"Yeah, just the one thing more," Tom responded.

"What?"

"Goodbye, Shorty!"

Chapter Seventeen

Nebraska, 1866

Well, that job didn't last long," Tom said.

"Thanks to you," Ben complained as they rode alongside the work-train cars on their way to Omaha. "And that smart-alecky goodbye of yours dang near cost me my horse." He looked over his shoulder and scowled. "That runt, Dan, he was gonna renege about selling me Blaze." He reached forward and patted his horse's neck. "They charged me more'n the horse is worth, but I ain't complaining."

"I figger they shorted me too, on my cash," Tom said. "Got a lot less'n what I thought I'd earned. I might've argued about it, but I reckon they had the books fixed up to show it their way, so I didn't fuss about it." He touched his hand to a back pocket of his jeans. "We'll hafta get by as best we can on what I've got."

"Whatcha got left?"

"Less'n thirty greenbacks."

"You got cheated."

They came to a scene familiar to Tom—a cart nestled close to a flatcar where Michael Donnell and his crew were swinging iron rails to men on the cart. Tom guided his horse past the cart and reined up near Donnell's position. At first, the big Irishman tried not to look at him, keeping his eyes and attention on his work. Tom continued to sit astride Duke and waited.

"All right," Donnell said at last, leaving his work and turning to Tom. "If you're wanting me to say I'm sorry about last night, I surely will." He didn't speak again for several seconds and then: "And not for what I was doing to Mr. Bonniwell, but I do feel the shame for young Bill."

"Shame enough to go around, but that's not why I stopped here," Tom said. "Ben and me, we're pulling out, but maybe you and a couple of others should do the same."

"I can't afford to, young lad," Donnell said. "None of us can." He paused. "It's Bonniwell, is it?"

Tom nodded. "He won't forget the licking you gave him."

"He's that kind, is he?"

"He was a surprise and a big disappointment to us . . . he ain't what he pretends to be," Tom said. "He'll likely try to get even."

"Our lot, I suppose, and we'll face it as best we can," Donnell said. "God go with you." He waved and turned away.

Tom guided Duke to the east once again and, side by side with Ben, rode to the end of the work train. As they passed the last car, both looked back.

"Well, here we are, danged near broke again," Ben said in a dour voice.

"But we got *two* horses now, and we got out of Yankee country," Tom reminded him.

"Something to be said for that, I suppose." Ben rode in silence for a while and then gave a little cough to gain Tom's attention. "I've been thinking. Here I am ten years older'n you and *I'm* always doing what *you* say we do."

"More like twelve, thirteen years older."

"Never mind 'bout that," Ben said impatiently. "I ought to be giving *you* the wisdom of *my* years."

"You do . . . at times."

"Yeah, like the time at the fire when I said 'Let's keep marching' and you said 'Let's run for the river.' "

"Well, I just knew the lay of the land a little better."

"Way I see it, for your time of living, I'd say you got gumption," Ben said. "I ain't putting myself down, but I do think you sometimes sense things 'fore I do."

"Let's argue the other side of it," Tom said. "Whose bright idea was it to go looking for them Indians when, if it'd been you, you'd have had better sense?"

Ben laughed. "Well, maybe that makes us even." He gently kicked the sides of Blaze to urge the horse to stay abreast of Tom's. "Now, I hate to ask . . . you got any idea of where we're going?"

"You?"

Ben laughed. "Not one at all."

"We're heading back towards Omaha . . . maybe see the sheriff 'bout them deputy jobs."

Ben smiled. "You anxious to see that Mary Beth girl?"

"Sure, that'd be nice," Tom admitted, "but you and a half dozen others done told me she'll likely set her sights on somebody of quality rather than a saddle bum like me."

"Being a person of quality means we gotta have not just money in our poke, but a bunch laying in the bank."

"First thing, we gotta find work. If the sheriff don't take us on, what little I got ain't gonna last long."

Riding alongside the roadbed of the railroad, they soon passed through the tents of cardsharps, swindlers, scalawags, and wayward women. They trotted their horses and ignored the counterfeit cries of welcome and sham promises of quick riches, beer and spirits, and pleasurable companionships.

As the railroad moved west, civilization of this sort had followed as well. Honest opportunists as well as those of a far different nature realized that the finished railway would be an avenue of commerce for many years to come. Tiny little towns were springing up along the way to service the construction crews and to reap rewards from train passengers in the days to come.

By midday they had come to a small settlement under construction, wooden buildings being erected amidst a scatter of large and small tents, a dozen or more Conestoga wagons, carts, and a corral with horses inside.

"This warn't here a month ago," Tom said. "They building a real town?"

"Grifter town, it appears to me," Ben responded. "Want to take a closer look?"

"I'm getting a little saddle sore," Tom allowed. "Let's do 'er . . . maybe get a bite to eat."

They guided their horses onto what would eventually be the central street if the settlement lasted. It was about fifty feet in length, with a two-wagon width. One frame building, with a noticeable lean, was nearly complete with clapboard siding, and workmen were on the roof pounding shingles to cover the wood panels. Two other sites were skeleton structures with more people hammering wall braces into place.

"Howdy!" Tom called to a portly bald man in a rumpled suit who seemed to be overseeing the work on the start of a fourth building. On site, two men were awkwardly attaching cross members to support timbers that were lined seven to each side and six across the front and back. "When did this town start?"

The man turned and looked up at them, an appraising glance that evaluated their horses, their saddles, their clothes, and the newcomers themselves. "Howdy back to you," he said coolly. "Just curious, or is there something you're looking for?"

"Curious, I guess," Tom replied, his affability fading as he tugged the reins to turn Duke away. "We'll leave you to your work."

"Hold on," the man said quickly. "Sorry if I sounded unfriendly." He pointed to the haphazard construction. "Watching the way my building is going up got me lathered up. It'll likely fall down 'fore they get the roof over it."

"No carpenters?" Ben asked.

The man walked closer and a chagrined smile appeared. "I got a blackjack dealer and a whiskey drummer hitting their thumbs more'n the nails. There's a fancy lady who ain't half bad at it, but she only works once in a while, when she takes a notion." He paused. "Either of you know how to saw or hammer?"

"I ain't bad at it," Ben said.

"And you?" The man directed the question to Tom.

"I know enough that you ought to tear down everything you've put up so far," Tom told him. "Don't look like there's a good footing for your building. Couple of them support posts look crooked."

"We poked those support beams down pretty deep," the man said defensively. "Ought to hold okay."

"Cement on bottom of 'em?"

"No . . . should there be?" the man questioned.

"Dirt ain't gonna hold. You got to dig 'em up again, pour cement, and anchor 'em good and strong. Be best to pour a line foundation fer the whole shebang."

"Sound like you two know about buildings?" the man said in the sense of a question.

"Enough to know you're putting up a problem," Ben told him.

The portly man sighed and then reached up his hand to Ben. "My name's John Wilcox."

Ben shook his hand. "Ben Haley . . . this here is my partner, Tom Patterson."

After the second handshake, Wilcox said, "I wonder if you gentlemen . . . would you step down and listen to a proposition?"

"What kind of a proposition?" Tom asked, remaining in his saddle.

"As you can plainly see, I need some help," Wilcox told him. He swept his hand to indicate the surroundings. "This whole town is having growing pains."

Ben swung down from his horse and held the reins in his hands. "What kinda place you building here?"

Again, Wilcox made a gesture, pointing to a cluster of tents. "We've been following the Union Pacific track-laying enterprise, providing services, entertainment and goods for the men and—"

"And fleecing 'em outta their money right and left," Tom cut in.

Wilcox shrugged. "Well, there's gonna be a lot of business

along this railroad while she's being built and after they've got her done. We're just not going to be working out of tents, but out of real buildings." He turned his head and gave a nod to indicate his suspect structure. "This here is going to be this town's first café, so I guess I'm taking a turn at being respectable."

"Café or saloon?" Ben asked.

Again, Wilcox shrugged. "Maybe a little of both."

Tom swung his right leg over Duke's rump and stepped down from his saddle. "You said something about a proposition."

"That I did, sir," Wilcox said. "I'd pay for you to either show these lunkheads how to build my place, or maybe do the work yourselves."

"Pay how much?" Ben asked.

"Well . . . I'd go as high as . . . eighty dollars."

"Eighty . . . that's for the both of us?" Tom wanted to know.

Wilcox nodded. "Throw in your meals . . . that'd be a good deal for you." He looked back and forth between Tom and Ben, searching their expressions for acceptance or refusal. "How about it?"

Ben rubbed the stubble on his jaw, feigning misgiving. "Well, we was just traveling through . . . we got things to do back in Omaha."

"It would only take a few days," Wilcox said. "Wouldn't delay you too long."

"What do you think, Tom?" Ben asked.

"I don't know . . . just eighty for the pair of us?" Tom said, understanding Ben's ploy. "Looks like we'd be held up fifteen, twenty days."

"Okay, fifty apiece," Wilcox said hastily. "I'll even let you share sleeping in my tent if you'd like."

"Nah, that wouldn't be necessary," Ben said and looked to Tom. "We ain't due in Omaha 'til the end of the month, so maybe we could do Mr. Wilcox here a favor."

"Seventy-five dollars," Tom said. "Guess that might do."

"Apiece?" Wilcox asked. "That's danged high!"

Tom touched the brim of his hat in a farewell salute. "Well, been nice to chat with you and—"

"Wait a minute," Wilcox said hurriedly. "I guess I can live with that."

Tom looked around. "Got some shovels?"

"You taking the job?" Wilcox asked.

"First thing is to dig up them posts and give 'em a cement foundation," Tom told him. "We'll make you the best building in town."

Chapter Eighteen

Nebraska, 1866

Eleven days later, the shell of the single-story building was completed. The siding had been tacked to the outside, the roof planked and readied for shingling, the door openings framed awaiting the doors, and a boardwalk laid at the front. Inside, the wall studs were starkly visible, and no ceiling planks had been nailed to the rafters. The floor was dirt, hard packed by the stomping feet of the workers, and by those who had come by to admire the progress.

Tom, Ben, Wilcox, and another man finished placing the stubby bar at one corner of the new facility, and they all strolled to the front and looked back at what had been created. Three rough tables and accompanying benches had been cobbled together from available lumber for seating patrons. One space in the open area that would serve as the kitchen featured another rough table for food preparation. A brand new stove, just arrived on the last supply train, was placed against the back wall with its flue pipe angled up and out through the rear siding.

"That 'bout does her," Ben mused. "All we can do."

"A fine job, boys," Wilcox said with a nod of approval. "There's finishing-up work in here to do and more in town if you're interested."

"Nah, it's time to ride on," Tom said. "And time to settle up."

"Yes, of course," Wilcox said with a nod. "We must get to that after a while."

"We was thinking . . . what about right now?" Tom questioned. He unfolded a piece of paper and handed it to the café proprietor. "That's seventy-five each for me and Ben."

Wilcox concentrated his attention on the hand-written figures on the paper, then folded it and placed it in his suit coat pocket. "This evening, we'll talk about it."

Tom and Ben exchanged a look.

"We're leaving after breakfast, tomorrow," Tom said. "There ain't gonna be no problem, is there?"

"Of course not," Wilcox assured him. "Come see me about six this evening." With a half-salute, he turned and walked toward the stove with a show of great interest in its features.

"Think he's putting us off?" Ben asked in a low voice.

"Wouldn't put it past him," Tom responded. "He's a little too slick, you ask me."

They walked out of the building and paused to survey the rest of the small village. The lean of the first building they had seen was even more severe than when they had arrived, and now it was beginning to look dangerous. Whatever it had been built to house, as yet there was no business occupying it. Men occasionally approached it, tentatively entered, and quickly came out again. Other building projects in the new town were proceeding slowly and sporadically, the amateur carpenters carefully copying the work they had seen from Tom and Ben.

During their stay, they had tried to gauge the character of John Wilcox. In contrast to the majority of the unsavory residents, he seemed well spoken and attentive to their needs. As time had passed, however, Tom and Ben shared a growing suspicion of him. There had been a couple of occasions when the man's civility seemed to slip, and a coarse and callous personality had been briefly glimpsed. Not with them, but with others he had shown flashes of malevolence. There had been spiteful words muttered under his breath after the departure of one man with whom he had just held a seemingly cheerful and friendly meeting. His words for the scarlet women of the tiny settlement were contemptuous, demeaning, and obscene.

"He's a smoothie with us, but I don't trust him one whit," Ben said as they walked to the area where they had left their bedrolls. "He's got some pals that look like they could cut your throat."

Tom nodded. "I saw a couple of 'em give us a look from time to time. He pays us . . . we clear out tonight 'stead of tomorrow."

"*If* he pays us."

"Oh, we'll get our pay," Tom assured his friend. "One way or 'nother."

Well hidden in grove of trees on a hill overlooking the fledgling community, Tom and Ben lay on their stomachs in tall grass to watch activities below. Their horses were tethered a short distance away, and their possessions were stashed at the same place.

"Look there!" Ben said softly. "We figgered right."

Tom nodded. Two rough-looking men came out of the rear door of the café structure, stepped into the gap between the Conestoga wagon parked at the rear of the building, and remained in the concealment that the narrow space provided. A minute later, John Wilcox came through the rear door and conferred with the pair for a short while, then re-entered his building. ·

"What time you make it?" Tom asked.

Ben shaded his eyes and looked for the position of the sun low above the horizon. "Figger it around five-thirty or so."

Below, the two men were examining the loads of their revolvers.

"They're waiting for us," Ben said. "Guess that means Wilcox ain't gonna pay."

"Never was fixing to," Tom said.

"You figger they're just there to back Wilcox or . . . ?"

"Or to gun us down," Tom finished Ben's thought.

"Would they do that in the middle of the danged town?"

"This town? Why not? Ain't nobody decent in this whole place. They're the same kind of thieving bunch what's been following the rail laying. Lord help any fool who stops over in this here hellhole."

"Think we can take care of them two?" Ben asked.

"Let's go give 'er a try."

They returned to their horses, where Ben took a lariat from the side of his saddle. Then, careful to keep out of the line of sight of the two men behind the café, they worked their way down the rise to huddle by the near side of the building.

"Now what?" Ben whispered.

"You know any songs?" Tom asked in a low voice.

"Songs?" Ben asked incredulously. "What do you mean?"

"You're dead drunk . . . laying against this wall and singing, not too loud, not too soft . . . and you're making them song words sorta mealy-mouthed."

"Why?"

"To get them two's attention. So they come 'round to run you off."

"Where'll you be?"

Tom pointed to the Conestoga. "Other side of that wagon."

"What'll happen to me?"

"Nothing, I hope. I'll knock 'em both in the head while they're looking at you."

"What if they shoot me 'fore you do that?"

"Well, I'll knock heads anyway," Tom said with a grin. "Nah, it'll take 'em a spell to make out what's going on, and that's all I'll need."

"Maybe there's another way," Ben whispered.

"What?"

"*You* be the singing drunk and *I'll* hide behind the wagon."

"What songs do you know?"

"Well, a couple of hymns I remember."

"Nah," Tom shook his head. "What else?"

Ben furrowed his brow in thought and then nodded. "I got one. Get yourself set."

Tom removed his wide-brimmed hat and knelt at the base of the building to sneak a quick peek around the corner. To his great satisfaction, both men were staring intently at the rear door of the building. He took a few seconds to evaluate each of the men, then rose to a crouch, replaced his hat, drew his revolver, and moved silently across the yard-wide space to hide behind the tailgate of the wagon.

He recognized the men; they were the same suspicious pair he had seen before. Hidden from view behind the Conestoga, he raised a hand and gave a signal to Ben.

His partner showed a flair for dramatics as he quietly retreated a few yards. He pulled his shirt half in, half out of his trousers, punched the shape out of his hat, and cocked it low over his forehead. Then he turned and began a staggering, noisy, foot-scraping advance as he began to sing in a surprisingly melodious tenor voice.

"Lissun to the mockin' bird . . . lissun to the mockin' bird . . . lissun to that doggone bird . . . and . . . howsat rest go?"

"What the hell is that?" one of the men behind the café swore.

"Some fool drunk," the other said.

"Boot his tail outta here, Carl, 'fore them two fellers show up," the first man said.

"Lissun to the mockin' bird . . . lissun to that birdie singing in the trees . . ." At the sound of hurrying footsteps, Ben began to hum his tune, then turned away and slumped against the building. As Tom hoped, the two hooligans came to the corner together.

"Get outta here, rummy!" shouted the one called Carl.

Tom moved quickly forward and slammed the barrel of his revolver on the crown of Carl's hat, not watching him fall as he turned to his accomplice. This thug ducked Tom's descending revolver and whipped around with his own revolver already coming out of the leather. With no chance to strike again, Tom was vulnerable.

From behind the hooligan, Ben's revolver came crashing down on the man's head and dropped the man senseless beside his inert companion. Tom and Ben knelt to check the vital signs of each of their victims.

"Mine's still breathing steady," Ben said softly. "Yours?"

"He'll live," Tom replied. "Think we need to tie 'em?"

Ben shook his head. "They won't come to for some time." He reached for one unconscious man's revolver and tossed it into a nearby clump of high weeds. "We'll get our pay and be long gone 'fore these birds are up and find their shooting irons."

Tom threw the other thug's gun into a different weed patch and, with Ben's help, dragged first one and then the second unconscious body well under the Conestoga wagon.

"Listen to the mocking bird?" Tom chuckled as he and Ben headed for the front of the building. "That's all the words you knowed?"

"All I could think of at the time," Ben admitted.

"I never heard you sing before," Tom said as they rounded the corner. "You sing pretty."

"When, since you knowed me, have I had anything to sing about?"

They walked into the unfinished café and headed straight for John Wilcox, who was standing behind the stub bar in a back corner of the building.

"Good evening, gents," Wilcox said jovially. "Right on time, I see."

"On time and ready to get our pay," Tom said.

The portly man tightened his lips and gave a dejected sigh. "Well, now, about your pay . . . I've been reconsidering." He gave a wide sweep of his hand to indicate the empty interior of his restaurant. "I'm not yet ready for business and, well, I'm going to need all my ready cash to get it up and running."

"You owe us a hundred fifty dollars," Ben said.

Wilcox glanced at the rear door and then raised his voice. "You'll have to whistle for it, my friends. I don't want any trouble so—"

Tom drew his Colt. "They ain't coming, John. They're taking themselves a little nap out yonder." He glanced to Ben. "Check his suit coat, I 'spect he's carrying a hideaway."

Ben walked behind the bar and ran his hands over Wilcox's clothing and in a breast pocket found a two-barreled derringer. "Here's a little nasty," he said and tucked the weapon into his jacket pocket.

"Find anything else?" Tom asked with a knowing smile.

Ben nodded. "He's a chubby one, but there's a bulge around his middle that don't feel like his own lard."

"Let's have the money belt," Tom demanded. "Figger a man like you wouldn't leave your greenbacks where anyone else could get to 'em."

"This is robbery," Wilcox protested. "I don't have but just a little—"

"Jerk it off him," Tom interrupted. " 'Less'n he does it himself."

With a muttered curse, Wilcox waved Ben away and undid the lower buttons of his shirt and unfastened the buckle of an underlying belt. He pulled it free and placed it on the bar counter. "There! Take your money and get out of here!"

Ben slid his right hand along the belt to the bulge and undid the overlapping fold to pick out the bills inside. "Lookee here," he said with a short laugh. "Whatcha got in here, John? I count eight, nine . . . no, there's more like a thousand dollars stuck in your belly belt." He laid the bills on the top of the bar and extracted a few silver coins to place beside them.

"We'll take our pay," Tom said and picked up two one-hundred-dollar bills from the bar, then reached for an additional fifty-dollar greenback. "And double it for our trouble."

"There's more," Ben said hopefully.

"Nah," Tom responded. "Leave him some cash to open up his new honest business."

"You won't get away with this!" Wilcox blustered, although his eyes remained fastened on Tom's revolver. "Someday—"

"Don't say another word, or I'll shoot you right in the gizzard," Tom cut in. "Come on, Ben. Let's ride 'fore I do the world a favor and pull the trigger."

Chapter Nineteen

Omaha, Nebraska, 1866

In the early afternoon, with Omaha just ahead, they reveled in the shared thought that the money in their pockets would buy comfortable beds in a well-regarded hotel. The nearness of significant civilization also meant relief from the past several days of Indian worries. Several wispy plumes of cooking smoke seen straight ahead meant good meals in a decent restaurant and, later, a drink or two of a quality whiskey in a cattleman's bar.

"We ain't working for the railroad no more," Ben said. "If the sheriff don't hire us, when this money runs out, what're we gonna do next?"

"We could hire out for more building stuff," Tom ventured. "We made good money at it, even if we did have to bust heads to get it."

"Well, we sure ain't real carpenters," Ben said. "Some of what we did back there wern't worth a lick."

"Yeah," Tom agreed. "Well, let's hope the whole kit and caboodle caves in on that conniving crook."

They passed a number of outlying ranches and farms, and, finally, they came to the city-limits sign at the edge of town. They rode past feed stores, cattle pens, ranch and farm supplies—all of the city fringe businesses that served the surrounding cattle and agricultural enterprises. Of special interest to them, there were many buildings providing support for the Union Pacific railroad project. There were manufacturing facilities where rail cars were being built, ore smelters, warehouses to shelter the incoming hardware from the East, stockrooms to store canned goods, and foodstuffs for the supply train to take to the railhead.

As they rode toward the heart of the burgeoning community, it was apparent that the prairie settlement was thriving. As the Union Pacific headquarters for the westward expansion, Omaha was attracting wealth. Business was flourishing, with new shops, restaurants, banks, theatres, hotels and rooming houses, and hardware, grocery, and dry goods stores. There was an influx of additional professional men: doctors, dentists, attorneys, land brokers, etc.

The surge of money had also brought a sleazier set of attractions. Grubby saloons, miserable hovels, and disreputable flophouses rose on the back streets of the low-end district.

"Glad we ain't sleeping in any of them cootie houses back there a piece," Ben said as they turned onto the main street and paced their mounts to flow with the traffic of individual riders, horse-drawn buggies, and wagons. "Had enough of them little bedfellows back in them dormitory cars."

"I never slept in a real bed," Tom said, a reluctant admission. "Always just a blanket on the floor or at best a canvas cot. Bedrolls and sleeping on the ground, that's been the most of it."

"Never on a mattress or a feather bed?"

"Nope," Tom responded. "Don't even know what a feather bed is."

"Too summerish for 'em now, but come winter, you'd be in sleeping heaven," Ben informed him.

"There's a hotel up there that don't look too shabby," Tom said, pointing to a two-story white building ahead. "It's on the main street, so maybe it'll be clean."

"One way to find out," Ben said and kicked his horse to a trot. "Let's see how much they'll soak us for."

Tom urged Duke to match Ben's steed until they reined up at the hitching rail in front of the hotel. Both dismounted and stretched away saddle stiffness, and then they walked to the double-door entry and pushed inside.

A bright, multicolored rug on the polished wooden floor of

a small foyer/sitting room furnished with a sofa and two up-holstered chairs gave a cheerful ambiance to the entryway. Further back, a front-facing short stairway led to a landing, then right-angled up a longer flight of steps to the second floor. Tucked in a space to the right of the stairway access, a high registration desk was backed by a pigeonhole cabinet for storing room keys, messages, and mail. Next to the right wall, a door opened into a room recessed beneath the staircase.

Through a portal to the left, there was a cozy dining room with eight square tables with white tablecloths. At this mid-afternoon hour, it was not yet open for dining, although kitchen sounds could be heard through an open doorway in the back wall.

"Good afternoon, gentlemen." A middle-aged man, slim, dark haired, well groomed, and proper in a midnight blue suit, came from the room behind the desk. "May I be of service?"

"Like a room for the night if it ain't too dear a price," Tom said as he and Ben walked to stand at the front of the desk.

"Sharing the room?" the desk clerk inquired as he placed a register on the top of the desk.

"Got one with two beds?" Ben asked hastily.

"Yes, we have rooms with doubles," the man answered. "Eight dollars . . . would that be all right for you?"

"Sounds okay," Tom responded. "That's eight for both of us?"

The desk clerk nodded. "Extra for the bath," he added. "Two dollars per person. The bathroom is at the end of the hall."

"Bath? That'd be nice," Tom exclaimed. "I'm for it."

"Ought to take one 'fore we climb in them clean beds," Ben said in agreement. "Maybe we'd better do 'er right away 'fore supper."

"I'll have a boy bring up water," the desk clerk said.

"That'd be appreciated," Tom responded.

"Sign for the room, please," the clerk said. He turned the register to Tom and then offered a pen.

"I can do 'er," Ben said and pulled the register to him. He

took the pen, dipped the tip into the ink jar, and laboriously entered both names.

"That will be a total of twelve dollars," the man said. "Stable for your horses out in back." He pointed to a hallway to the left of the stairway. "There's an entry door at the back of the hall."

Tom took his wallet from his rear pocket and counted out the bills for the room. "Charge extra for the stable?"

"Fifty cents for the feed," the clerk said. "Rolled oats in the trough at the entrance."

Tom took another dollar from his wallet and added to the bills on the desktop. "That do 'er?"

The clerk nodded, swept the bills from the desk, and placed them in an unseen drawer below. "Welcome, gentlemen. Let me get the keys to your room." He turned and took a pair of door keys from a box marked 223 and handed one to each of his new guests. "Enjoy your stay with us."

Tom and Ben nodded their thanks, returned to their horses at the front of the building, unhitched them, and led them through an alley to the stable at the back of the hotel. Each of them took the time to remove saddles and bridles, and then they brushed down and fed each animal.

Carrying their belongings and weapons, they re-entered the hotel through the rear door and walked through the hall to the lobby. They went up the steps of the stairway two at a time and strode the upstairs hall to Room 223. Tom unlocked the door and, with a sweep of his hand, ushered Ben in ahead of him. Closing the door behind him, Tom took a long look at the bed-chamber they had rented for the night.

It was a light and airy room; the wallpaper displayed a beige background striped with repeating narrow columns of entwined green vines and tiny pink flowers. The walnut headboards of two single beds were butted against an inner wall, with a central table and a three-foot space separating them. Each bed was covered by a white, check-patterned coverlet with the bulge of a plump pillow beneath at the head end.

The outside wall featured two tall windows, one opened at

the bottom to allow a flow of cooling air into the room. To their left, against a wall, a small dresser with a mirror was flanked on either side by two tall chiffoniers. Just inside the door, at the wall to their right, there was a wide table with another mirror and a towel rack above it. On the table's surface, there were a soap dish, a graniteware pitcher, and a matching wash basin.

"Fancy," Ben said. "Mighty fancy."

"Oughtta be, for twelve dollars," Tom said. He walked toward the bed, touched his fingers to the coverlet, and pressed down three times. "Looks like a girl's place."

"You stay off that mattress 'til you wash up," Ben said in stern admonishment. "Who's going down the hall first?"

"Might as well be me," Tom said with a wide grin. "I do got a hankering to lay down for once on a real bed."

"Get to it . . . and clean out that tub 'fore it's my turn!"

With their bodies scrubbed clean and their clothing flapped out the window to rid the trail dust of many days, Tom and Ben came jauntily down the stairway. At the bottom of the steps, they sauntered to the desk, where the clerk was engrossed in a paperwork task.

Tom gave a little cough for attention, then said, "Hi, there, Mister—"

The desk clerk looked up with a smile. "Bancroft. Clyde Bancroft at your service, sir."

"Dining room opens when?" Tom asked.

Bancroft glanced at the grandfather clock in the corner of the lobby. "Six o'clock," he said. "Five more minutes."

"Serve a good meal here?" Ben inquired.

"Very good, sir," the clerk assured him. "My missus does the cooking and my daughters do the serving."

"Whole place is a family affair, is it?" Tom said with an approving nod. "You run a nice place, gotta hand it to you."

"I appreciate the compliment," Bancroft said. "And we do keep the price reasonable."

"We may just stay a day or two more," Ben said with a cheerful fervor.

"Mind if I ask you a question?" Tom asked.

Bancroft turned his attention to Tom. "Hope I can give you an answer."

"We ain't just drifters," Tom began, "and we got us a line on some work hereabouts, but if that don't pan out, you got any suggestions?"

"Lots of work in town, mainly with the U.P. if you're interested," Bancroft suggested. "Might give them a try."

"Just finished up with the track crew out west," Tom countered. "Guess we coulda stayed on with them, but we kinda had our fill of the outfit."

Bancroft chuckled. "Had your fill of General Jack, I suspect." Then he shrugged. "Whole town's got work for those looking for it. U.P. runs most of it, but there are independent suppliers that you might sign with. Wages are pretty good."

"We'll certainly give that a try in the morning," Tom said with a little nod of appreciation.

Bancroft looked past Tom and gave a nod of his own to indicate the dining room. "Supper is ready, gents. Now open for business."

Tom was savoring the very last bite of his apple pie when the opening of the hotel's front door caught his attention. He swallowed and touched Ben's shoulder to direct his attention to the tall man who was striding toward the desk.

"Hey, there's Sheriff Tucker," Ben said.

"Let's finish up and let him know we're in town," Tom said and took his napkin from his lap and placed it on the table. "Go say hello while I settle up."

"He seed us, looked right at us when he walked in," Ben said and wiped his mouth with his napkin.

They were seated at a table close to the entrance to the dining room. The other tables were mostly occupied, only a couple empty as diners had finished their meals and left. Around them, there was a low volume of men and women in conversations and the occasional sound of silverware on china plates.

"Evening, Clyde!" the sheriff hailed the clerk loudly. "Looking for two desperados who might've come in!"

Tom reached out his right hand to Ben's arm, to stop him from rising.

"Haley and Patterson, that's their names!" The lawman's voice was clearly heard in the dining room and hushed all talk and froze the movement of spoons, forks, and glasses. "Heard they might be registered here!"

"He knows we're right here . . . why's he talking so loud?" Ben whispered.

Tom shook his head and waved a hand to silence his friend.

Bancroft said something, but not loud enough to be understood.

"Not in their room?" the sheriff bellowed. "Well, out on the town I reckon!"

Bancroft turned his head and eyes toward the dining room. "Sheriff, they're right—"

"Well, I'll be back in about an hour!" the burly lawman interrupted. "Got a wire from some feller named Wilcox in some ramshackled burg up the road saying that those two jaspers robbed him of his money!"

Again, Bancroft spoke, his words growing louder: "Sheriff, I'm trying to tell you—"

"I know those two! Right friendly with them, I was!" the sheriff cut in once again. "Thought highly of them! Helped me and my deputies to keep the peace! Even offered 'em a job! Now, I don't rightly believe some scalawag's story about 'em being robbers, but if they're in town, I'd have to arrest them! It'd be trouble for everybody! Have to put them in jail, maybe take a month or two to straighten it all out! Of course, if they was to get out of town 'fore I come back, it just might be best 'til things blow over!"

"I think I get your meaning, Sheriff," Bancroft said. "What should I say if I should see them?"

"I'd tell 'em that they'd be better off somewheres outside

of Nebraska Territory for a while! Don't think that Wilcox story will hold up very long. He'll probably be in jail 'stead of them." He turned and walked back toward the front door. "I'll be coming back in an hour or so." Without another word, he opened the door and walked out to the street.

"All that shouting was for us?" Ben asked. "Mean what I think it means?"

Tom nodded. "I reckon it means I ain't going to get my chance to sleep in no real bed tonight."

They rose from their chairs and, without waiting for one of the Bancroft daughters to bring the check, Tom laid more than enough money on the table to cover the cost.

Chapter Twenty

Clay County, Kansas, 1866

Just had to take that extra hundred dollars," Ben chided. "That made us robbers."

Tom shrugged at the reprimand. It was early morning as they rode west of Manhattan, Kansas. Almost a week had passed since they had left Omaha at night, and it had been bedrolls instead of mattresses for their sleep each evening. With the miniscule railroad wages plus the purloined extra cash, they possessed the largest sum of wealth that either had known in their entire lives. Despite Ben's complaint, neither was worried about the Wilcox robbery charge.

"'Spect it was already stolen money," Ben continued when he heard no response from Tom. "It warn't no actual stealing on our part. Way I figger, we had it coming."

"You do go on," Tom said with some exasperation. "You badger the both of us, keep saying that now we're outlaws, then you start jawing about how we ain't no such thing. Which is it, Ben?"

"You saying I talk too much?"

"Don't mind the talking when it makes sense, but it gets a bit to me when it's just working the same thing over and over."

Ben looked away to study the countryside, obviously miffed.

Tom suppressed a smile at the manner of his companion, knowing that Ben's pique wouldn't last more than a mile or two and he would became talkative once again. Even though he was smart in his own way, Ben could rag on a subject on occasion. He also, however, could bring up matters of interest and importance from time to time, as well. Tom truly enjoyed his companion's company; he was a loyal, true, and trusted friend.

Tom recognized that Ben had most often been a steady hand to quell Tom's youthful, rash actions. Now, as he grew older, Tom also recognized that impulsiveness was a basic part of his own character and would always remain so. Sometimes it worked to his advantage, and other times it did not. Ben, on the other hand, was a conservative man who often worried. He preferred traditional paths and, when Tom chose a diverse direction, the worry came quickly.

"Town ahead," Ben said, breaking the silence.

"Good! Money's burning a hole in my pocket 'bout as big as the one in my belly! How about a real sit-down breakfast?"

"Hoping you'd say that," Ben responded.

Twenty minutes later, they rode past outlying houses and ranch-supply and service facilities into a modest-sized western Kansas town. There were commercial businesses located on either side of the central street, and others on a couple of cross streets. Among them were a grocery store, a barbershop, a land office, a boot and shoe store, a stage stop, and a small hotel. Five business buildings carried the name of the town painted on their front walls: Murphyville Grain and Feed, Murphyville Mercantile, Murphyville Saddle and Harness, the Murphyville Tavern, and an imposing brick building with a rooftop sign, the Murphyville Bank.

"Guess we're in Murphyville," Ben said wryly.

"Well, there's an eating place," Tom said. "Plain old Mom's Café."

"Right next to the undertaker's," Ben noted. "Hope that ain't a bad sign."

Mom's Café was a narrow, one-story structure with a mortuary on its right and a gunsmith's shop on the left. A short hitching rail directly in front of the restaurant was fully occupied by horses, as was the one in front of the gunsmith's building. There was, however, an empty hitching rail in front of the mortuary.

"Good sign, ain't no burying business going on," Tom observed.

With a laugh between them, they hitched Duke and Blaze in front of the undertaker's establishment. As they stepped onto the boardwalk, Ben stopped to stare through a large window at an expensive, manufactured casket with the upper half opened to display a thickly padded white lining.

"Ain't that a pretty?" Ben asked solemnly. "Wonder if either you or me will have one that fine when the time comes."

"We here to eat or to mope about burying?"

Ben turned away with a sheepish grin. "Never knowed nobody carried to glory in nothing so fancy."

"Just hope the food ain't so bad that you'll need one," Tom said. "Come on."

They took the few steps to the front of the café, opened the door, and entered. The breakfast business was good; the five tables next to the right wall were fully occupied and the counter to the left with only three stools vacant. The patrons were men of many ages, shapes, and sizes. Some wore business suits, others wore overalls, and most wore long-sleeved shirts above their jeans or cotton twill trousers. It was noisy, with prattle of many conversations, the clinking of cups and glasses, the scrapings of dishes, and the clatter from the kitchen as pots and pans were moved about.

"Right down here, young men!" shouted a buxom, middle-aged woman behind the counter as she pointed to the three empty stools. "Sit yourselves down!"

As Tom and Ben walked down the center aisle, eyes turned to appraise them, and most of the men they passed smiled or gave a welcoming nod.

"Seems a friendly little town," Tom said as he and Ben sat on the last two stools of the counter. From where they were seated, they could see into the kitchen over a chest-high dividing wall topped with a wide ledge. An older man and a woman of similar years were hard at work in the steamy enclosure. The man was at the big cookstove, managing bacon and ham frying in one skillet, eggs frying in a second and boiling in a pot while he turned flapjacks in a third frying pan. The old woman was alternating between placing plates of food on the high ledge and washing dishes in a tub to her right.

"What'll you fellers have?" the buxom waitress asked as she turned from another customer. At their hesitation, she pointed at the schoolhouse-style blackboard hanging above the back counter. "Give you a minute to look it over." She turned to the high ledge and, as the old woman placed a couple of plates atop it, grasped one with her left hand, placed the second in the crook of her left arm, picked up a heavy coffee pot with her right hand, and hustled toward the tables.

Tom and Ben studied the bill of fare scrawled in white chalk on the blackboard until the waitress returned to the counter. She took two large mugs from the back shelf and placed them in front of the pair. "Well, what'll it be?" she asked as she poured black coffee into each mug. "You wanted coffee, right?"

Both nodded.

"Use cream or sugar?"

Both shook their heads.

"I'll take them ham and eggs," Ben told her. "Hard fry on the eggs." He hesitated and then spoke again. "And a dish of that stewed fruit . . . prunes?"

She nodded.

"I'll take the hot cakes and a side plate of bacon," Tom said. "Make that bacon real crispy."

"Coming right up," the waitress said and hurried away.

"Nice town," Ben said. "Betcha a nice place to live."

"I suppose," Tom agreed.

"Think we could find work here?"

Tom shrugged. "I suppose."

"Maybe I should ask?"

Tom nodded. "I suppose."

Their food arrived a few minutes later, and they ate slowly, savoring the good taste of it. By the time they finished, many of the townsmen had arisen from their tables, paid their bills, and left the café. Several remained over after-breakfast coffee, talking business, weather, and local gossip.

"You boys from around here?" the waitress said as she placed the bill in front of Ben.

He pushed the small slip of paper to Tom.

"Just passing through," Tom told her. "Down from Omaha."

"How's that railroad coming along?" she asked.

"Getting there," Tom said. "Laying rails a couple of miles a day. Sometimes more."

"We was working on that railroad," Ben interjected. "One day, they laid over ten miles."

"Is that a fact?" the woman questioned. "Lordy, that's a marvel, ain't it?" She regarded them with an evaluating stare. "You fellers were doing the heavy work?" she asked with some skepticism.

Ben shook his head. "We was riding sentry for the outfit, keeping eyes out for Indian war parties."

"That sounds like a pretty fair job," she said.

"Not so good in some ways," Tom countered. "They was slow to pay, had us living in grubby boxcars, food was nothing good like it is here."

"Well, thank you, sir, for saying so," she said. "We do try to please."

"We like your town," Ben said. "Any work 'round here?"

She shrugged and then turned her head to nod past them. "Might ask Frank Bowman over there." She raised her voice. "Hey, Frank! Could you slide over here and talk to these boys?"

Tom and Ben turned to follow her gaze to a nearby table and saw a big-shouldered, middle-aged man who sat a half-head taller than his two companions, who were sitting across from him. The big man broke from his conversation and looked at the waitress. "What about, Emma?" he asked.

"Come over and let them say," the woman said.

The man rose from his chair and spoke briefly to his two cohorts, then ambled across the center aisle to seat himself on the stool next to Tom and offered his large hand. "Frank Bow-man," he announced. "Your names, young gents?"

"Tom Patterson, and this is my partner, Ben Haley," Tom said and shook hands.

"We just rode into town," Ben said, reaching across Tom to take his turn shaking hands. "Kinda taking a liking to the place and was wondering if we could find work here."

"Kinda work you do?" Bowman asked.

"Most anything," Ben continued. "Working cattle, fence-hole digging, horse shoeing, law enforcing . . . that sort of thing."

"Law enforcement?" Bowman questioned. "That a fact?"

"Rode sentry for the Union Pacific," Tom told him. "Helped the Omaha sheriff and his deputies on occasion."

"From the sound of you . . . you're Rebs?" Bowman asked.

Tom stiffened. "If that's a problem—"

"Didn't say it was," Bowman cut in. "Union myself, but I don't hold no grudge . . . unless you all are diehards about it."

"Way I see it, we got licked, and now that's over and done with," Ben said. "We need to get on with putting things back together."

Bowman sat silently for a few moments. Tom estimated the man's age somewhere under fifty; under a salt-and-pepper thatch of dark hair, his face had rather blunt features and was wrinkled more by sun and weather than by age. His smile seemed to be a ready occurrence and his manner, while businesslike, was genial. He seemed fit and strong, with only a slight pooch in the plaid shirt above the silver buckle of the wide leather belt that threaded the loops of his cotton twill trousers.

"Truth is, boys, me and my missus are full up with our own hands out at our ranch," Bowman said. "I understand Walt Perry might have a spot or two."

"What about this fellow Murphy?" Ben asked. "See his name on buildings all over town."

Both Bowman and Emma laughed.

"Been buried more than fifty years," Bowman told them with a huge smile. "I don't 'spect he's hiring." He sobered and gave a nod to Tom's holstered revolver. "Not too many townsfolk 'round here carrying their sidearms. Mostly ranchers carry rifles in their scabbards or maybe lay them in a wagon bed."

"They're a comfort when we're traveling," Tom said defensively.

"You said you rode sentry for the railroad and helped the law in Omaha," Bowman said. "Does that mean you're both handy with those firearms?"

After a glance between them, Tom and Ben nodded.

"Interested in work as lawmen?" Bowman wanted to know.

"Whatcha getting at, Mr. Bowman?" Ben asked.

"Well, I don't know that I should be talking about this to a couple of fellows just riding through," the big rancher said. "You could be a couple of outlaws on the run for all I know."

"Like Ben said . . . whatcha getting at?"

"Assuming that you two *are* just a couple of young fellows looking for a place to settle, and assuming that you're honest men . . . well, there's a situation here in Murphyville that you might be right for."

"Go on," Tom said.

"Ever steal anything?" Bowman asked.

Ben looked shocked, but Tom nodded and touched the revolver in his holster. "Took this Colt off a Yankee soldier after the war was over and he decided it wasn't. He and a bunch of other bluebellies came riding roughshod over us when we was living in a hard-luck camp." He cocked his head toward the front door of the café. "And the horse I'm riding out there . . . I took that off him too. When he come figgering to kill me and Ben, I knocked him hard in the head 'cause it was him or us." He took a few moments before he continued. "Maybe you'd call that stealing."

"Did you kill him?" Bowman queried.

"Nope," Tom said. "I gave him a hell of a headache, that's for sure."

"You didn't have to tell me that story," the rancher said. "But I'm glad you did." He looked from Tom to Ben, then back again. "What would the sheriff in Omaha say about the two of you if I'd wire him this afternoon?"

"Well, go right ahead!" Tom said in some exasperation. "We'll even give you his name." He shared an annoyed glance to Ben. "Look here, Mr. Bowman, you been asking all these questions . . . now, how about you answering some of ours? What's this about?"

"Fair enough," Bowman responded as a sad smile touched his lips. "We got a town marshal, Jim Nolan, here in Murphyville. Been with us a long time." The smile disappeared. "Jim's a good lawman, a good man, and a good friend. Now, he's sickly . . . he's got a cancer and not long left to live."

Tom and Ben waited for Bowman to continue.

"Jim being unable to do his marshaling . . . we got a couple of jobs open enforcing the law here in our town. Would you two be interested?"

"What as? Deputies?" Tom asked.

Bowman nodded. "We've sent out word looking for an experienced lawman to take over Jim's job, but we haven't had any luck so far. While we've been looking, we tried to get some of our locals to help us out, but none have any background or interest in that line of work."

"I'm not so sure we do," Ben put in. "And I'm a little worried that you'd pick two strangers just off the road."

"I *will* check with the sheriff up there in Omaha, and if he vouches for you, and if you're willing, we'd make it worth your while," Bowman said.

"And what if he says he don't quite remember us all that well?" Tom argued.

"Well, truth is, we're a little desperate," Bowman told him. "If he has nothing bad to say about you, it's a chance I think I'd be willing to take. Town looks peaceable, but we got some local problems brewing, and we're worried about our town, with some of the hard cases we see coming through from time to time. Since the end of the war, lots of men are down on their luck, and they're not above turning outlaw." He rose from the stool. "You fellows give it some thought. If you decide to ride on, that's fine. If you want to talk about it, come see me." With a nod, he turned and returned to his table, picked up his hat, and bid a goodbye to his friends. He strode to the front of the café and pushed through the door to the outside.

"Come see him?" Ben questioned. "See him where?"

"Over at our City Hall," the waitress told him. "He's our mayor."

"And where's City Hall?" Tom wanted to know.

"Next to his bank," she said. "You can't miss it."

"He own anything else?" Ben questioned with some derision.

"Quite a bit more," Emma said with a lilt of mockery in her voice. "He came by it all fair and square." Her smile widened. "Murphy was his wife's great granddaddy."

Chapter Twenty-one

Murphyville, Kansas, 1866

T hink he wired Omaha?" Ben asked as they walked toward the redbrick bank building up ahead. This side of it, they came to a one-story white frame building with large double windows taking up the most of the frontage, and an entry door to the right. On one window, in gilt letters with black shadow edging, were the words MURPHYVILLE CITY HALL.

"Just been a couple of hours, doubt if he's had the time," Tom responded. "Might as well go in and find out."

"I ain't just talking you into this, am I?"

"I like the lay of the town myself," Tom replied. "We move on, who knows if we get a better offer?"

"One more thing," Ben said and lightly gripped Tom's arm, a slight restraint. "Settling down in one place is okay for me, I'm getting a little long in the tooth. What about you? You're a young buck, and maybe you want to see the world." He chuckled. "I've seen 'bout all I need to see."

"You got a point," Tom agreed, "but settling down here may not be all there is. Maybe, if we get the jobs, it'll just be for a few months, or a year, or maybe five or six. And if it don't work out fer us, we move on." Then he gave a short laugh. "'Sides, you ain't to the geezer age yet."

"Well," Ben said as he mused. "There's something else—"

"Thought you said one more thing?"

"You really want to be a lawman?" Ben said, ignoring Tom's jibe. "Pay's just fair, and it can get to be a danger every now and then. Like the man said, some hard cases coming through."

"Best offer we got," Tom countered. "Let's go in."

Tom opened the outer door and waited for Ben to enter in front of him. Inside, to the left, a long, waist-high walnut rail ran to a building-wide divider wall across the center of the interior space. At the end of the wide aisle straight ahead, an open door revealed a partial view of a meeting room at the back of the structure.

"Can I help you?"

Tom and Ben turned to a handsome middle-aged woman seated at a desk in front of a large open office area on the other side of the railing.

"Can I help you?" the woman asked again.

"They're here to see me, Wilma," Bowman said and rose from his chair at a large walnut desk at the back of the office area. He walked to the hinged gate in the rail and opened it. "Come in, unless you've come to say no."

Tom flicked a glance at Ben.

"Guess we're here to talk it over," Ben said. "Not quite ready to say either way."

Bowman nodded and gestured them inside the rail. "Like you to meet my secretary, Mrs. Stevens," he said with a nod to the woman at the desk. "Takes the best shorthand meeting notes I ever did see."

The woman smiled at the compliment, murmured her greetings, and then turned back to the paperwork on her desk.

"Have a chair," Bowman said as he took his seat behind his desk. He waited until Tom and Ben were comfortable in the pair of matching wood chairs facing the desk. "Had a chance to talk it over between the two of you?"

Ben nodded. "First things, first," he began. "Your Marshal Nolan . . . sick as he must be . . . is he still the head honcho as far as keeping law and order?"

Bowman tightened his lips in a slight grimace before he answered. "He tries. Some days he's good, but those days are getting few and far between."

"Still paying him his wages?" Ben asked.

"Of course," Bowman responded.

"That's the way it should be," Ben said as he and Tom both

nodded their approval. "That being said, how's the town fixing to pay the pair of us? And if you care to say, what would that amount be?"

"We paid our deputy thirty-five dollars a month and provided him room and board," Bowman said.

"Paid?" Tom posed a question. "You still got a deputy working?"

Bowman shook his head. "Had the one, but he took off and headed for Kansas City. Okay fellow, but it wasn't really his calling."

"Is that what you'd pay for each of us?" Ben asked.

"We could manage that," Bowman replied.

Ben looked to Tom and then returned his gaze to the town's mayor. "Here's what Tom and I talked about. You make me chief deputy, and Tom reports to me as regular deputy. It'd be nice if you'd pay me five dollars a month more, but that's up to you."

"*Chief* deputy at more pay?" Bowman inquired. "Why is that important?"

"Ben was my sergeant in the war," Tom interjected. "He's got the age and the know-how to be in charge." He gave an apologetic shrug. "With what you say 'bout your Marshal Nolan and him being in tough shape, Ben would have to do most of the thinking and acting about Murphyville law and order."

"I see your point," Bowman admitted.

"Something else," Ben said. "If your marshal is as bad off as you say, there's gonna be a time sooner or later when you'll need someone to take his place. I heard you say you been scouting 'round for some *experienced* lawman to come in from the outside."

Bowman nodded.

"If'n we give your offer a try for a while," Ben continued, "you can be the judge of what kind of a job we do." He took a deep breath. "If we do well, I say I'd get first call as the town marshal and Tom becomes *my* chief deputy."

Bowman took a few moments before he responded. "For a couple of drifters just passing by, you do have some mighty high-demand ideas."

"Seems reasonable to us," Tom said and started to rise. "We'll be—"

"Hold on, I'm still thinking it over," Bowman interrupted. He pointed at Ben. "That'd be forty a month for you and"— he switched his gaze to Tom—"and thirty a month for you."

"You'd be cutting my pay?" Tom questioned.

"I can drive a hard bargain too," Bowman said with cheerful smile. "Gentlemen, like I said, we're kinda in a tight spot, what with no law to speak of . . . so maybe you got us over a barrel." He was silent for a few moments more and then nodded. "All right, gents. That's seventy dollars for the pair of you on, let's say, a three-month trial period. Room and board like I said, and we'll give Mr. Haley here first consideration for the marshal's job when Jim's time comes around. That suit you?"

Ben caught the lift of Tom's eyebrows that he recognized as an affirmative signal. "I guess maybe we got us a deal."

"Well, we'll see how you all work out," Bowman reminded them. He looked past his two visitors to his secretary. "Make out a couple of employment papers, Wilma; make it for three months," he called. He rose from his chair. "Let's walk over to our jail, and let me show you where you'll be working."

Tom and Ben followed as Bowman led the way to the rail gate where he, again, held it open for them to pass through. Bowman took an unexpected turn toward the meeting room rather than toward the front door. "We can go out the back," he said, striding ahead. "Jail's right behind us."

He led them through the meeting room door, past a long council table positioned parallel to the divider wall and four rows of wooden chairs placed to face it. At the back of the room, he opened a door and stepped out into the sunlight. Tom and Ben followed the mayor into a grassy space between City Hall and the back end of a substantial stone building. Bowman walked past a privy to the solid wood rear door of the jail building, took a key ring from his trouser pocket, and opened the door.

In single file, he ushered them into the right-hand walkway of the cell area of the jail. Tom turned to watch as Bowman swung the door closed. He noted the deep notches in the stones on the inner sides of the door and a heavy steel bar propped against a wall nearby.

There were two unoccupied cells to their left with a brick wall separating them. Each held two wood-and-canvas cots as sleep accommodations, but nothing else. The bars on the front of the cells were close set, no greater than four inches apart. Any circulation of outside air to this section of the jail would come through three high and slender horizontal windows in the wall to their right.

"Since Jim's been sick, he hasn't been up to jailing any of our troublemakers," Bowman said as he paused at the closed door at the front end of the cell area. "If he was able, we could probably use a couple of more cells."

"Town don't look that rowdy," Tom ventured.

"It's growing," Bowman said, "and having growing pains."

He opened the door and waved them through.

The jail office was a large room, the interior width of the building. At one side, a large unoccupied desk and chair, undoubtedly the duty station for the ailing marshal, had several wooden file cabinets behind it. On the other side, a smaller desk was tucked into a corner under a rack of rifles and shot-guns. The two narrow windows in the front wall on either side of the thick wooden door were outfitted with bars on the out-side and hinged heavy wood shutters on the inside.

Tom walked to one of the windows, pulled together the shutters to cover the window, and nodded as he noted the nar-row slits cut clear through the hickory slabs.

"Rifle ports—Jim's idea," Bowman explained. "Makes the place a fort if we have a prisoner that folks want to lynch." He shook his head. "Thankfully, we haven't had that problem as yet."

"You never know," Ben said. "What about in the back?"

"Secured," Tom said. "Steel bar. Saw it when we came in."

Ben strolled to the gun rack and took down one of the brass-framed rifles. "Lookee here, Tom! One of them new Winches-ter carbines! Takes them new-fangled cartridges." Ben's eyes roved over the facility. "Marshal knows his business, looks like. Say he's been here quite a spell?"

"Going on nine years," Bowman told him. "Come out from Missouri after his missus passed away. Wanted some place new with no memories."

"You talked about room and board," Tom asked as he folded the shutters back from the window. "Where do we—"

"Marshal Jim's got his own house," Bowman interrupted. "We can set you up with a couple of rooms at Mary Kelsey's rooming house. She keeps a clean place and serves a good breakfast and supper." He paused. "Catch your lunch with Emma. We don't pay for lunch, but they'll give you a nice discount."

"Which one is Mom?" Tom asked. "Emma or the old lady in the kitchen?"

Bowman laughed. "I guess it's the old cook, Jess Atkins. He came to town and started the place and called it Mom's. Emma and the older lady, Miss Wanda, they just work there."

"What'll I do about sitting down at Marshal Jim's desk?" Ben asked. "If I do, will he take it wrong?"

"I'll talk it over with him this evening," Bowman responded. "He won't mind. He knows how it's going to go." He walked to the big desk, opened one of the drawers, and drew out a pair of shiny badges. "These are yours for the time being."

"I still kinda wonder at you hiring us on," Ben said as he accepted one of the badges and looked at it in his hand. "Like you said, a couple of drifters."

"Well, I'm not quite the dunderhead you may think me to be," Bowman said with a wide smile. "Sheriff Tucker up there in Omaha wired me back telling me what fine, upright fellows you are."

"He said that . . . 'bout us?" Ben asked.

"Oh, and something else," Bowman said. "Something about somebody named Wilcox who got himself shot to pieces a day or two back. What's that all about?"

Tom took a moment before answering. "A lowlife rascal I thought would come to a bad end. Sounds like he did."

Chapter Twenty-two

Murphyville, Kansas, 1866

Tom had awakened early in his room at the Kelsey boarding house, the morning sun just a little below the horizon, which he could see through the window. The few clouds in the sky had turned rosy, then blended subtly through many hues before flattening into the warm constant light of a fair, late-summer day.

He had remained in the bed for another hour, luxuriating and burrowing into his first real mattress—a shame to waste such comfort by sleeping on it.

A real bed! So this is what they feels like!

Into his mind flashed a myriad of remembered cots, grimy pallets, thin blankets on hard wooden floors, and the vermin-infested bunks in the dormitory car.

There was a knock at his door.

"Get up, lazy." Ben's voice was a good-natured jibe. "We're meeting Frank Bowman after breakfast. I'll be at the dining table."

After he heard Ben move away, Tom leaned on one elbow and looked around the room. It was small and spare, with beige painted walls, a brass bed, a chest of drawers, a chiffonier for his clothes, and a washstand with a basin and a large water pitcher.

Somewhat reluctant to leave the heavenly soft mattress, he arose, made the bed, and did a stand-up bathe at the basin, scrubbing his face and body with soap and cold water from the pitcher. After shaving and combing his hair, he put on the new shirt he had purchased the day before, pulled on his new

147

pair of jeans, and slipped his stockinged feet into his old and comfortable boots. He pinned his badge on his shirt and stood for a moment to see how it looked in the small mirror over the washstand. He allowed his reflection to smile back at him in satisfaction, then reached for his gun belt, donned his hat, and left the room.

He strapped the gun belt around his waist as he came down the steps to the hallway and turned toward the large dining room. He was not surprised to see his landlady, Mary Kelsey, preparing the long table for her lodgers' breakfasts. A stout, gray-haired woman in her late fifties, she was moving with a quick step despite her weight. She looked up at Tom as he entered the room, her still comely face showing a bright smile.

"Morning, Mrs. Kelsey," Tom said.

"Good morning, young man. How many times I told you yesterday that it's Mary," the woman chided.

"Yes, ma'am," Tom told her. "Where's Ben, my pard?"

"Had his ham and eggs already and gone on. Said he'd meet you at the jail," she responded. "Good to have some law back in the town."

"Shame about Marshal Nolan," Tom said.

"Poor man hasn't much time left in this world," she said solemnly, then smiled again. "Breakfast?"

"No offense, ma'am, but I best get on," he told her. "Shouldn't be late on the job my first day."

"Nonsense! Sit down! You can't do your marshaling on an empty stomach!"

"I'll eat twice as much tonight," he countered cheerfully. "Honest, it's my first day."

"Go on, then," she said in mock indignation. "No use wasting my good food on someone just gonna sit there raring to go."

With a farewell wave, Tom turned back into the hallway and went out through the front door. He hurried to a corner and strode up a back street to the jail.

" 'Bout time," Ben said as a greeting as Tom entered the office and closed the door. "Frank's due any minute now." He was seated at Marshal Nolan's desk, leaning back in his chair with both hands clasped behind his neck.

"I ain't late," Tom responded.

"Ain't early, either," Ben said. "Skip breakfast?"

Tom shrugged, and then nodded.

There was a single rap at the door and Frank Bowman opened and walked through it, leaving it open as he spoke: "Good morning, gentlemen."

"'Morning to you," Tom and Ben spoke in unison.

"Come with me," the mayor said. "Going to give you a walking tour of our town and introduce you to folks." He stepped back through the open door and waved his new lawmen to join him.

Ben rose from his chair and, with Tom, followed him outside. Tom paused while Ben locked the door, then both flanked Bowman as they walked the side road to a corner where they turned and headed toward the main street.

"I spoke to most of the council, and I've got a majority who gave me an approval on hiring the pair of you," Bowman said as they walked.

"Good to hear," Ben said in response. "We gonna meet with any of 'em?"

"Maybe meet a few today," Bowman told him. "All the rest come the next council meeting."

The first business establishment they entered was the Murphyville Bank, where Bowman's employees deferentially greeted him. The mayor introduced his rotund and balding bank manager, William Moran, and then a young, slender and affable chief teller, John Delaney.

"Glad you're here, fellows," Delaney said. "It's a good little town, one that's going to grow. You'll like it here."

During the morning, the trio moved up one side of the business street and down the other, Bowman introducing Tom and Ben to men and women they met on the boardwalks and to proprietors, clerks, and customers in the stores that they entered.

In the Murphyville Mercantile, Tom and Bowman were engaged in a genial conversation with the store's manager, Alfred

Neal, when the man's eyes shifted to the front door as the tingling bell above it announced a new arrival.

"Excuse me a few minutes, gents," Neal told them. "I'm holding some merchandise for that rancher and his wife that just come in."

"We're about to leave anyway," Bowman said as the manager hurried away.

"Looks like Ben ain't in no hurry," Tom observed with an indicative nod of his head. "Who's the pretty lady?"

Bowman turned to follow Tom's gaze. "That's Mrs. Martin Richards. Rachael Richards."

Standing at a counter across the large room, Ben was holding his hat in his hand, all smiles as he attentively listened to the words of a slender and attractive woman as she awaited a young girl who was loading two large sacks with her purchases.

"Hope she ain't got a jealous husband," Tom observed with a laugh. "Look's like Ben's tongue's is about to hang out."

Bowman chuckled. "He's safe. She's a widow lady, lives on her ranch a little way out of town."

"Widow? Pretty young for that."

"Local lady, married one of our young men about ten years ago," Bowman told him. "Marty was leaning off his horse to open a corral gate when something spooked his mare and she bucked him headfirst right into a post. Freak thing that shouldn't have killed him, but it sure did."

"That's a sad story," Tom said. "Nobody ever knows what's coming for ya."

Bowman nodded and, with a glance across the store, he caught the eye of Ben and beckoned with a subtle motion of his right hand. Ben gave a head bob of his own to acknowledge, but made no effort to leave the side of the attractive lady. Instead, he reached across the counter to take the two bulging sacks from the clerk and, with a gesture for Mrs. Richards to precede him, he followed her toward the front door.

"Well, if that don't beat all!" Tom exclaimed. "You don't know 'bout it, but Ben's one of them widower fellers himself. Lost a wife and a baby back 'fore he enlisted in the army."

Bowman smiled. "He's just one of many hereabouts who find the lady attractive."

"Too bad about the others," Tom said cheerfully.

They waved their goodbyes to the storeowner and walked outside where they found Ben standing just off the boardwalk, watching the departure of a horse and buggy.

"Well?" Tom said to get his friend's attention.

Ben turned. "Well, what?"

"Looks like you found another reason to put down roots in Murphyville," Tom said with a wide smile on his face.

A sheepish smile came to Ben as well. "Could be, could be."

Chapter Twenty-three

Murphyville, Kansas, 1866

Death came for Marshal James Randolph Nolan less than three weeks after their arrival in Murphyville, and before either Tom or Ben had a chance to meet and visit with him. He had not been well enough to come to the jail; he had been bedridden with Dr. Schroeder in regular attendance, and with an elderly widow keeping watch and administering laudanum daily. Although Nolan's last, gasped request had been for a return to Missouri to lie near his late wife to share eternity, the heat of the lingering summer required an immediate burial in the town's hilltop cemetery. As compensation, the townspeople had chipped in to purchase the undertaker's fancy coffin for the departed.

"You're now acting marshal 'til the trial contract is up," Bowman said to Ben as they walked down the hill from the cemetery. He waved to his wife as she drove past in her buggy. "I expect we'll make it your job for keeps at that time."

"That's okay with me, Frank," Ben said. "I reckon it'd be kinda disrespectful to take over for Marshal Nolan too soon."

"That was a mighty fine send-off," Tom said as they walked on the side street toward the corner and then turned onto the main avenue. "I thought the Baptist feller did the best preaching . . . but the other feller was pretty good too."

The Methodist minister, Reverend Peter Wallace, and the Baptist pastor, Reverend Ernest Durfee, had conducted the memorial service in tandem. Both men of the cloth used the church, and they graciously scheduled separate Sunday services at noncompeting times for their own congregations.

When the trio reached the front door of City Hall, Bowman unlocked it and gestured for Tom and Ben to precede him into the building. On the other side of the dividing rail, the mayor took his seat behind his desk, and Tom and Ben sat in the chairs facing him.

"I can free up some money now that Jim's gone," Bowman said in a solemn voice. "Ben, you'll get Jim's salary, at sixty dollars a month and Tom, we'll give you forty. Fair?"

"Very fair, sir," Tom said as Ben nodded assent.

"More money means more law problems," Bowman told them. "I've got a ticklish situation here that's been smoldering for some time." He leaned back in his chair and stared up at the ceiling. "We've got two saloons in town, and I used to own one of them." He sat erect and looked straight at Ben. "Things are quiet and peaceable at the Tavern . . . but the Sunflower Saloon is a real den of iniquity."

Ben and Tom nodded in unison.

"We were there last Saturday night and had to break up a fight that had got nasty," Ben said in strong agreement. "Drunk as skunks, them two cowboys was. Got some saloon girls in there that was egging 'em on."

"Somebody's gonna get shot there one of these days," Tom put in. "We tried to talk with the owner, but the bartender said he was gone home for the night."

"Russell Lockhart," Bowman said with an acknowledging nod. "Some time ago, I sold the Murphyville Tavern to a second cousin, Jacob Miller," Bowman told them. "Runs the place okay, he and his bartender don't allow customers drinking themselves silly, and, at the first sign of cutting up, they're both hardy enough to put a stop to any tomfoolery."

Tom and Ben waited for Bowman to continue.

"Now, Russell and Edgar Lockhart are a pair of scalawags living a couple of miles southwest of town. Russ has got himself a scrawny common-law wife, a real harridan from what I hear," the mayor said with a shake of his head. "The bunch came here about three years ago and got themselves a ranch." He gave a sort of a grimace and then spoke again. "Never knew much about them 'til one day Russ and Ed showed up in town, bought the building from old man Williams, and turned it into a bar." Again, he shook his head in dismay. "No telling where they got the money. From what I've since heard about them, they could be in cahoots with some very shady people. Russ and Ed, they may have run with some outlaw gangs. They could've stole it off a stage or a train, robbed a bank, or maybe it's moonshine money because word is they run a still out there around their place."

"Heard tell their bar whiskey will scald a cat," Ben joked, and then he spoke seriously: "Be a good idea to head out to their ranch, wipe it out, and send the whole bunch packing, but we ain't got no such authority once past the city limits."

Bowman nodded. "We had a council meeting a few days ago and most wanted me to close down the Sunflower, but a couple of the Lockhart cronies are now on the council, and they practically accused me of malfeasance." He smiled at the questioning expressions on his lawmen's faces. "Saying I had an unlawful interest in closing that saloon because I had ties with my second cousin at the Tavern. Saying it would be a conflict of interest."

"That don't hold no water as I see it," Ben said. "What's they or either of them Lockhart fellers gonna do about it if you *do* close 'er down?"

"I'm afraid they could make the case," Bowman admitted. "I've already talked it over with Judge Cunningham and he warned me to be very careful in dealing with the Lockhart brothers."

"And I reckon that does concern us, don't it?" Ben asked. "That's why we're here and why you're telling us, ain't it?"

Bowman nodded. "They're also saying I'm using the law to harass the patrons of the Sunflower. Saying that, on my orders, you and Tom are deliberately jumping their customers to drive their saloon out of business."

After a minute of silence, Ben gave a slow, comprehending nod. "You're saying we gotta stay outta the Sunflower and let them drunks do whatever they want to do?"

Bowman shrugged. "Anything short of a brawl or a killing, I guess that's about it."

"How about outside the place?" Tom asked. "Drunk and disorderly, public nuisance, that sort of thing?"

Bowman pursed his lips and slowly wagged his head. "Even that might be construed as harassment." He sighed. "Sorry, boys. Our hands are tied."

"Maybe not," Tom interjected. "I got me an idea, but it may be one you ain't gonna like."

"Well, say it," Bowman said after a few moments. "What's this great new idea?"

"You can quit as mayor," Tom said.

Bowman's facial expressions began with surprise, then showed incredulity, consternation, and, finally, anger. "What in the hell are you saying?"

"What *are* you talking about, Tom?" Ben asked, his voice ripe with irritation.

"Ain't no conflict of interest if Frank ain't got no say-so anymore," Tom said with an easy smile. "No offense, but you really need to be the mayor? You got a ranch, a bank, and a couple of more businesses here in town to run. Ain't that enough to keep you busy?"

"I think it's impertinent of you to—"

"I ain't sure what that word means," Tom cut in, "but don't you see that with you outta the picture, the law can do whatever it needs to do, and they can't make no claims that we're taking your orders?"

"I'm your boss, young man," Bowman sputtered. "I'm the mayor of Murphyville, and I've got plans for making it a wonderful place for people to live."

"And you're the only man in town who can do that?" Tom questioned. "They got you over a barrel, and they got Ben and me over a couple of 'em too." He paused. "You think folks here won't pay attention to them wonderful plans you got if you say 'em out loud when you're just one of them pillars of the community fellers?"

For a long time, no one spoke.

"I like being mayor," Bowman said, breaking the silence. "I guess that's why you made me so mad." He drew a breath and released it in a sigh. "Thinking on it, I expect you're right. I've had a long run of it . . . maybe it *is* time to resign. It would be the smart thing to do." He sighed again. "There are some good men here in town who would like the job."

"If Tom's right," Ben said with sudden insight, "be best if you don't have no say in picking one of 'em. They'd be saying he was your stooge."

"I see your point," Bowman acknowledged. "I'll meet with the town council, resign, and call for a special election."

"When are you planning to do this?" Ben asked.

"Might as well do it as soon as possible," Bowman said. "Give me time enough to wrap up some things." Then a sly smile came as he faced Tom. "One thing you may not have thought of, young man."

"What's that, sir?"

"The new mayor just might not want the pair of you when your contracts are up," Bowman told him with a impish grin.

"That's a fact," Tom agreed. "Still, we was looking for work when we showed up here, and I reckon we can still find it somewheres else down the road."

"I don't expect that'll be a problem," Bowman said. "Folks around here seem to like you and Ben. I think you'll be here for quite a spell if you so choose." He swept his eyes around the City Hall office as if looking at it for the last time, and then focused on Tom. "You got a lot of audacity, son."

"Is that something good?" Tom asked.

"Could be, if you use it well," Bowman told him.

"Then whatever it is, maybe it's good I got it."

Chapter Twenty-four

Murphyville, Kansas, 1866

The election for mayor was held on the first Tuesday in October, one month after Frank Bowman announced his resignation to the town council. Four of the councilmen, including one of the Lockhart cronies, put their names in nomination, but the winner was Hiram Keats, the lanky, middle-aged proprietor of Keat's Grocery Emporium. Although there was not, as yet, a newspaper in Murphyville, Keats had a handpress in the back of his store that he used to print circulars on his grocery specials. He also printed a one-page handbill of weekly news off the telegraph that he sold for a nickel.

During the week prior to the election, he allowed all other candidates to print their election qualifications on flyers for which he charged a similar amount. It was this magnanimous gesture to his rivals that won him community praise, admiration and, ultimately, the title of mayor.

"You boys were doing a good job for Frank," Keats told Tom and Ben as they sat in the same chairs across from the new mayor behind the large desk in City Hall. "I expect you to do the same for me."

"Awaiting your pleasure, Mr. Mayor," Ben responded.

It was not yet eight o'clock in the morning, and the summons had come to the Kelsey rooming house while Tom and Ben were still lingering over their coffee mugs and chatting with their landlady. As they had entered City Hall for the first time since the election two days ago, they had been pleased to see Mrs. Stevens still at her desk. They had nodded their good mornings to her and Mayor Keats and taken their seats for their first new employer-employee meeting.

"First thing I want you to do is straighten out that depraved lot at the Sunflower Saloon," Keats instructed.

"Close 'em down?" Ben queried.

Keats frowned as he considered the question, and then he shook his head. "No, not yet. We'll be obliged to give them some time to change their ways, but I want you to ride them hard and see if we can't clean up that cesspool."

"There's already talk coming from them scalawags that you being the mayor ain't gonna change anything," Ben told him.

"Well, I'm the new broom, so we'll see," Keats told them. "Let's see how they like my sweeping." He looked up at the big clock on the wall to the right of his desk. "Might be the right time to have a chat with them before they open for today's business."

Tom and Ben strode purposefully along the boardwalk, crossed a side street, and arrived at their destination at the edge of the city limits.

"Me being the marshal, maybe I oughtta do the talking?" Ben asked.

"You usually do," Tom said with a rueful smile. "Okay if I put in my two cents' worth ever so often?"

Ben returned a mocking smile. "You usually do." He rapped firmly on the closed door of the Sunflower Saloon, waited, and then repeated the action.

"We ain't open yet!" a muffled shout came from the dark interior of the building. "Come back in an hour!"

Tom looked up at the sun and estimated the time at about ten o'clock. Ben nodded his agreement and went to work on the door again—this time harder and louder.

The door jerked open and the saloon owner stood in the doorway, squinting in the slant of morning sunlight. "Oh, it's the pair of you," the man said scornfully. "Bowman's boys."

"Call us the Keats boys now, Mr. Lockhart," Ben said with

equal disparagement. He and Tom stepped inside, shouldering the saloon man aside. "Mayor Keats want us to have a little talk with you."

"Why don't you come right on in?" the saloonkeeper said sarcastically. "What the hell you want to talk about?"

Tom turned to look the man over. Russell Lockhart was in his late thirties, slightly over medium height, with a once-husky physique now turning steadily into flab. He was slightly bald, and this morning, his remaining brown hair was spiky and uncombed. He looked like it had been a bad night for him, and he was likely still wearing yesterday's clothing. It was also disagreeably apparent he had neither bathed nor shaved.

"Okay, you got a good look, so what do you want?" Lockhart demanded.

"Where's your brother?" Ben asked.

"Out at the ranch."

Tom took a few steps away from the confrontational pair and swept his gaze around the barroom, seeing the chaos and the litter left from the night before. In the cold, gray light, it was a dismal sight. The floor was grimy with tracked-in dirt that was swirled with cigarette and cigar butts, and it was caked with spilled beer and whiskey. Playing cards and empty and half-empty glasses and steins still remained on the tables and on the bar. Chairs were scattered far from their tables, and two were overturned.

Along one wall, a long bar was scummy with beer and liquor spills dried on the unwashed surface. The back bar, with two beer barrels at its center, was in disarray. There were empty whiskey bottles lying on their sides among the upright ones, many of which were uncapped. On the wall above the back bar, a large painting displayed a nearly nude woman, her shapely back to the viewer and her winsome face smiling provocatively over her bare shoulder.

"This here is a foul place," Ben said as he brought an intent look to the unkempt saloon owner. "You and your no-good brother coddle to a rough crowd that comes in here. It ain't just the local bad boys . . . you seem to be the first place saddle tramps head for when they's passing through."

"Looks like it's a couple of saddle tramps in here doing some loud talking," Lockhart said derisively.

"It's lawmen that are doing the talking," Ben responded. "Here's what Mayor Keats wants you to do. Clean it up, run it right, or you're out of here in thirty days . . . maybe less."

"That ain't fair!" Lockhart protested angrily. "You're all in cahoots—"

"First time we come in here to stop a fight or hear somebody's been cheated outta their wages, we close you down," Tom cut in as he rejoined them.

"We'll see about that," Lockhart muttered and stepped belligerently close to Ben. "You cross me and my brother, it'll be a sorry day for you." He shifted his gaze to Tom. "And that goes for your wet-behind-the-ears deputy too."

Ben's right hand shot out, his palm slamming into the bar owner's chest, sending him reeling away. "Don't crowd me, mister! It ain't just this sorry spot we're keep an eye on. There's some funny business going on out at that ranch of yours."

"My ranch ain't in your jurisdiction," Lockhart said as he reached to a table to regain his balance. "Nothing out there's any of your business."

"I hear of any suspicious shenanigans out there, you'll get a visit from the sheriff over at Clay Center," Ben said.

Lockhart touched his right hand to his chest. "I ain't forgetting you coming in here and knocking me around. You'll pay for that!"

"Fine, swear out a complaint," Ben prompted. "I'm sure it'll be appreciated by the folks at City Hall." He turned to Tom. "Come on, let's go."

"We'll be coming 'round night after night to see how it goes," Tom said. He took another disgusted look at the squalid saloon. "Lord knows why any fool would come in here anyhow."

"You come in, you're looking for trouble," Lockhart threatened.

"You give it, we'll give it back in spades," Tom said. "Clean this pigsty up, and you might see if you can find a bath some-wheres for yourself. Lordy, you do stink to high heaven."

"You've been warned," Ben said. "But I kinda hope you don't listen, 'cause I'm itching to run the likes of you out of business, out of town, and out of the county, and, by thunder, you can bet I'll do exactly that!" Without waiting for a re-sponse, he and Tom went out through the saloon's front door. The last one out, Tom made sure to slam it hard.

"See you back at the jail," Ben said. "I'm going to stop by the grocery store and talk to Hiram." With a casual wave, he stepped off the boardwalk and crossed the street, pausing to let a wagon pass, and then continuing toward Keat's Grocery Emporium.

Tom's spirits were high as he walked along the main street, nodding and speaking to passersby along the way. As frontier settlements go, he considered, this one was still quite small, so getting to know most of its citizens had been an easy and com-fortable endeavor. As in any community, there were a few low characters, such as the Lockharts, but most of the inhabitants were decent, friendly, and willing to help in any way to make Murphyville a thriving town.

"Hi, there, Tom!" A friendly shout came from the open-sided shed of the blacksmith's shop. Timothy Adams, a tall and burly man befitting his strenuous vocation, stepped away from his forge. He laid his fire tongs aside and walked out into the cool air of early fall. "Seen you coming from the Sun-flower. Closing 'em down?"

"Not today, but maybe later if they don't mend their ways," Tom said as he stopped to visit. "From what I've seen, skunks can't change their stripes."

"You're a bit new in town, so don't you go taking 'em too lightly," Adams cautioned. "Fellow from over there near Bald-win said he's known them Lockhart boys since they was tad-poles. Seen 'em hogtie and cut up a neighbor's dog just for the fun of it." He shook his head. "Said he ain't never seen any-thing as mean and ornery in his life."

"Some folks born that way, I reckon," Tom said. "Seen a few pure evil men in my life, and I never knew how they was made."

"Their pa was just the same, and the old lady maybe even worse," the blacksmith told him. "Russ has got himself a wild thing of a wife who's a little daft in the head. You don't want to mess with her, neither."

"She would have to be touched in the head to put up with the likes of him," Tom said.

"When they first hit town and opened that Sunflower Saloon, they put on a show like they was law-abiding people, but them of us who knowed about 'em, we knowed better."

"How did Marshal Nolan deal with 'em?" Ben asked.

"Jim was good with a gun and had eyes in the back of his head, seems like," Adams said. "That had 'em spooked as long as he had his health. He was a tough man, and they knew he'd gun for 'em if he needed. I do believe they was scared of him."

"Sounds to me like those cowards ain't no real threat," Tom said. "Ever know 'em to put a hurt on something other than a tied-up dog?"

"Been a couple of fellers stopped in at the Sunflower that no one ever saw ride on out of town." Adams took a few moments before adding: "Ed Lockhart brought me a horse for shoeing that I swear I saw one of them fellers was riding a few days before."

"Anything you could swear to in court?" Tom asked.

Adams shook his head. " 'Fraid not."

Tom touched the brim of his hat in a farewell salute. "I thank you, Tim, that's fair to know. I gotta get on to the jail, but me and Ben will look into it."

"Just focus them eyes in the back of your head," the blacksmith said as he walked back to his forge and hand-pumped the bellows to bring it back to white heat.

Tom strode at a fast pace to the jail, unlocked the front door, turned the handle, and walked into the office. He crossed the room, took off his hat, and put it on the hat rack, then settled into a chair behind his desk. He went through a few papers including some Wanted notifications, reading each with a slow determination to understand the content.

"Gotta get somebody to help learn words better," he said aloud.

The door opened and Ben came through it. He doffed his hat and took his chair behind his desk. "Told the mayor that we laid down the law to Lockhart."

"Make him happy?"

"Said to keep pressuring him."

"I talked to Tim Adams," Tom said. "Had some interesting things to say about our Lockhart friends."

"Something we don't know?"

"Told me they was likely bushwhackers," Tom told him. "And we best stay on our guard."

"I'm always on my guard," Ben assured him.

"How about when you're seeing Widow Richards home after church services on Sundays?"

"I keep my mind on my business," Ben countered.

"Any chance you might be thinking less 'bout business and more about keeping the lady company?"

Ben was visibly uncomfortable with the possibility and gave a shrug instead of a retort.

"I ain't aiming to put a damper on your courting—"

"Who said I was courting?" Ben cut in sharply. "Just 'cause I'm doing a widow lady a favor—"

"A very young and pretty widow lady I might say," Tom broke in. "All I'm saying, be careful for yourself . . . and careful for the lady too."

Ben didn't speak for a long time; then he slowly nodded. "Never figgered I was putting Miz Rachael in harm's way." He paused. "Maybe I could get someone else to see her home." He came to his feet and, with no further word to Tom, walked to the cell-area door, went inside, and closed it behind him.

Tom's gaze remained on the closed door for a few moments,

and then he took the Colt from his holster and opened the cylinder. He checked the loads, spun the cylinder, and snapped it back into the frame.

" 'Cupid' sure ain't my middle name," he said, then opened and spun the cylinder once again.

Chapter Twenty-five

Murphyville, Kansas, 1866

Thanksgiving had come and gone, and in the first week of December, the Sunflower Saloon remained in business. To the vexation of the saloon owner, the night-after-night intrusions of the town's new lawmen had tamped down the rowdiness of its patrons. Russ Lockhart had vented his anger each time at both Ben and Tom, but he seemed to be especially vehement in his comments to the former, vowing retribution.

"He sure don't cotton to you," Tom commented to Ben with a grumble of derision. "Maybe you remind him of somebody who bloodied his nose once upon a time."

They were sitting in Mom's Café over midmorning coffee, taking a break from patrolling the streets. It was cold outside, the prairie winter covering the sky with low-hanging, dark globular clouds emitting occasional showers of fine snow to portend a likely blizzard to follow.

"Funny thing about it, they've all of a sudden been minding their manners for a few days now," Ben said. "Hard to figger. Maybe they're gonna mend their ways and become model citizens."

"They're biding their time," Tom countered. "You mark my saying so, they're sidewinders waiting to take a nip at us."

Ben was correct about the surprising cessation of rowdy behavior and near mayhem at their town's trouble spot. Whatever the reason for the saloon's reformation, the small town had been transformed into a peaceful and tranquil community.

With no appreciable wrongdoing occurring at the Sunflower, misbehavior in Murphyville had subsided in this pre-Christmas period. There were a few minor transgressions: an occasional fistfight and a couple of instances of public drunkenness. One case of indecent behavior by a demented octogenarian had been dismissed due to the man's age and mental condition.

"You getting serious, you and Mrs. Richards?" Tom teased, changing the subject.

The previously perceived danger of Ben's weekly trips to the woman's ranch had been attenuated when, shortly before Thanksgiving, she had leased the ranch to a man and his family while she took up residence in a house in town.

"Eat your pie and fill that gossipy mouth," Ben grumbled.

"I'd like to know about that too," Emma said as she refilled both of their coffee mugs. "That pretty widow lady's been needing a good man to keep her company for quite a spell."

"Ain't you got customers to help?" Ben asked

"Gotta find out all the details to pass along," the buxom waitress said merrily. She gestured to the near-dozen diners at tables and at the counter enjoying late breakfasts or midmorning snacks. "Everybody's talking 'bout it."

"Emma, I thought better of you," Ben said in exasperation. "Making sport of me is one thing . . . but it ain't right for the whole town to talk about Miz Rachael."

"Why, you all ain't done nothing to be 'shamed of," Emma said, feigning innocence. "Or have you?"

Before Ben could protest, Emma moved quickly down the counter to fill other mugs with coffee.

"We're just having fun with you," Tom said. "You once told me you might marry again someday if you found the right lady."

"It's too danged early for marrying talk," Ben groused. "It's true that I'm enjoying some female company for a change, and I think she likes having a man again to talk to."

"Nothing wrong with that," Tom voiced his agreement. "She's still young, and losing her husband the way she did was a shame . . . a shame like you losing your wife and baby."

"She and me, we don't talk about our losses," Ben said, his tone still showing irritation.

"Well, what do you talk about?" Tom persisted.

"We talk about what a big buttinsky you are and how come a young smart aleck like you ain't yet got 'round to sparking one of the local gals," Ben said angrily.

"Maybe I'm picky," Tom said cheerfully. "Ain't yet seen one that strikes my fancy."

"Maybe it's them who's picky 'bout you and got a doggone right to be," Ben responded. He rose from the counter stool, pulled his mackinaw around him and clamped on his hat. "I'm heading back to the office. You take your time 'bout coming back 'til you show me and Miz Rachael some respect and not talk 'bout her in this here danged public place." He tossed a greenback on the counter and stalked out of the café.

"Got his goat, I guess," Emma said a few minutes later as she returned to stand in front of Tom. "We shouldn't tease him . . . I think he and Rachael would be a good thing."

Tom nodded. "Him and me, we been together through the war and ever since. Man his age needs to stop running with a young buck like me and settle down. Ben needs a good woman and that Miz Rachael might—"

A distant and muffled popping sound cut him short.

"What the hell?" he said and turned toward the front door.

Then the popping sounds came in a flurry, and Tom knew exactly what he was hearing. "Damn! That's gunfire!"

The front door slammed open, and an excited young man stood in the doorframe. "It's the bank! They're robbing the bank!"

Throwing on his coat, Tom drew his Colt and sprinted to the door, roughly pushing the young man inside. He turned to the café patrons and shouted, "Everyone stay inside and take cover behind something! Don't be a target!"

He slammed the door behind him and broke into a run across the central street, nearly getting trampled by a riderless horse galloping past. Moving swiftly and staying close to the front wall of each building he passed, he worked his way toward the Murphyville Bank at the far end of the street. The gunfire was now clearly heard, the multiple explosive reports indicating that a number of guns were active. As he came closer, he stepped between two buildings for cover as he surveyed the scene.

A dead horse and a dead man lay in the middle of the street while five horses tethered at the bank's hitching rail were whinnying, bucking, and straining to pull free. A dark-clad man was hunkered down behind a water trough with his back to the bank and aiming his fire across the street. That, and the gunfire coming from the bank, turned Tom's eyes to spot two shooters, one on either side of the stage station. He couldn't identify the men, but he was sure neither was Ben.

He dashed from his position and cut into the next open space where, to his relief, he found Ben peering around the corner of the City Hall building adjacent to the bank.

"It's Tom! Coming behind you, Ben!" he called.

Ben twisted his head to confirm and then waved for his deputy to join him. "We got ourselves a mess."

"Tell me," Tom said as he knelt to better see past Ben.

Ben pointed his gun barrel across the street. "Them two is hands out at the Mark Jeffries ranch: Jess Aldrich and Pete Cowan. Guess they saw what was happening and started shooting." He cocked his head toward the jail building. "I was coming the back way when I heard it."

"Robbers still in the bank?"

Ben nodded. "Can't hardly blame them Jeffries cowboys, but it might've been better if they'd just let them robbers go on their way. I don't know anybody was shot inside the bank, but it's a worse situation now."

"They'll be coming out shooting," Tom said gravely. "Likely using anybody they can as shields."

Ben nodded. "And they'll take 'em with 'em to make their getaway." He shook his head. "I don't like the odds of hostages coming back alive."

"Can you get a shot at the guy at the water trough?"

Ben shook his head. "See a piece of him from time to time; not a clear shot."

"I'll cut around behind the bank and get another angle on him and, maybe, on them coming out."

"Go now!" Ben instructed. "They may be coming out any minute!"

Tom gave a wave and hurried toward the rear of City Hall. With reasonable caution, he cut across the space between it and the jail and sprinted past the back of the bank building. He positioned himself at the front corner of the bank, his Colt cocked and steadied against a brick edge.

The gunfire was now sporadic, the gunmen outside and inside the bank apparently unable to find a fair target. From Tom's position, he had a line on the shooter behind the water trough; the man was completely unaware of his vulnerability. With the two ranch hands and Ben behind cover, Tom held his fire, however, not considering it wise as yet to reveal his advantage.

"In the bank!" It was Ben's voice. "This is Marshal Haley! Ain't no need for any more killing. You're bottled up in there and there ain't no way out!"

"Go to hell, Ben!" came a shout from the bank's interior. "We're coming out with two of your fine citizens in front of us! You shoot, they die!"

"Biggs?" Tom muttered softly. "Leon Biggs?"

The front door of the bank was pushed open and the frightened bank teller, John Delaney, coatless and in his shirtsleeves, was thrust outside with two men close behind him.

"Hold your fire!" Biggs shouted. "We're coming out, and this feller's first to die if you shoot!"

"Across the street!" Ben yelled. "No shooting! Do what he says!"

There was a surge at the door as Biggs and two others came through it, shoving a second hostage past Delaney.

"Good Lord!" Tom breathed. "Preacher Ernie's wife."

A slight, middle-aged woman in a long coat and a winter bonnet stumbled ahead of the trio of outlaws. She was confused and obviously terrified as she looked right and left for help.

"Biggs!" Ben's voice was scornful. "Even you ain't low enough to use a woman—"

"We're going for our horses!" Biggs shouted. "We get a mile head start and then we let 'em go! You come too soon, they're dead!"

"You got no call to hurt them folks, Biggs!" Ben responded.

"You got my word 'long as you do what I say."

"What good is that?" one of the cowhands yelled.

"Shut up!" Ben commanded. "Nobody talks but me."

"How about it, Ben?" Biggs challenged. "You let us go?"

The two huddled groups shuffled to the horses, and the bandits began to untie the reins.

A gunshot barked and then another!

Instantly, the outlaws began to shoot wildly and the men at the stage station returned fire. In the ensuing confusion, the young bank teller threw himself toward the frightened woman hostage, shielding her as they fell to the ground, a ball ripping into his back as he did.

Tom's first shot took out the outlaw who had risen from behind the water trough. A second ball aimed at Biggs caught a different bandit, who'd had the misfortune to move into the missile's path. A shot from across the street dropped another while three of the remaining desperados swung up onto their horses and madly spurred them into a frantic attempt to escape. Tom fired twice at the fleeing horsemen, one shot finding a rider who cried out at the impact yet managed to stay on his mount while doubling over with pain. A few moments later, the trio was out of pistol range, riding hard into the December-brown prairie under the dull light of the winter day.

Tom holstered his Colt and ran to the hostages lying on the ground. He knelt beside them as, from across the street, the two cowhands were also rushing toward the fallen pair. To Tom's relief, the bank teller slowly turned his head to show a weak smile and then rolled off the sobbing woman. "Did I do all right?"

"You did a brave thing," Tom told him. "How bad are you hurt?"

"I don't know," the young man replied. "Feels like somebody hit me with a club."

Tom looked up at the two grizzled cowhands who now stood over them. Behind them, people were pouring from the buildings, a crowd heading toward them. "Get Doc Schroeder and hurry."

"I see him coming," one of the cowboys said, and he pointed to an older man in a short, heavy coat and a stocking cap, his medical bag swinging from his hand as he hurried their way. Behind him, more of the townspeople were emerging and heading toward the scene of the shooting

Tom turned his attention to the still-hysterical woman. "You're all right, Mrs. Durfee, just banged up a little, but it's all over. Calm down, now."

"Are they gone?" she asked tremulously.

"Long gone," Tom told her. "You're safe now."

The doctor arrived and pushed past the two onlookers, looking first to the woman. "She all right?" he asked Tom.

"Scared, might be bruised a bit," Tom told him. "John took a shot for her . . . bravest thing I ever seen."

The doctor was already stripping the man's shirt from the wound and examining a long bleeding furrow. "Deep graze, but not punched in." He took off his own heavy coat and laid it over the bank teller. "You're damned lucky, John." He looked up at the crowd that was gathering. "Couple of you men help me get him down to my office." He bent to the bank employee once again. "How about inside? Anyone hurt in there?"

The agonized teller shook his head. "No, sir, we all were doing just what they said. No trouble 'til the shooting started." He shivered. "I'm cold and I hurt."

"We'll get you inside and give you something to take the edge off the pain," the doctor assured him.

Tom scanned the men and women who had circled around the wounded man and distraught woman. The bank manager, William Moran, had just come from the bank and was looking around nervously. Frank Bowman and Hiram Keats were standing together as somber late arrivals from City Hall. Two women had Mrs. Durfee between them, holding, comforting, and calming her.

Tom looked at all the faces of the men, a frown coming to his own. He turned to the two ranch hands that had participated in the gunfight. "Where's Ben?" he asked.

Both men looked into the crowd, their faces puzzled. "I thought he was here," one said.

Tom came to his feet immediately and pushed his way through the crowd, his hands swift and forceful as he thrust both men and women out of his way. He broke into a trot on his way to the corner of the City Hall building where he had last seen Ben.

He dashed into the space between the buildings, where he came to an abrupt stop. "Ah, Ben," he cried aloud. "No, no, damn it, no!"

Ben Haley was slumped down, his back against the concrete base of the building, a scarlet seepage pooling chest high on the left side beneath his open mackinaw. His revolver lay in his lax hand, his hat blown a few feet away by the swirling frigid wind. The same gusting breeze was fluttering the strands of red hair away and back again over the face, where his eyes stared without sight.

"Ah, Ben," Tom sighed as he took him into his arms and pulled him close, laying his cheek next to Ben's, feeling not only the cold of the weather. "Why you?" he said as his tears began. "Why you?"

For a long time, he rocked his mentor, his companion, his friend. Gradually, he became aware of those who had followed and now stood in silence around him.

"Tom, let us take him now," Frank Bowman spoke softly as he stepped up beside him. "It's beginning to snow."

Chapter Twenty-six

Murphyville, Kansas, 1866

The storm blew swiftly over into Missouri and Iowa, and it left only a light covering of snow on middle and eastern Kansas. The temperature of the following dawn, however, dropped to below zero, restricting outdoor activities. In the immediate hours after the robbery, the bodies of the bandits felled in the gun battle had been uncaringly enclosed in rough pine coffins and indifferently left outside at the rear of the mortuary.

Ben's body, after a medical examination at Tom's insistence, was carefully and respectfully laid out in the undertaker's shed behind the mortuary to await the order for a quality casket to arrive from Kansas City. All of the deceased would remain above ground until the rock-hard earth could thaw sufficiently for the gravediggers' shovels.

The threat of a possible blizzard on the robbery day had quashed the thought of pursuit of the bandits, and even though Tom argued for an immediate chase, he was reminded it was not a town marshal's call.

"Jurisdiction be damned," Tom had railed at Mayor Keats and the others gathered at the bank. "We're letting murderers get away while we're jawing about it!"

"We've sent word to Sheriff Kerry over in Clay Center," Keats had responded. "Even if he is willing, there's little chance he can find people to ride as a posse in this weather."

"Then I'll go myself!" Tom declared in anger.

"Wait 'til the weather clears," Frank Bowman said. "There are things in town we need to tend to."

"It's your bank's money, Frank!" Tom argued. "They're getting away with it."

Bowman nodded. "I'm appallingly aware of that, Tom. But if it's bad weather for us, it'll be so for them. They'll have to hole up somewhere."

"Or maybe keep riding clear out of Kansas," Tom said with bitter disdain.

"It's getting late, Tom," Keats said, his voice commanding. "Be dark soon and nothing anyone can do. Let it go at least until tomorrow"

Sleep had not been a consideration: Tom had spent the long hours of darkness sitting in a chair in his boardinghouse room. The night had been filled with warmhearted remembrances, yet plagued with far too many self-recriminating memories.

Why did I talk him into coming west? Why did I talk him into working for the railroad? Why did we take this damned job?

As dawn lightened the winter day, he left the building while his landlady was busy preparing breakfast in the kitchen, avoiding what would surely be the well-meaning and sympathetic comments that would hurt more than soothe.

Tom tucked his face deep into the sheared wool lining of his heavy mackinaw as he walked the deserted main street of the frozen town. For the third time since yesterday's robbery, he pounded at the door of the Sunflower Saloon and ignored the CLOSED sign hanging on the door. He shaded his eyes from the snow-bright light to peer through the door's small glass window into the building. He was turning to leave when a movement in the saloon's shadowy interior caught his eye. Again, he pounded on the door with renewed force and rapidity.

"Saloon's shut up!" a voice shouted. "Can't ya read?"

"Open up!" Tom called. "Right now, or I'll open it for ya!"

After a few moments' hesitation, the shadowy figure moved toward the door, unlocked it and jerked it open. Wearing a rumpled and dingy nightshirt, the sleep-haggard bartender, Maynard Granger, blinked and recoiled from the cold. "What do you want, Marshal?" he exclaimed.

"Either of the brothers here?" Tom asked.

The stout, grizzled man partially closed the door against the frigid weather and left it open only a few inches. "Ain't here. Been gone to their ranch a few days ago."

"Sure they warn't here yesterday?" Tom asked accusingly.

The bartender didn't answer immediately, his eyes widening as a momentary twitch of expression revealed evasion. "Naw, they been gone days ago. Like I said, we've been closed."

"Funny time of the year for saloonkeepers not to be working," Tom said. "Christmas coming, folks wanting to get all cheery and likkered up. Don't seem likely."

"Heard tell the missus was feeling poorly, that's why they shut down and went home," the man responded. "Tom, it's freezing cold . . . I want to get back to bed."

"You lying to me, Maynard?"

Again, evasiveness flickered in the man's face. "Honest, Marshal. I ain't lying."

Tom shrugged, and as he turned away, he heard the door close behind him.

Man can't lie worth a damn!

"What's going on here?" Mayor Keats asked.

Across the room, Mrs. Stevens looked up from her paperwork, intrigued by the mayor's question, to regard the three men who were seated facing the mayor.

"Tom thinks the shot that killed Ben was deliberate murder," Bowman spoke in response. "Tell him, Tom."

Tom rose from his chair and turned, presenting a right profile to the mayor. "When I left Ben, he was standing just like this at the corner of this building." With his left hand, he drew down an imaginary line to represent the corner a few inches to his left side. "He was taking cover behind this wall, taking a peek 'round the corner to watch what was going on."

"What are you getting at?" Keats asked.

"Bear me out on this." Tom crooked his left arm behind

him and pointed to a spot nearly to his back on the left side. "Doc tells me the shot came in here and dug a line straight forward into his heart."

"Go on," Keats said.

"All the shooting was in front of him," Tom said, and then touched a point on the side of his chest. "Shot from the gang would've hit him here if they'd seen a piece of him."

"Maybe he turned around and—"

"No, sir, Mr. Mayor," Tom cut in. "Not unless he stepped out from cover and turned his back to them outlaws . . . and Ben warn't no fool to do that."

"Those other men were shooting," Keats persisted. "Maybe a stray ball might've done it."

"Maybe," Dr. Schroeder put in. "The angle would've been wrong for them too, but nobody can say for sure."

"Something else," Tom said as he walked to a chair and sat down. "The shots that started the shooting shebang came from Ben's direction." He paused. "Ben's gun hadn't been fired."

There was a long silence, only the crackle of the fire in the stove sounding.

"Then what's the conclusion, gentlemen?" Keats asked.

"Somebody in this town shot Ben," Tom said. "Used the bank robbery to bushwhack him."

"And you, gentlemen?" Keats asked Bowman and the doctor.

"We think Tom is right," Bowman said as Dr. Schroeder nodded.

"And I know who," Tom said bitterly.

"But you can't prove it, can you?" Keats asked.

"Not a chance," Dr. Schroeder interjected quickly. "Even if Tom's right . . . and I'm almost sure he is . . . there's no way we can lay it to the Lockharts."

"So they get away with it?" Tom asked, his face grim.

"All we have is suspicion," Keats said.

"Maybe that's all I need," Tom contended.

"I'm going to remind you that you're a lawman," Keats said pointedly to Tom. "I can imagine what you might want to do, and who could blame you?" He shook his head. "But there's no going after them without proof."

Tom started to speak, than clamped his lips closed.

"What about the bank, Frank? How much did they get?" Keats said, changing the subject.

"A little less than sixteen thousand," Bowman responded, then cast a glance toward Mrs. Stevens. "Like to keep that figure just among us."

She nodded.

"And the men that got away?" Keats asked.

"Sheriff Kerry over at the county seat will be forming up a posse soon as weather lets up," Tom said, then added: "But maybe by then, they'll be gone."

Later, outside the jail, Tom looked up at the sullen gray clouds as if hoping to spot the sun near its zenith. It appeared to him to be past noon, and he felt that the cold weather might have warmed a few degrees. He had returned to his room and now was swathed in extra clothing. He had pulled his second pair of jeans over his longjohns and wore a couple of flannel shirts instead of one. There were three pairs of woolen socks in his boots, and he had exchanged his wide-brimmed hat for a borrowed fur cap that tucked down over his ears. He had wrapped a thick wool scarf over his lower face, leaving a mere slit for his eyes. Instead of gloves, he wore mittens to keep the fingers warmly together rather than separated.

"I must look a rolypoly," he muttered through his scarf. "I'm as wide as I am tall."

Tom lumbered toward Duke, raised his left leg, and guided his boot into the stirrup. He lunged up and swung his well-padded body into the saddle, tapped the horse's sides with his heels, and guided the stallion toward the edge of town. Even with layered clothing and the fur cap, he was already feeling the bitter cold. He watched the vapor of his breath through the scarf and kept his breathing slow and shallow. If Ben had been here, he'd have warned that this journey was another foolish notion, that it would be smart to wait for a livable temperature.

"C'mon, Duke," he whispered softly. "Let's get it done and back 'fore it turns cold."

He walked the horse slowly, looking down at the snow-covered roadway. In spite of the weather, there had been enough traffic to leave a muddle of hoofprints and wagon-wheel tracks. Other residents of the town and of the country surrounding had their wintertime errands to run, needs and reasons to be abroad despite the below-zero conditions.

Fifteen minutes later, a quarter-mile away from the edge of town, he found what he was looking for—hoofprints in the snow of two horses crossing over the roadside ditch and angling toward the southwest. He guided Duke across the gully and onto the flat prairie to follow the tracks. He stayed wide to the side so as not to disturb the dark furrows left by the horses' legs as they moved through the crystalline white landscape.

He traveled for a distance and came to the periphery of a small, wooded area of leafless trees, dark against the glaring background. He slowly nodded his head, knowing that the tracks leading into and wending a path through the thicket were in a direct line toward the Lockhart ranch.

Leon Biggs and his pal were, and maybe still are, holed up there. Maybe with Russ and Ed, they'd all been in cahoots in the robbery from the very start. Tom touched his upper teeth to his lower lip beneath his scarf as another thought came to him. *Maybe robbing the bank had been Biggs' idea, but maybe murdering Ben and me was the thinking of the Lockhart brothers.*

Tom sat quietly for several minutes to contemplate his next actions. *If they're really there, including Russ and Ed, it'll be four or maybe five to my one. Too many.*

His horse nickered, and he knew it was a protest against the standstill in the arctic chill. "I know, I know," he said softly, his glove stroking Duke's neck below the mane. "Ain't fit for man or beast." He tugged the reins and turned Duke away. "Stay warm by the fire while you can, gents," he said aloud. "When I come back, it'll be colder in your graves."

Chapter Twenty-seven

Clay County, Kansas, 1866

Four days later, the morning arrived with a cloudless blue sky, a bright sun, and a gusting, warming wind. The muddy roads in and out of Murphyville quickly dried, and they were soon heavy with traffic, mostly commercial wagons and a few personal buggies and buckboards. Horsemen also were mid-morning travelers, and it was a pair of them who found the snow-crusted body of a dead outlaw a short distance from town in a field alongside the road that led to Manhattan. The corpse was loaded onto a farm wagon and brought into Murphyville, where another pine box was cobbled together to store the remains with the others behind the mortuary.

"Hope it don't blow away no more tracks," Sheriff Marvin Kerry said as he rode beside Tom, the posse trailing behind. Three of the six men riding with them were two sheriff's deputies and a deputy marshal also from the county seat, Clay Center, twenty miles away. The other three were from Murphyville, volunteers the sheriff had approved as levelheaded and reliable men. Kerry had deputized Tom as a member of the posse despite repeatedly voicing his misgivings about bringing along a person with such a deeply felt grudge. "You sure we're heading the right way?"

"Tracks led that way three days ago," Tom said. "We should've been here sooner."

"So you've already told me more'n once," the senior lawman said. "Maybe you got Eskimo blood. I sure don't, and none of these posse fellers do neither."

"Tracks was headed right for the Lockhart place," Tom said.

"You've said that before too," Kerry reminded him.

They came to the top of a rise in the prairie, and the hoof prints they had been following disappeared in the wide stretch of brown turf that the wind had laid bare. The sheriff raised his right hand to halt his posse, and he stood in his stirrups to scan the landscape ahead. With a shake of his head, he settled back into his saddle and turned to address his followers.

"We can try to pick up the tracks again, but I'm thinking they're mostly blown away," Kerry told them. " 'Sides, looks like there's been a slew of riders out here going different directions." He sighed. "We'll start with the Lockhart clan, since you're so all fired het up about them, and see if we can find anything there."

Kerry raised his right hand again to wave his posse forward and led the group across the windswept terrain toward the distant woodland. As he followed, Tom's eyes focused on the brown grass as they moved along, seeing a few indentations that were likely what remained of the tracks he'd seen before, but not as many to show a definite trail.

When they entered the woodland, Tom's spirits lifted. He urged Duke forward to ride beside Sheriff Kerry. "Wind didn't blow 'em all away," he said, pointing to the rutted path in the snow.

"I see 'em," Kerry acknowledged. "I see something else too." It was the sheriff's turn to point as the tracks veered sharply to the right. "If it was them, it looks like they're headed for the road."

"That still goes close by the Lockhart ranch," Tom said.

"Or maybe they was on the way to Hutchison," Kerry countered. "I said we'd check on Ed and Russ. Let it be." He guided his horse to follow the marks in the snow, the posse following. "Do I understand you and Ben knew one of the holdup men?"

"Leon Biggs," Tom responded promptly. "He was in our company during the war and worked on the Union Pacific rail-laying outfit while we was there. Boss ran him off as a troublemaker."

"No friend, then?"

Tom gave him a withering look. "Leon Biggs is as bad as they come."

"Had to ask," the sheriff said.

They came to a narrow farm-to-market road now cleared of snow by the midday sun. The trail they'd been following abruptly ended in the churn of the dried mud in the lane, plenty of hoofprints going left and right amidst the wagon-wheel grooves.

"Looks like ever'body in the county's been out here running up and down," Tom said in complaint.

"Everybody's getting out after the cold spell," the sheriff said. "Here comes the Jarvis family right now."

Sure enough, a farm wagon was approaching with a man in a heavy coat handling the reins of the pulling horse. On the high seat, a warmly dressed woman sat beside him and two children, bundled against the cold, rode behind them in the wagon bed.

"Howdy, Sheriff!" the man called. "What's going on?"

"Bank robbery in Murphyville the other day," Kerry said as the man hauled on the reins to bring his horse to a halt.

"Land's sake!" the woman exclaimed. "Anyone hurt?"

"Or killed?" the man asked.

"Bank teller, John Delaney, was hurt—not too bad," Kerry said, then paused. "Marshal Haley was killed."

"Lordy! How awful!" Mrs. Jarvis fretted. "That's just terrible!"

"What about the bank robbers?" Jarvis asked. "They get away?"

"Couple of them," the sheriff replied. "That's why we're out this way. See anybody riding past the last few days?"

"We was pretty well tucked in during the cold," Jarvis replied. "They'd have been fools to be out in that weather."

"We kinda wondered if they might've holed up somewhere around here?" Kerry said as a question.

"Not with us, that's for sure," Jarvis said and followed it with a chuckle.

"Richard Harley Jarvis!" the woman said sharply. "A robbery and a killing ain't no time for making light of things!"

Jarvis sobered quickly. "You're plumb right, Ma. Meant no disrespect." He snapped the harness reins and clucked the horse into a walk. "Gotta get to town and back. Looks like the weather ain't gonna hold. Good luck and hope you catch them fellers."

With a farewell wave to the family, Sheriff Kerry led the posse in the opposite direction, moving at a brisk trot that continued for more than a mile until they reined to a stop at a turnoff that led to a ranch complex two hundred yards to the left. The access road ended at a low, rambling log main house with a front porch, a flagstone front walk, and a barn, a corral, and a couple of small sheds around and behind it.

"Careful as we go in," the sheriff cautioned. "Possibly they're there. Probably they ain't, but keep your eyes peeled."

"Tracks coming in and out, Sheriff," one member of the posse said.

"That don't tell us nothing special," the lawman responded. "Just the same, walk your mounts slow and easy."

As the eight men on horseback moved toward the ranch buildings, Tom and two others drew their revolvers. Other posse members positioned their hands close to their holsters or to the butts of their rifles in their scabbards. There was no sign of outdoor activity at the ranch ahead, and neither was there movement in and around the outbuildings.

"Halloo, the house!" Sheriff Kerry shouted as he reined his horse to a halt and held up his right hand to bring the others to a stop. "Halloo, the house! Sheriff Kerry coming in, posse at my back!"

They waited.

"Halloo, the house!" Kerry shouted again. "Russ! Ed! We're coming in!"

They waited a minute more, and then two men came out of the front door of the ranch house and stepped down from the porch. They sauntered to the end of the walk and stopped to stare at the intruders.

"Whatcha want here, Sheriff?" Russ Lockhart demanded.

"Don't get your dander up, Russ!" Kerry called. "We're checking house by house for some dangerous men. Might even be holding guns at your back. We're here to help if we're needed."

"Ain't no guns at our back," Russ Lockhart shouted. "Don't need no damned help, so best you and your bunch be on your way."

"Don't see it that way!" Kerry shouted. "We'll come in and take a look, then we'll be on our way." Without waiting for another exchange, the sheriff tapped his heels to his mare's sides and started her trotting toward the ranch, the posse hurrying with him. They rode into the bare-earth area at the front of the ranch house and reined up to look down upon the Lockhart brothers.

"What's he doing here?" Russ Lockhart demanded, his look fastened on Tom. "Town marshal ain't got no authority outside of town."

"He's deputized as a part of my posse," Kerry said.

"What's this all about?" Ed Lockhart asked in a surly tone. "Why you riding in on us?"

Tom studied the younger of the Lockhart brothers. Edward Lockhart was slightly taller than Russ, with a skinnier frame. He had a very ugly face, badly pockmarked by an apparent childhood bout of smallpox. In contrast to his older sibling, he was given to nervous behavior, his eyes blinking continuously, his body swaying in constant minor to-and-fro movements.

"Bank robbery in town," Kerry told the pair. "We think them that didn't get themselves killed might have come this way."

"That's news to us, Sheriff," Russ said with a show of surprise and interest. "None of our townsfolk hurt, I hope."

"Marshal Haley killed, and the bank teller's shot but gonna be okay," Kerry responded. "We're looking for two men who got away. You see anyone like that the past few days?"

Russ shook his head, but he cast an oblique look at Tom

with a smirk that quickly came and disappeared. "Well, that's a shame. I'm sorry to hear it."

"Them fellows wouldn't have lasted long in the kinda weather we've been having," Kerry said. "They came this way, we figger they needed a place to get out of the cold."

"You talking our place?" Ed questioned.

"Mind if we check inside?" Kerry parried. "The barn, the sheds?"

"Check the privy if you got the notion," Russ said, a wide smile now on his face. "Look around all you like. We ain't been hiding no bank robbers."

"And I don't like the idea of you busting in like you think we did!" Ed blustered.

Kerry twisted in his saddle to address his men. "Will, you, Jim, and Chester take the house. Matt, you, Jake, and Marty take the barn." He fixed his eyes on Tom. "You stay with me."

"My old lady's inside," Russ objected. "You don't go barging in—"

"Knock on the door and tell her to get decent if she ain't," Kerry interrupted. "Be polite, but don't get careless. Keep your pistols at the ready if there's anyone hiding in there."

"See here, Sheriff," Russ said in anger. "You got no call to—"

"Now, you see here, Lockhart," Kerry cut him off again. "You and your brother ain't hiding them criminals, then you got nothing to worry about, but if you've been aiding and abetting, we'll see about that for sure."

Under the hostile and watchful eyes of the Lockhart brothers, the designated members of the posse dismounted and, with handguns drawn, started their examinations of the house and the surrounding buildings. There were loud, swearing protests from a feminine voice inside the house, but no shouts of alarm from the men or revolver reports. After ten minutes, the posse members returned to the front of the ranch house to remount their horses.

"Nobody inside other than that danged woman," Will Cartwright said as he swung into his saddle. A tall, slender, self-confident young man from Clay Center, he had quickly established himself as an easy companion to the others in the posse. "Saw a passel of dishes there by the wash pan . . . maybe more than enough for just the four of 'em."

"Them's a couple days' dishes," Russ said with a dismissive gesture. "My old lady's on the lazy side."

"Or maybe you had visitors," Kerry parried.

"That's accusing talk, and we ain't taking that lightly," Ed said sharply, his shoulders hunching on his hard-said words. "You seen all there is to see here, so what about you all moving on down the road?"

"You watch your steps, gents," Kerry warned. "We've been watching you and we're gonna watch you closer. You had a hand in any of this, we'll find out sooner or later."

"Merry Christmas to you, Sheriff," Russ said with sarcastic cheer. "And the same to you, Deputy Marshal." Without waiting for a response, he turned on his heel and, with a curt cock of his head to bid his brother to follow, he walked to the ranch house with Ed close behind.

"Betcha Santa puts nothing but coal in their stockings," Will Cartwright said with a wide smile. "Whooeee, what a shoddy bunch!"

Chapter Twenty-eight

Clay County, Kansas, 1866

Sheriff Kerry led his posse along the country road for the remainder of the day, making a stop at each ranch along the way. Most of the ranch families were cordial and cooperative in the searches of their homes, buildings, and land; only two were churlish and resentful at what they considered intrusion.

"Getting late and getting colder. We could head into Murphyville for the night," Kerry announced to his group. "Or, next place we come to, if they let us, we'll ask permission to bed down in their barn and a get a good start in the morning. Hope you all brought enough to keep you warm and something to fill your stomachs."

"Maybe we can get the folks there to fix us a little something for supper," Will Cartwright ventured.

"We'll be lucky if they give us the shelter of their barn," Kerry countered.

"How about coffee?" Cartwright persisted. "Could we ask for that?"

"How about you let me do the talking and we'll see," the sheriff said brusquely, although his tone was not severe.

At sunset, the posse turned their horses into the front area of a ranch house. It was an attractive dwelling, with white clapboard siding, a front porch spanning the width of the building, and the main entry door off to one side of two centered mullion-paned windows. Back of the home, there was a small, empty corral, a modest-sized barn, a couple of sheds, and an outhouse. From a fireplace chimney at one end of the house, a plume of smoke drifted up and dissipated into the air.

"I know these folks," Kerry informed Tom. "Bert and Nadine Baxter. Nice young couple . . . got a couple of kids, little boy and a little girl. Came here from Ohio about two years ago."

"Pretty lonely out this far from town," Tom said. " 'Specially for the young 'uns."

"I guess you haven't been out this way," the sheriff responded. "There's a passel of folk living hereabouts. Small store up the road apiece where they can get their day-to-day goods and groceries without having to come into town 'cept every now and then. One lady out here does the schooling for the young ones."

"You're right about me being a stranger to these parts," Tom admitted. "Never yet had much cause to come this far in this direction."

Kerry swung down from his mare and handed the reins to Tom to hold while he walked to the front door of the ranch house and knocked. From his short distance viewpoint, Tom saw the door open only a few inches and could see the face of a young woman. He could hear bits and pieces of the conversation, enough to determine that the woman was tense, her part of the talk in clipped answers and uneasy responses to Kerry's questions. The sheriff tipped his hat to the woman and walked slowly back to take the reins Tom handed down to him.

"Kinda funny," Kerry said as he swung up on his saddle. "Nice girl, always friendly." He sighed. "Short-tempered this time. Asked us to please not bother."

"No sleeping in her barn?" Tom asked.

"Really put out even at the idea," Kerry told the posse. "Said she had some sick kids and didn't need us roaming around, making noise and keeping 'em from their healing sleep."

"See her husband?" Will Cartwright asked.

The sheriff shook his head. "Said he was sick along with the kids."

"Strike you as strange, Sheriff?" Tom asked. "I could tell she was edgy when she was talking. Maybe that was her being scared making her testy."

"Like maybe there was somebody with a gun on her, you're guessing?" Kerry said with a nod. "For that reason, we ride out of here just like we was heading on down the road." He turned his mare and waved the group back onto the country lane.

"If they're in there and we storm that house, it ain't just the bad guys who are gonna get hurt or killed," Tom warned.

The sheriff nodded again as he swiveled in his saddle to address the posse members. "Who's our best shooters?"

"I'm not bad with a rifle," Will Cartwright answered.

The sheriff turned to Tom. "I ain't seen you shoot, but I hear you're okay with a handgun."

"I can do a rifle too," Tom said.

"You ever kill anybody?" Kerry asked.

"In the war," Tom admitted. "Not that I brag on it."

"You, Will?"

"Same," the man said. "No offense, Tom, but I was shooting gray coats."

"None taken, Will," Tom said.

"Well, if what Tom is saying is what *I'm* thinking," Kerry told the posse, "we'll ride on a mite farther, then Tom, Will, and me can double back on foot and see what we can see at the Baxters'."

"What do you want us to do?" a posse member asked.

"The rest of you stay put 'til if and when we need you," Kerry informed the group. "You hear shooting, come after us, but come easy so you don't get caught in a crossfire."

"If Biggs is really in there," Tom said, "he'll shoot the man, the woman, and the kids just 'cause he thinks they're a bother."

"Mean critter, I take your meaning," Kerry nodded.

They rode for a short distance before the sheriff halted the group's progress. "This is far enough," he said, and he stepped down from his horse, tied the reins to a sapling, and took a rifle from his saddle scabbard. "Come on, let's go."

Tom and Cartwright dismounted, tied their horses beside the sheriff's and, with rifles, followed Kerry back down the road. In a few minutes, they came to a tree-lined curve just out of sight of the Baxter ranch.

"We'll cut through the trees and into that tall brush, and then move up close on the house," Kerry instructed. "You boys did military, so I don't need to tell you not to jiggle the bushes so them in the house can see."

"We don't rightly know there's anybody in there, do we, Sheriff?" Will asked.

"We'll get in close enough to wait and watch," Kerry replied. "I hope, for the family's sake, we're barking up the wrong tree."

The sheriff waved Tom and Cartwright to follow, and the trio moved into the scattering of trees on the left side of the road. The twilight sun was casting long, deep shadows, and the three men stayed within them, crouching low as they crept toward the Baxter ranch house.

As they came within a hundred yards of the dwelling, Tom, Cartwright, and the sheriff took off their hats and crawled stealthily forward. Each man, mindful not to disclose his presence, slid his body into gaps in the undergrowth without a telltale movement of the tops of the tall prairie grass.

They wriggled to the cover of an earthen mound not more than fifty yards from the front of the house and chose it as their vantage position.

"Wish we had some field glasses," Tom whispered as he peered over the mound.

On the left, beside him, Cartwright fished a rifle scope from his jacket, handed it to Tom, and whispered, "Mount's broke on it, but I figgered it might come in handy."

"Let me see it," Kerry said in a barely audible voice. "Good thinking, Will."

Tom passed the scope to the sheriff, who inched his head higher over the mound, then placed the scope to his right eye and adjusted the focus. "Pretty dark in the house, but I can make out the furnishings, pictures on the wall, that sort of thing."

"See anybody yet?" Tom asked.

Kerry shook his head and handed the scope back to Tom. "You take a squint at it. Maybe young eyes can see better'n mine."

Tom adjusted the focus to his right eye as he peered through one of the two tall windows left of the front door. He too could see the dim-light images in the living room area: an upholstered chair, a china cabinet with a display of dishes and glasses, and the back of a wooden rocking chair.

"Anything?" Kerry whispered.

"Not yet," Tom whispered in response. "Wait a minute! I see something going on!"

In his field of view, he saw the Baxter woman thrust suddenly and violently across the room. She nearly fell, but recovered her balance and, in a soundless pantomime of terrified obedience to an unseen menace, she nodded and settled into the big upholstered chair. A moment later, two youngsters ran to the protection of her arms as she drew them close to her. Tom couldn't see who had pushed her, but he could see that the woman and her children were frightened of someone just a few feet away.

"They're in there," Tom said in a low voice. "There he is! Biggs!"

Through the scope, he saw the unpleasant face of the outlaw peeking around the inside corner of a window, his expression stern and wary as he stared directly in Tom's direction.

"Don't move," Tom cautioned. "He's looking right our way."

"Can he see you?" the sheriff asked.

"He'll see grass move if I duck . . . maybe I just look like another bush long as I'm holding still." He paused. "He might be figgering we might come back and do just what we're doing."

On his left, Cartwright clicked the hammer back on his Spencer. "I can see him," he said. "I can get a head shot."

"No good," the sheriff spoke in a hush. "We get one, we've got a second man inside to do the killing. We've got to get 'em both in our sights."

"What's the chances of that?" Tom asked.

"Chance I think we got to take," Kerry countered.

"So what do we do?" Cartwright asked.

"We wait," Kerry said. "Wait and hope we get a clear shot at both at the same time."

"He's turned away," Tom said as he lowered the scope and lowered his head. "I can't see him."

"Neither can I," Cartwright added.

They lay behind the mound and took turns peering into the house through the rifle scope as the daylight faded into dusk, and then into night. The Baxter woman rose to light an oil lamp and then returned to her chair to clutch her children tight against her. On four occasions, each of two outlaws moved briefly into view and out of sight again. Then a different man moved slowly, laboriously within the frame of the window.

"That one there . . . that's Bert," Kerry informed them as he looked through the scope. "Looks like they've busted him up a bit." He handed the scope to Tom.

"He's lucky Biggs didn't shoot him instead," Tom muttered as he raised the scope to his eye. "How long we been here?" he asked. "Couple of hours?"

"About," Kerry confirmed.

"Rest of the posse is gonna get worried 'bout us," Cartwright said. "Think one of us ought to go back and tell what's going on?"

"I told 'em to stay put," Kerry said. "They'll stay . . . at least, they'd better."

"I don't think we're ever gonna get them badmen together in our sights," Cartwright said.

"We gotta hope so," the sheriff responded.

"Been thinking on that, Sheriff," Tom said. "I agree with Will. We ain't yet had a chance to see one of 'em real good, much less both at the same time."

"You got a different idea?" the sheriff questioned.

"Say you or Will gets a shot at one man, takes it, and maybe even gets a kill." Tom paused. "Then what happens?"

"You're talking, Tom," the sheriff prompted. "You tell us."

"There'll be a few seconds for the one that's left to figger out what just happened . . . and then the shooting will start for sure." He paused again. "And that Baxter family will be smack dab in the middle of it."

"Go on," Kerry prompted.

"It could be even worse," Tom said. "What if you take your shot and you miss. Now you got two shooters that knows we're out here."

"You're driving to something, so tell me what," Kerry said.

"It's dark enough now . . . I move up right next to the house and wait," Tom told them. "You get a shot and takes one down, I go in and pop other one 'fore he knows what's happening."

"Fat chance!" the sheriff scoffed.

"And if we miss?" Cartwright asked.

"Then I take down the both of them," Tom said.

"Too risky," Kerry said. "Close hand shooting by you or them might get one or more of the Baxters."

"Let me tell you something, Sheriff," Tom said, his voice solemn. "You take a shot and you miss, they'll take hostages. They'll likely take the young 'uns . . . easier to carry and less to struggle." He fell silent for a few moments. "And Biggs will kill the ma and pa if they try to save their kids."

Kerry's dark silhouette was very still, no movement of head to indicate what he was thinking.

"Time's a-wasting," Tom said. "Do I go?"

"Okay," the lawman said with a sigh. "I think it's a fool thing to do, but you know the man and likely know what he'll do. You better do it right."

"And if I don't?"

"I'll likely say some kind words over your grave." His silhouetted head nodded toward the ranch. "And theirs."

Chapter Twenty-nine

Clay County, Kansas, 1866

Tom waited until a cloud came over the quarter moon, and then he used the same stealth to retreat to the thicker and higher undergrowth that ringed the ranch house. Crouching low, he circled to the side of the ranch house and crept closer to the front porch.

When he reached the cover of the porch-front shrubs, thankful he hadn't been seen, he burrowed beneath them. From his ground-level point of view, he couldn't see the outlaws or the house residents, but through the bushes he could see an occasional shadow as someone passed between the lamp light and the windows. He gauged the space between his position and the front door: two steps up and five feet of the porch floor.

If he crawled across that porch, would the creak of boards give him away? Too risky!

At this position, he could hear clamorous voices within the house, although the words were unclear. There were loud and enraged utterances from the captors and, barely heard, the plaintive pleas of the captives. To Tom, it sounded like something had escalated the outlaws' anger, and the fury was mounting to a dangerous level.

Something's about to happen!

He rose to his hands and knees, gathering for a lunge toward the door. He drew his revolver, and then hunched down quickly as a shadow was cast through the window onto the floor of the porch. Tom's eyes fastened on it and he saw, to his immense relief, it remained.

A shattering of glass masked the crack of the rifle shot and the shadow lurched out of sight. Tom sprang from his crouch, leaped to the porch, and dashed to the door. He threw all of his weight against it and crashed it open as he fell to the floor of a central hallway. On his side, he fired two shots in the direction of the still-standing outlaw near the window and, seeing the man fall from the corner of his eye, looked frantically, desperately, for Biggs.

And couldn't find him!

Survival instinct made him roll to his right just as a ball fired from the far end of the dark hallway slammed into the floor inches from him. He felt another fan past as he lunged through the kitchen doorway with a protective wall partition between him and Biggs' repeating gunfire.

The woman's horrified scream confirmed Tom's dread. The Baxter woman broke away from her husband and little girl and dashed into the hallway. Bert Baxter reached out and pulled her, fighting him, back into the living room.

"Damn you, Patterson! I've got the boy, and I'll kill him!" Biggs shouted.

"You got a posse around the house," Tom lied. "There's no way out! Let the boy go and give yourself up!"

A flash in the dark with the boom of Biggs' handgun was the answer, the ball speeding into the partition near Tom's head.

"Tell 'em to give me clear passage or I'll put a shot in his little head, that's a fact!" Biggs bellowed.

"Let him go!" the hysterical mother cried, struggling against her husband's arms. "Don't hurt him!"

"Listen to her," Tom said, keeping his voice calm. "No need to hurt nobody else, Leon. He's just a little kid and—"

"Shut up! I'm getting outta here, and the kid stays alive long as nobody tries to stop me."

Tom's eyes had adjusted to the dim light, and he could see the dark silhouette of Biggs and the small child who was squirming against him. Tom covered the hammer of his revolver with one hand to muffle the sound as he cocked it. "You ain't taking that boy out of here," he said with grave intensity. "You got a chance to walk out of here alive, but not if you hurt that young 'un."

"Go to hell!"

"Don't!" Nadine Baxter shouted, and she tore away from her husband's hold.

Tom aimed and fired.

There was another gunshot from Biggs' revolver, but it was a wild ball that grazed past the youngster's head and into the ceiling of the hallway. The boy fell from the outlaw's slack arms with a piercing cry of pain and terror as he landed hard on the pine floorboards, his wails bringing his mother into the hallway with a frightened cry of her own.

Tom leapt from his position to catch her by the arm and swung her behind him as he faced the dark figure staggering toward the back of the hallway, his gun held in his drooping hand as he headed slowly for a rear exit door.

"Biggs!" Tom called. "Don't try it!"

Behind him, he heard the footsteps of Sheriff Kerry and Will Cartwright pounding on the porch and into the hallway.

The silhouetted Biggs lurched against the wall and, using it for support, he turned and slowly raised his weapon.

The sharp bark of a gun close behind him sounded, and the black shape in the gloom of the corridor was whirled about by the impact of the ball, the gun dropping from his hand as he crumpled to the floor.

Tom looked over his shoulder to see Sheriff Kerry with a wisp of smoke curling from his revolver. He gave a nod as he lowered the weapon and holstered it.

"Stay back," Tom said to the woman as he walked quickly forward. With his gaze concentrated on the still body of the outlaw, with his revolver remaining in his right hand, he reached with his left to scoop the crying child away, then rose and carried the boy to his weeping mother.

"He's all right," Tom assured her as he handed the youngster to her, his eyes never leaving the man on the floor.

And because of that, he was surprised at the stinging slap of the woman's hand on his face.

"You could've killed Jimmy!" she accused. "You could've shot my boy instead of that badman!" Racked with sobs, she knelt down and clutched both of her children tight to her.

"But I didn't," Tom countered. He looked to Bert Baxter who was standing at her elbow. "Take them into the kitchen while we take care of things."

"I'm sorry for that," Bert Baxter apologized. "She's just, well, she's upset."

"I know," Tom said with an understanding nod. "Don't blame her at all."

Baxter took his sobbing wife and crying children through the door into the kitchen and led them to a table at the back, where he seated them and took turns at comforting each.

Tom walked back down the corridor to kneel down and examine Biggs' body, searching for signs of life. He shook his head and rose.

"This one's still alive," Cartwright said as he knelt beside the second outlaw, the sheriff already moving into the living room. "Hurt pretty bad, but he's saying things."

"Biggs is dead," Tom said as he hurried to join them. Cartwright edged away to allow Tom and Kerry to kneel on opposite sides of the wounded man.

"What's your name, fellow?" Kerry asked in a consoling tone. "Can you tell us your name?"

"Johnson," the outlaw said in a barely heard rasp. "Kenny."

"Kenneth Johnson?" Kerry supplied the given name.

"Am I gonna die?" Johnson whispered.

"You're hurt pretty bad," Kerry told him. "You need to make your peace here, before you go to your maker."

"I ain't a really bad feller," the wounded man whimpered, his protest giving his voice a little more strength. "I just fell in with Leon and the others to make a little—"

"Them others?" Tom cut in. "Were the Lockhart brothers in with you?"

Sheriff Kerry gave a glance of irritation to Tom and bent close to resume his questioning. Before he could speak, the outlaw choked and a gush of blood streamed from the corner of his mouth.

Cartwright unfastened the neckerchief from his throat and handed it to Kerry, who used it to wipe away the blood away. The outlaw lay still for a long time, and then his eyelids fluttered and he began a slow nod.

"You're saying 'yes'?" Tom persisted.

The man tried to speak, but the words were inaudible.

Both Tom and Kerry leaned forward, their heads nearly touching as they bent to listen to the suffering man's whispered words. Johnson's lips continued to move; the speech lasted for no more than a few seconds, and then the man's lips opened and did not close again.

Tom leaned back. "He's gone."

"What was he saying?" Cartwright asked. "Praying?"

Tom shook his head and fixed his gaze on the sheriff. "You heard, didn't you? Damn it, tell me you heard!"

The sheriff bobbed his head once. "Enough of it."

"Will it hold up . . . in court?" Tom asked fervently.

Kerry gave a slow and deliberate nod. "Maybe so. Deathbed confession, we both heard it. Be different if it had been just one of us."

"Heard what?" Cartwright said peevishly.

Kerry rose to his feet at the sound of horses' hooves approaching the ranch house. "Posse is here. I better go tell 'em things are okay," he said and then returned his gaze to Cartwright. "The Lockharts were in on the robbery from the very start . . . and Russ was the one who shot Ben Haley." He looked to Tom. "We'll arrest the brothers on our way home tomorrow."

Chapter Thirty

Clay County, Kansas, 1866

The early-morning sunlight lasted only a short while. Gray clouds gathered to hide the sun, and intermittent flurries gave a forewarning of another snowfall.

Bert Baxter had taken his family to a neighbor's for the rest of the previous night, his wife and children still upset and leery of spending the dark hours in the house. Tom and another member of the posse had boarded the broken window, repaired the front door, and stoked the living-room stove and the one in the kitchen to restore heat to the dwelling.

All of the men had accepted Baxter's offer to stay in the house for the night, sleeping on the living room and kitchen floors rather than mussing and muddying up the bedrooms. Up early, at dawn, the posse members had made a clean sweep of every inch of the house to make it suitable for Baxter to fetch his family back home again.

The bodies of Biggs and Johnson were roped securely over their horses and kept out of sight in the barn as Bert Baxter returned with his wife and children in the buckboard. The wife had offered her thanks to the posse members, but she had avoided Tom.

As they left the property, the riders positioned themselves in a tight line to shield the cadaver-burdened horses from the view of anyone in the house.

"Woman told me she was sorry she slapped you," Kerry told Tom as they rode side by side. "Embarrassed to say so to you."

"No need," Tom responded. "She was more right than

wrong." He paused, remembering the event. "It was plumb dark back there in that hallway. Could've gone bad."

"You did what you had to do," Kerry said. "Don't go laying blame on yourself."

"Find any of the bank money?" Tom asked.

"Biggs' saddlebags were in the house," Kerry replied with a nod. "I haven't counted it, but it looks like quite a lot."

"How we gonna handle it at the Lockhart place?" Tom asked, changing the subject.

"Go in careful like," Kerry told him. "They'll be wary seeing us coming back." He twisted about in the saddle and raised his voice to address the posse. "When we get there, you boys watch out. Step down off your horses and keep 'em between you and the house in case them Lockharts don't want to be arrested."

"Sheriff, this is my best danged horse!" one of the men sang out. "Maybe I'll put Bess behind me!"

Everyone laughed.

"Chester, you're wide enough we could hide five men behind you," Kerry quipped. "And old Bess there too!"

Again the laughter came, although it now seemed tinged with anxiety.

"Now, here's what I'm saying," Kerry said as the merriment subsided. "Russ and Ed may come along just as easy as pie, but, from what Tom tells me, they're hot tempered. We stay out of pistol range, and if there's shooting starting, we'll spread out around the house and bide our time 'til we see a good way to corral 'em."

"Don't forget, there's that crazy woman in that house," Will reminded the group. "I ain't wanting no woman-killing on my conscience."

"From what I hear, that woman is meaner than the men," Kerry responded. "She may be the one to start shooting."

"Well, do we shoot back?" another posse member asked.

"Let's cross that bridge when we come to it," Kerry said. "Just watch your step."

The flurries evolved into a constant fall of lazy-floating

snowflakes as the posse rode on and, in time, came to the short road to the Lockhart ranch. They turned down the lane and, as the sheriff had instructed, stepped down from their horses and walked with the animals between them and the Lockhart ranch complex.

Kerry, walking with Tom at the head of the procession, came within hailing distance of the house, where they stopped near a large, leafless white oak. Kerry handed the reins of his horse to Tom and stepped close to the thick trunk. Cupping his hands to his mouth, he shouted: "Russ! Ed! This is Sheriff Kerry again! Come on out! We need to ask some more questions! Come on out and let's palaver!"

They waited.

A few minutes later, Kerry loudly repeated his words and, again, they waited.

"You ain't going in, are you?" Tom asked.

"I look like a fool?" Kerry responded. "No, like I said, we wait."

Five minutes passed, then another five.

At last, the front door opened and a slatternly woman, with uncombed hair and wearing a wrinkled housecoat, came out and took three steps forward. She raised her hand to shade her eyes to peer through the falling snow. "What do you want, Sheriff?"

"Mrs. Lockhart?"

"What do you want?" the woman repeated.

"We need to talk with Russ and Ed."

"They ain't here!" she shouted.

"They was here yesterday!" Kerry countered.

"Ain't now! Gone! You run 'em off and they left me all alone!"

"Which town they heading to?" Kerry queried.

"Them skunks? If I knowed, doncha think I'd tell ya?" the woman screamed, her voice scornful.

"I'm sure you won't mind if we come in and see for ourselves," Kerry bellowed.

"Thought you got eyes full before!"

"Well, we'll do it again!"

Kerry turned to Tom and the others. "Now is when we watch our steps. Mind what I said about keeping your horses between you and the whole place."

As he had done before, Kerry assigned specific buildings of the ranch for pairs of deputies to investigate. With revolvers drawn, cocked and ready, Tom and the sheriff approached the house with their eyes fastened on doors and windows. In spite of the use of their horses to provide inconsistent protection, Tom realized how vulnerable they were. Leaving their horses near the entrance to the home, they passed the swearing woman and entered the front door warily.

Tom experienced a few moments of trepidation in the time it took his eyes to adjust to the inside gloom. It was an incredibly grubby living room, jumbled with old and mismatched furniture. The floors hadn't seen a broom in ages, and litter was strewn everywhere, piled deep in the corners.

Tom's eyes, however, were searching the dark doorways of adjacent rooms for movement.

Cautiously moving and crouching near any article of furniture that might provide some cover, he and the sheriff went through the house room by room, and they found neither Russ nor Ed. They came back into the living room and walked out the front door, where the Lockhart harpy was waiting.

"Well, didn't I tell ya they was on the vamoose? Whatcha say now, lawdogs?" She spat the words at them.

"I say you ought to clean the place 'fore you catch something," the sheriff shot back.

The other men were returning, holstering their guns as they grouped at the front of the house.

"Nobody here," Cartwright said. "We looked everywhere and they ain't here."

"Get off our land!" she bellowed. "You got no call to come 'round and go traipsing through our place!"

Kerry ignored her and motioned for the men to remount

their horses. While the woman shouted obscenities, the posse trotted their steeds back on the access lane and headed back toward the main road.

"Should we have searched for more of the bank money?" Cartwright asked, urging his horse to ride abreast of Tom and the sheriff.

Kerry shook his head. "Russ wouldn't leave his share laying around with that daft shrew."

"We'll find it on 'em," Tom put in. "Sure as shooting."

"Ain't nowhere in my jurisdiction left to look," Kerry said sagely. He glanced up at the sky. "Snow's getting pretty heavy. Looks like the weather's gonna take another lick at us." He gave an apologetic gesture to Tom. "I'm calling it quits, Tom. We'll put out Wanted notices south of here, maybe over to Colorado or down to New Mexico."

"You're giving up?" Tom asked angrily.

"No sense in keeping these men out in the cold no longer," Kerry answered. "We'll take the bodies back into Clay Center and you and your men can head back to Murphyville." He paused and gave Tom an understanding look that might have been compassion. "Somewhere, boy, somebody's gonna catch up with 'em."

"That somebody's gonna be me," Tom said bitterly.

Tom spoke briefly to the three men from Murphyville to tell them of the sheriff's decision. "You all can head for home," he said in conclusion.

"I've been cold for two full days," said a young man, Marty Wheeler. "You coming?"

"I'll be along in a while," Tom replied. "Head on out."

After the Murphyville men trotted their horses away, Sheriff Kerry touched Biggs' saddlebags he had thrown over the pommel of his saddle. "You want to take the money back to the bank?"

"You being ranking officer, I'd rather you keep it for now," Tom responded. "Bank can make do for a few days."

The sheriff nodded. "I'll hang on to it. Soon as the weather lets up, I'll get it back to Murphyville."

"Snow's coming harder," Tom said. "Best get home."

With an acknowledging half salute, Kerry led the Clay Center posse members away.

Tom tapped his boot heels against Duke's sides and urged the stallion into a trot. His fellow townsmen were nowhere to be seen, and the sheriff and his followers were now dark, vague figures barely visible in the thickening snowfall. He kept his pace until he saw the riders ahead turn off on a side road to Clay Center. As they disappeared into the whiteout, he reined Duke to a stop, turned, and headed back toward the Lockhart ranch.

Chapter Thirty-one

Clay County, Kansas, 1866

Tom turned Duke off the road and into the thicket of trees that faced the Lockhart ranch from about a hundred yards away. The crystal flakes came down steadily, and the accumulated snow on the bare branches above had formed a partial canopy over the woodland. Tom found a stand of close-growth fir trees that formed a wall against the elements. It was an evergreen recess within the surrounding wooded area that could shield Tom and his horse against the cold wind and hide him and his horse from the house.

Tom stepped down from his horse, tucked the wool collar of his heavy coat tight against his neck, and pulled his stocking cap down to cover his ears. On a clear day, this vantage point would have given a view of the ranch with only a few slender tree trunks in the foreground. Today, with the snow steadily falling, and the wind gusting and swirling it, visibility was intermittent.

For over an hour, Tom kept his vigil. Despite the negligible shelter of the evergreens, the deepening cold invaded his body, especially numbing his feet and his hands. Behind him, Duke was nestling into the fir trees, lifting his fore and hind legs and stamping his hooves repeatedly.

"You feeling it bad, same as me, ain't ya, feller?" Tom said to the animal. "Maybe we're being plumb stupid out here."

He walked to the edge of the woods and looked out into the blur of the cascading heavy snow that obscured the features of the area. The outlines of the dark ranch across the way were indistinct, almost erased from view by the storm. Tom's surrounds were now completely monochromatic, vaporously glistening and eerily luminous with a cloud-hidden sun spreading an overall diffusion.

He started to turn away when, in the hush of the sound damping snowfall, he heard distant voices approaching from the west. The words were indistinguishable, but the tenor of them was anger: shouted curses and bellowed vulgarities.

"Russ and Ed ain't too fond of snow neither," Tom said to himself and to his horse in grim humor. "Guess we guessed right, after all."

He swung up on Duke, took off his mittens, and tucked them into a pocket of his saddlebags. He blew on his hands, then rubbed them vigorously to bring back feeling. Fingers still stiff and tingling, he opened his coat and drew his revolver, checked its load, holstered it, and pulled the rifle from the saddle scabbard. He dug his heels hard into Duke's sides and trotted his stallion out of the woods on a line to cut between the arriving Lockhart brothers and their ranch.

Gauging the appropriate place to intercept, he reined up and stood tall and alert in his saddle stirrups, peering through the white veil of falling snow. He could hear the voices clearly now, an apparent argument between the two as-yet-unseen riders as they rode toward him.

"Damn you, Russ! We like to froze to death out there in that lousy moonshine shed!"

"You ain't in jail, are you?" Russ's voice questioned. "Warn't I right 'bout them coming back? They must've have caught Biggs and Johnson! Must've ratted us out!"

"We gotta light outta here! Right away!"

"Shut up, you fool!" the invisible Russ commanded. "We would freeze to death out there in this storm. We'll go when it's—"

The voice abruptly stopped and, at the same time, the dark shapes of the two riders on horseback appeared in a swirling cloud of snow, where they reined their mounts to an immediate halt.

"Who's there?" Russ Lockhart called.

Tom stepped down from his saddle into the deepening snow and gave Duke a sharp slap on the rump, the blow galvanizing the horse into a brief gallop that ended in a standstill some twenty-five yards away. "No sense you getting shot, Duke," Tom said under his breath. He raised the Winchester to a port position.

"What the hell's going on?" Russ Lockhart shouted. "Who are you? What do you want?"

"You're wanted for murder, Russ!" Tom declared in a loud voice. "You and Ed both! Also for bank robbery and hiding out fugitives!"

"You can't prove nothing like that!" Ed Lockhart said.

"We surely can and we surely will!" Tom yelled. "Step down from them horses and hold your hands up high. Make a move to your guns and I'll shoot you dead."

"Where's ever'body else?" Russ questioned.

"He's by hisself, Russ!" Ed shouted, his tone exuberant. "Damned fool is all by hisself!"

Tom dropped to his knees, anticipating gunfire instead of compliance, and raised the rifle to his shoulder.

True enough, one handgun made a popping sound in the snow-insulated atmosphere, followed by another. Tom had no idea which of the Lockharts had fired first, Russ to his right or Ed to his left. He was surprised and unprepared for a few moments as the pair spurred their horses into a full gallop, Russ breaking right, Ed coursing to the left.

The horseman on the right disappeared into a wind-driven screen of obscuring snow, so Tom swung the barrel of the rifle left to track the black figure now turning his mount into a curving charge directly toward him. Ed was leaning out of his saddle, the revolver in his right hand bucking with the recoil of the first and second shots he fired at Tom.

Tom pulled the trigger of the Winchester, and Ed's body lifted from the saddle and rolled over backward as his horse sped out from under him.

Tom threw himself flat into deep snow just as Russ' horse blasted out of the blinding storm and thundered right over him, a flying hoof crashing against the Winchester and sending it airborne to bury somewhere in the snow. He heard the explosive reports of Russ Lockhart's revolver, but he didn't know how close any of them had come. He had no hurt from either horse hooves or gunfire, and he rolled onto his back and snatched the Colt from his holster. He sat up and watched Russ Lockhart wheel his horse, snow spraying at the turn, and then charge again toward him.

Tom scrambled to his feet and lunged out of the way, twisting in his dive to fire back over his shoulder, a wild shot more from his alarm than from deliberation. The ball found a target and Tom winced at the result; Lockhart's horse screamed in pain as its forelegs buckled and it fell on its side, the hind legs kicking sporadically in the air in final agony.

Russ had been spilled a few yards away, the impact lessened by the cushion of deep snow. In the near whiteout, Tom saw him spring into a crouch and scuttle away toward the ranch house where the front door had opened and the Lockhart woman was peering out into the snowstorm. Tom took careful aim and fired a warning shot into the side of the house a few feet away from the doorway. With a scream and a curse, the woman slammed the door shut. Lockhart, alarmed by the shot, veered away from the house and ran, still crouched, toward the barn.

Tom rose to his feet and started wading after him, his boots crunching in the snow. Lockhart was struggling through a waist-high drift, twisting his torso to look back. He came to the cover of a parked farm wagon, ducked behind it, and fired a shot at his pursuer. The shot whistled a foot or more to his left, but Tom held his fire as Lockhart faced forward and resumed his hasty, floundering shuffle toward the barn.

"No backshooting for me," Tom muttered. "Alive to hang or a ball in his front, plain for all to see."

Lockhart continued his frantic and awkward progress toward the barn. He reached the big double doors, pulled the one to his right ajar, and slipped inside.

Tom knew all too well that the advantage now belonged to his quarry. Lockhart would quickly climb to the hayloft, and from the loft door he would have the sniper's advantage of looking down on the hunter.

Mindful, Tom moved as quickly as he could through the drifts, and leaped for the protection of the wagon.

Sure enough, a ball angled down and punched into the snow near his knee, and, to his dismay, a second thumped close against the wagon bed.

A rifle shot from the sound of it! Tom thought with dismay. *Must've had one in the barn! And he's sighted it!*

He cocked the Colt and aimed a shot at the loft door opening, surged forward, and fired three times more as he labored through the snow toward the corner of the barn. Even with his barrage of distracting gunfire, a speeding ball from the loft fanned past inches from his face. With relief, he reached the corner and stepped around it and out of Lockhart's sight.

"Empty," Tom said under his breath as he released the cylinder from the Colt. He reached in an inner pocket for the loaded spare and, with cold fingers, fitted it back into the frame of the revolver. With one chamber left empty to safely rest the closed hammer, it left five loads in the others. "Hope that's enough and powder ain't wet," he muttered.

Tom eased around the corner and flattened himself against the front face of the barn. For Lockhart to get a shot at him, he'd have to lean out of the loft door and present himself as a target. Tom, with his Colt held high, cocked and ready, inched his way along the barn wall toward the double doors. Through the dense fall of snow, he saw Lockhart's head and shoulder appear in the upper door as he peeked around the edge of the opening.

Tom reared back against the barn wall as the report of a revolver sounded flat in the sound-deadening snowy world. The passing ball was so close that it tugged fiercely at the collar of his mackinaw. The figure above ducked back inside before Tom could trigger a returning shot.

"Handgun," Tom said aloud. "Close quarters, now."

Expecting another shot from above at his vulnerable position, Tom risked a full charge to the partly open barn door and, with the sound of two pistol reports sounding, he swung around the door and into the darkness of the barn.

It took precious moments for his eyes to adjust from the white glare of the outside to the gloom of the barn's interior. He hoped Lockhart would still be right above him on the wide loading area just inside the loft door. Or, Tom reconsidered, he might be moving silently down the long arm of the L-shaped loft that extended the length of the barn over the four horse stalls.

Tom crept into a dim recess of the first horse stall and crouched low and motionless—waiting, watching, and listening. At the end of the line of stalls, a horse was restless at the explosive sounds and the intrusion of humans into the barn. Somewhere, above or on the ground level, Lockhart was doing the same—waiting, watching, and listening.

At the back of the barn, a buggy was parked at one side of the central aisle. Across the aisle, doorways opened into murky storage rooms and, on the wall, bridles, harnesses, hand tools, shovels, and spades hung from nails and pegs. Beneath the smaller items, a single Western saddle rested on a small waist-high stand.

Five minutes passed.

"Patterson," Lockhart's voice was weary. "I'm giving up. I'm coming down." He paused. "Don't shoot me."

"Drop your guns," Tom spoke in little more than a whisper, and immediately moved silently to a different corner of the stall.

The rifle dropped with barely a sound into a pile of hay in the center aisle, followed a few seconds later by a revolver. A minute later, Lockhart's legs appeared as he descended the ladder from the loft. As he reached the ground level, he turned slowly, his hands raised.

Tom's finger tightened on the trigger of his Colt.

"You gonna kill me?" Lockhart asked.

"Thinking about it," Tom responded.

"You're the law. That ain't right."

"You don't give a damn about the law," Tom said softly. "I 'spect Ben warn't the first you ever shot in the back."

Lockhart shrugged.

Tom eased the pressure off the trigger and waved the revolver to motion Lockhart out of the barn.

"You taking me in . . . in this snowstorm?"

"It's falling gentle, now," Tom told him. "We won't have trouble."

"You killed Ed?" Lockhart asked.

Tom nodded and reached for a coil of rope on a wall peg. "You can tie him on his horse."

They walked out of the barn, Lockhart holding both hands shoulder high and Tom a careful five feet behind him. They retraced their paths through the now gently falling snow to the body of Ed Lockhart. Under Tom's stern command, Russ retrieved Ed's horse, then struggled to lay his lifeless brother behind the saddle and rope the corpse securely.

Tom took a few steps to regain his own mount and swung up onto the saddle.

"Mount up in front of him," Tom instructed.

Lockhart turned his head toward his ranch. "I need to tell the missus."

"She'll be fine, let's go," Tom said impatiently.

"No, she won't," Lockhart said firmly. "Sometimes, if I'm not there, she gets a little funny in the head."

Tom sat his horse in silence for a long time and, finally, shrugged. "Call her to the front door, that's all. You ain't going inside or outta my sight."

Lockhart nodded and reached for the reins of the body-burdened horse. He led the animal to and tied it to the hitching rail at the front of the ranch house. Tom stepped down from the saddle and waved his captive forward.

At the front door, Lockhart reached for the doorknob, checked the move, and raised his right hand once again. "Can I put 'em down, Patterson?"

Tom stepped close and, with his left hand, patted each side

pocket of Lockhart's coat. "Stick your hands in your pockets and don't pull 'em out. I'll shoot if you do."

Lockhart sighed, nodded and thrust his hands into the pockets, then shouted, "Nora! Come to the door!"

There was no response from inside.

"Nora!" Lockhart bellowed. "You gotta come! I gotta leave!"

"There's shooting out there!" the woman's voice was muted.

"It's all over now!" Lockhart shouted. "I come to say good-bye!"

The door opened and the pathetic, frazzle-haired woman stood in the doorframe. "You leaving me, Russ?" The voice was plaintive, almost childlike, a whining plea. "You going off and leaving me for real?" Her pause included a whimpering sob. "What's going to happen to me?"

"Ain't got no choice, Nora. I just gotta—"

It happened suddenly, so abruptly that Tom had no idea of it. Lockhart's words ended with something resembling a shriek, so high in pitch that Tom thought it was the woman's scream. It was Lockhart, however, who hunched violently forward and stumbled back. Tom saw too late, the woman strike again and again with the butcher knife to her husband's mid-section.

Lockhart wheeled toward Tom with his eyes wide in fear and agony as he staggered a few steps and fell, blood gushing from his stomach and coloring the snow.

Tom trained his Colt on the woman as he bent to Lockhart and watched as the man looked up. Then the eyes stared, with no life behind them, and a second Lockhart died that day.

"Drop it!" Tom said as he rose.

The woman nodded and let the bloodied knife fall. "He said he was gonna leave me," she said in a curiously keening voice. "Going off and leave me, wouldn't even hug and kiss me goodbye." She turned her eyes to Tom and, in her ravaged features, he briefly saw what remained of a younger and different face. "Who's gonna take care of me now?"

Chapter Thirty-two

Murphyville, Kansas, 1866

The snow lasted through Christmas and on the second day following, Ben's ride-to-glory casket had arrived on the freight wagon from Kansas City. Two days later, Murphyville's only church was overcrowded for the funeral, the women and the elderly occupying most of the pews, and the men standing in the side aisles or at the back.

Tom had sat in the front row with Frank Bowman and his wife, Mayor and Mrs. Keats, and Sheriff Kerry. The lawman had come over from Clay Center to attend, to return the bank's recovered money, and to conclude some law enforcement business. On the opposite side of the aisle, the widow Rachael Richards sat quietly and dabbed at her eyes occasionally as Reverend Wallace and Reverend Durfee took turns delivering the eulogy.

After the burial at the cemetery, Mayor Keats asked Tom to join him, Sheriff Kerry, and Frank Bowman at his City Hall office.

"It don't fit right with me now, and it ain't never gonna fit," Sheriff Kerry said as they all settled into their chairs. The lawman's face was ruddy with his unbridled annoyance as he turned his gaze on Tom. "Who gave you leave to go back there?"

"You did, Sheriff," Tom said mildly. "I was still a deputized posse member."

"And two men are dead who might not have been," Kerry said harshly. "And we got a murdering crazy woman in a loony bin."

Tom didn't respond.

In the days since Tom had brought the Lockhart bodies into Murphyville on a single horse during a snowfall, Kerry had been busy. He and his deputies had made a repeat visit to the Lockhart ranch and taken Nora Lockhart into custody. She had come meekly, and only vaguely confirmed Tom's account of what had happened.

"How did you know they'd come back?" Kerry continued his brusque interrogation. "And, damn it, if you did know something, why didn't you tell me?"

"Call it a hunch," Tom replied. "One I don't think you'd have believed."

"A hunch?" Kerry curled his lip. "That don't wash!"

"Sheriff, I ain't meaning to put you down, but maybe I was seeing things that you wasn't," Tom countered.

"Don't give me that, you young—"

"All right," Tom interrupted, irritation now in his voice. "You ever been in the Sunflower Saloon?"

"A time or two," the sheriff answered testily. "What's that got to do with anything?"

"Notice the painting over the bar?" Tom asked.

"One with the gal with almost nothing on? Hard not to," Kerry admitted.

"Did you ever chance to look at the lady's face?" Tom asked, a smirk appearing.

Kerry didn't answer, but the three men shared puzzled glances.

"That was Nora Lockhart," Tom told them.

"Nonsense!" Kerry exclaimed. "That crazy woman?"

"I've seen her, and I don't buy that either," Bowman put in.

"If you looked close, under them sags and wrinkles, there was what was once a very pretty lady," Tom said. "She probably ain't that old, but living on booze and who knows what else, it changed her. Changed her bad." He paused. "But not to Russ Lockhart."

"What are you saying?" Kerry asked.

"When you and me was looking through the house, I seen

other little pictures, little tintypes. They was everywhere, sitting on tables and dressers, that showed what she used to be." Again, he paused to explain. "Russ and Ed, they were leaving quick as they could, all right. I 'spect they figgered the jig was up if we had caught the others . . . my hunch was, Russ was coming back for her."

"Why?" Kerry was incredulous. "She hated him, you saw that! The witch stabbed him to death!"

"I never saw that coming, and neither did he," Tom confessed. "When I was taking Russ to jail, standing back in the snow behind him, maybe she thought I was Ed." He shook his head at the memory. "When he told her goodbye, she didn't understand. She thought he was leaving her behind."

For a long time, no one spoke.

"Lord Almighty," Mayor Keats murmured at last.

"I don't know how, in her crazy mind, she felt about him, but Russ loved her when she was young and pretty," Tom said. "And, whether you believe it or don't, I guess he still did."

A few minutes after Sheriff Kerry said his goodbyes, mounted his horse, and headed back to Clay Center, Tom walked with Keats and Bowman back to the mayor's desk. The two older men were quiet and contemplative, each obvious in their ruminations of what they had heard.

Tom unpinned his badge from his shirt and laid it on the desk. He reached in his pocket and laid a key beside it.

"What's this?" Keats asked.

"I'm calling it quits," Tom said.

"No need of that," the mayor protested. "Sure, Kerry is a bit upset with you, but it worked out okay."

"It won't never be the same with him," Tom said. "He ain't one to forget, and it'll be a problem 'tween him and me."

"I can straighten that out," Bowman said. "Just let me—"

"I've locked up the jail." Tom cut him off and touched the key. "I've packed my gear, and I'm out of the rooming house."

"Why, Tom?" Bowman asked.

"Town's quiet now, Frank," Tom said. "Good time for me to move on. Something I want to do."

"Move on to where?" the banker asked.

"Heard tell there was some work to do down in Texas," Tom replied. "Ain't been back since 'fore the war."

"What kind of work?" Bowman asked. "Cattle?"

Tom shook his head. "Riding guard again. Fellow I knowed from the railroad bunch got in touch. Said they was paying good money for them that was handy with a gun."

"On the right side of the law?" Keats asked.

Tom shrugged. "I surely hope so."

He let them walk him to the front door. He shook their hands and said his goodbyes before he went outside to untie Duke's reins from the hitching rail. He stepped a boot into a stirrup and swung up into the saddle, then turned the horse onto the street. He rode Duke at a slow walk as he looked from side to side, nodding to passersby on the boardwalks.

At the edge of town, he cut off the main street and followed a rutted dirt road up to the top of the gentle hill where headstones and flat memorial granite plaques marked the graves of those who had lived and died in this frontier town. He rode Duke to the turned-earth site where two laborers, hired by the undertaker, were setting a round-topped headstone in place. Both men stopped their work and looked up as he rode near.

"Someone close to you?" one man asked, his manner reverential.

"Closest friend I ever knew," Tom replied.

He leaned forward to read the legend chiseled into the stone.

BENJAMIN HALEY

TRAIL ENDS
ANOTHER BEGINS

1832–1866

Tom leaned back and touched the brim of his hat in a smart and final salute to the headstone. He turned Duke away and then guided the horse toward the dirt lane. He rode slowly down the hill until he and his stallion reached the main road. He looked up the hill once more, then jabbed his heels against the sides of the stallion to urge the animal into a gallop.